HIS GRACE'S GOVERNESS

SAVING THE SPINSTERS
BOOK ONE

JACKIE KILLELEA

To God and my dear and loving parents,
who never cease to believe that I can
accomplish what I set my mind to.

CHAPTER 1

MARCH 1817
LONDON, ENGLAND

*E*leanor fought back tears as she tore down the busy London side streets toward her townhouse, maid in tow. The interview had gone terribly. She stepped around a pile of horse dung as her mind went over the matron's cruel words, the bustling carriages a blur around her.

You're much too young to be a governess. You won't know how to handle children, that's for certain.

Eleanor had attempted to explain that she did, in fact, know how to handle children, but the matron hadn't budged, telling Eleanor—in no uncertain terms—to seek employment with another agency.

Eleanor huffed as a tear finally fell, rolling down her cheek in a lone streak. She swiped in away, eyes burning from the smoke-heavy air. She had to get a job—had to. Her heart thunked low in her chest as she pushed her feet faster across the uneven ground, skirts swishing with wild movements around her legs. A quick glance over her shoulder told her that her maid kept up.

Despair welled in her stomach. It hadn't been easy looking for a position in the past—

"Eleanor!"

She stopped dead in her tracks, her maid colliding into her with enough force to make her stumble. Eleanor righted herself, and Mary did the same, her dark eyes apologetic. "Sorry, miss."

Before Eleanor had time to respond, *he* was upon them.

"Eleanor," he said again, a smirk on his face. He guided her to the side of a nearby brick building, out of the way of passersby.

Mary stayed nearby, but not near enough for Eleanor's liking. She supposed the girl couldn't be faulted for not knowing of the man's reputation.

"Mr. Phips." Eleanor's voice remained cool. "How are you today?"

His lips raised even higher, forming a self-satisfied smile. He waved a hand. "Never you mind that. I'm going to pay a call on you tomorrow. We'll go for a ride in my barouche."

Eleanor met his brown eyes, furrowing her brows at the unwarranted confidence there. "Pardon me, sir, but I do not remember you asking."

He leaned his shoulder against the building. "Please, Eleanor, do away with the pretense. I've seen the way you look at me. There's no need to play chase when it's clear I've already caught my prey."

Anger and disgust swirled in Eleanor's mind at his awful comment. "I'm no animal caught in a snare! You have done no such thing, and I—I've not given you permission to use my Christian name, sir."

He leaned his head closer and grabbed her wrist. The hair on Eleanor's neck stood. Abominable man.

"Aren't you?" he whispered, a knowing look on his face. "I've heard that you've been looking for employment. You see, I wanted to offer you a position. Now, what was it? I've quite forgotten. A cook? No, I have one of those... A laundress? No, although it would be enjoyable to watch you iron all of my cravats—then again, I like your dainty fingers the way they are. Your hands would be ruined if you were to be a laundress. Oh —I remember!" He tilted his head toward hers, his foul breath brushing her face. "I wanted to offer you a rather more...superior...position."

He waited, seeing if she would ask him what it was, but Eleanor feared she already knew the answer. His smirk dimmed for a moment, then came back as he looked around, then whispered, "Be my wife, Eleanor."

Eleanor stumbled back, eyes wide. Her cheeks burned as though she had a terrible fever. Though better than what she'd anticipated he'd say, it still wasn't at all what she'd expected.

"Y-Your wife?"

He brought her hand to his lips and kissed it. "I could give you everything, Eleanor. You would never have to seek employment like a plain spinster."

She snatched her hand from his grasp, frowning. "Mr. Phips, we would never suit. I-I don't love you..." She backed away a few steps, but he moved forward, eyes glinting.

"You would grow to love me, Eleanor. I would take you to all the events your heart could desire. You would be the talk of Town, and every man would wonder how I'd gotten you."

Eleanor shook her head. The man was utterly mad. She tilted her head to the side, taking a small step back. She placed a gloved hand on his arm. "I do wonder, Mr. Phips..."

His eyes became affixed to her hand on his dark-grey coat. Eleanor didn't bother asking a question, only swiveled around and ran, calling out for Mary to follow.

Eleanor dashed down the street, occasionally glancing over

her shoulder to see if he followed. He didn't, as far as she could tell. She turned down a corner she wouldn't normally and took a right where it would be a left, keen to lose him, just in case. Why did the one man who offered for her have to be Mr. Phips? She finally slowed her steps but continued to move in haste, her thoughts as swift as her steps.

As it was, she was caught quite unaware by a rebellious cobblestone, protruding from the ground slightly higher than the rest and eager to trip unassuming passersby.

When her toe collided with the unmoving stone, Eleanor fell without grace toward the well-worn ground. She squeezed her eyes shut—already envisioning the rough earth rushing up to meet her—and braced herself for the impact.

Strong arms caught her before she met the earth, pulling her to the side. One supported her beneath the arm, and the other steadied her at the waist. Her eyelashes fluttered open in surprise. Blinking, she refocused on a startling pair of green eyes, so close to hers that she could see the little specks of gold hidden within them. They reminded her of a warm spring day, the kind where the sun shines brightly through the trees and dapples the soft ground beneath with light.

"Oh!" The bright set of eyes she had been so caught in belonged to a man. A handsome man.

Her gaze flicked to the ground as she regained her bearings —something easier said than done. Her senses were numbed by the intoxicating scent of warm spices that seemed to come from his person—a delicious blend of clove, sandalwood, and something else. She met his stare again and took in his kind face, framed by a strong jaw and a head of thick auburn hair.

He wore an expensive green silk waistcoat and black tailcoat, a crisp white cravat wrapped around his neck. The gold chain of his watch hung from a pocket in his waistcoat, the expensive metal managing to gleam even with the cloudy sky hindering its full potential.

They stood there, staring at each other for an indeterminate amount of time, and the bustle around her seemed to quieten. The sound of a passing carriage, however, managed to pierce through her reverie and bring her back to the present.

"Are you all right, miss?" He released her. His voice was soft and rich, colored by a hint of concern.

She lowered her eyes to her skirts and brushed out the wrinkles while her cheeks warmed.

"Y–Yes, thank you." She gave him a small smile.

He nodded, and his eyes held hers for a moment, as if peering through to her soul. A ghost of a smile lifted the corners of his mouth before disappearing. "Think nothing of it."

He bowed, leaving her to bob a quick curtsy before he turned away and continued down the cobbled street.

Eleanor pinched the once-soft fabric of her dress. When she'd been fitted for the pale-pink gown, the lace trimming had been bright. Needless to say, the cotton had seen better days, whereas the man had been so dapper in his fine jacket and waistcoat.

No wonder he left so quickly. He must have thought her a street urchin.

Eleanor groaned. How embarrassing!

She looked after him for a few moments, failing to banish the image of those piercing eyes from her mind. She could've sworn she'd seen a somber look in them. A tiredness, perhaps?

Despite their short encounter, a spark of energy had also leapt between them. Something she'd never experienced previously. The world had slowed, if only for a blissful moment. Her heartbeat still pranced in her chest from the interaction.

Eleanor! She scolded herself.

There were much more important issues to think upon. One of which being how she must now search the newspaper for a position. She sighed and shook her head, turning back toward her townhouse where her problems awaited.

Her maid, whom she had momentarily forgotten, scurried to her side. "Are you well, miss?" Her wide eyes filled with worry as she squeaked out the words.

Eleanor patted her arm. "Yes, Mary. Thank you."

This seemed to appease the maid. The girl's slight shoulders eased. Though she seemed fresh-faced, Mary, along with the few remaining servants at the townhouse, were being pressed beyond their limits. The familiar sense of guilt gnawed at Eleanor's insides. Things had to change, and soon.

Eleanor began to plod back home, trying to distract herself from the weight upon her shoulders and the intriguing green eyes she had beheld only moments before. Merchants sold their wares from crowded shop corners. The pounding of horses' hooves on the street rang through the air. Men and women dressed in the finest fashions walked arm in arm.

A woman passed, pulling a crying child by the hand. "Don't cry so, Susan, Mr. Whiskers will come back."

The girl's response was lost as they walked farther away.

Across the street, a man called to all listening ears, "A shilling a piece!"

The city was alive around her, yet Eleanor could not feel the rumble of life within. A sigh fell from her lips as a sense of melancholy draped around her.

As she walked toward her home, the rows of beautiful houses mocked her, reminding her of her family's straitened circumstances. With pristine red brick and well-swept walkways, their spotless windows stared at her stared at her like eyes, cold and unfeeling, with an air of superiority. She arrived at the front steps of her family's townhouse, the stone cracking and crumbling away in places. Dirt filled the cracks in the bricks, and the door's dark-green paint chipped away with every small breeze. The neighbors could not be pleased with having to reside next to what they surely deemed an eyesore. Though Eleanor would have liked to fix the house's facade, there were more pressing issues to be addressed within.

The door opened to reveal the aged butler, Crand. When he gave her a warm smile, his eyes crinkled at the corners. "Welcome home, Miss Clairbridge." He spoke in a kind manner with a raspy edge to his voice.

She returned his smile, albeit feebly, and stepped past his frail figure into the foyer. "Thank you, Crand." Her smile waned as she glanced around the entry room, noting the threadbare rugs and the peeling wallpaper that lined the narrow hall. The unpleasant smell of tallow candles reached her nose, and she fought hard not to grimace. She understood the necessity of cutting costs but didn't believe she'd ever become used to the scent of them.

Eleanor well remembered bounding through these halls, once so full of warmth and light, as a child. Something akin to a frown pulled her lips as she recalled hiding behind the plum-colored curtains that framed the now-clouded windows in games of hide and seek, her father acting as though he didn't spy her shoes peeking out from beneath. Now, her father, the Baron Saint Helens, was gone. That light had faded. The halls were no longer full of laughter, the curtains were no longer a hiding place, and Eleanor was long past childhood.

She handed Crand her cloak and bonnet.

"How was your walk, Miss Clairbridge?"

Should she reveal the finer details of her stroll? Eleanor thought the better of it. "Eventful, but pleasant all the same."

She regretted lying to Crand, but she didn't want him to worry about her, and he would if she revealed her true thoughts and emotions. Crand had always watched out for her, sneaking her biscuits from the kitchen and cheering her up when she had taken a tumble, which had been a frequent occurrence.

The corner of his mouth quirked up, and he raised a brow but remained silent on the matter. Instead, he bowed, his wispy white hair dancing with the motion. "Very good. Would you like me to call for some tea, miss?"

She hesitated before shaking her head. "No, thank you, Crand. I believe I'll visit my mother in the drawing room." She attempted to muster up a blithe look and nodded her head to him in a gesture of appreciation before turning toward the grand staircase at the end of the foyer. She strode to it and began up the stairs adorned by worn red carpet, her hand skimming over the banister, smooth to the touch from years of use.

Mama was bound to have already sent for tea. Perhaps there would be a few biscuits left for Eleanor to nibble on. Her stomach gave a quiet grumble, and she placed a hand over it. Yes, a few biscuits would be just the thing.

Beyond the stairs and a short walk down the hall, Eleanor reached her destination. She pushed the drawing room's door open and stepped inside. She was greeted by the scarcely furnished area, flooded with light from the windows that illuminated the dusty air within. They'd had to sell most of the furniture to pay the remaining servants, and what money they'd had left had been used to buy food. The room's large size made the lack of furniture even more evident. The wallpaper was in a similar state as that in the hall, and the fireplace to the right of the room held only the weakest of flames.

Eleanor shivered as she entered, the room hardly warmer than outside. No matter that spring had arrived, winter's chill held on with all ten fingers.

Her mother sat before the fireplace in her favorite chair, embroidering. A thin blanket covered her lap. Eleanor couldn't imagine it did a very good job at keeping her warm. Her violet-colored dress fell limply around her thin frame, and her greying hair was tucked away into her lace cap. Only a few strands poked out here and there. Her face held a somber expression as she added stitches to her work, an air of sorrow in her resigned movements. She looked up and gave a tender smile.

"Are you all right, Mama?" Eleanor bit her lip.

Her mother waved her hand. "You've asked me this same question before, dear, and my answer remains the same. I am perfectly content."

"I wouldn't ask if you didn't look so..." Unsure how to phrase what she'd seen in her mother, Eleanor allowed her words to fade.

"You mustn't worry about me, dearest. It's my job to worry, after all. Now, how was your walk? You did bring Mary with you, didn't you?"

Eleanor took the cushioned seat across from her and warmed her hands by the fire. "It was enjoyable and, yes, I did. I ran into Mrs. Witherby, who was eager to speak to me of the latest fashion plates." She plucked a biscuit from the tea tray that was sitting on the short table between them and took a small bite. "She always has such..." Eleanor paused, searching for a kind word. "...lively conversation." If only she might have had a more peaceful walk, one that fulfilled its intended purpose. She shivered as the image of Mr. Phips's glinting eyes entered her mind, unbidden.

"What a dear woman she is," Mama said. "A more cheerful person is seldom found."

Eleanor nodded with a faint smile and took another bite of the biscuit, the treat soon turning to sand in her mouth. Her mind was occupied with other things, such as how much longer they could afford to keep on the servants.

Mama acted as though they were better off than they were, but she knew Eleanor had seen the ledgers. Mama couldn't hide the numbers—the truth. The day Eleanor had stumbled across the leather-bound books had been stamped into her mind—an ink stain that could not be removed, no matter how much milk she used. Red ink marred the pages, and she'd seen how deep in the thicket they were.

Her mother caught on to her pensiveness and the worry in her eyes. "Dear...I'm sorrier than you'll ever know that you feel you must seek a position as a governess. Your poor father—may he rest in peace—never meant for this to happen." Her mother closed her eyes for a moment. Eleanor had heard this story before. She even recollected her father speaking of the matter when he was alive, but she let her mother go on. "I remember the night he told me of those investments. He said they were reliable."

She seemed lost in memory. "The previous baron was a terrible gambler. Even this townhouse was in shambles when we first married," she explained, gesturing to the room. "My dowry helped to repair this home to its former glory, of course. After that, your father and I never worried that our finances would take a turn. He wanted you to have a season, marry well, and never have to worry about money the way we did." A tear slipped from the corner of her eye. "If only he hadn't been taken so soon... He never once doubted investing in those crops. Never once. And who could have foreseen the blight they'd be struck with?"

Eleanor dipped her chin. "Of course." Her father had been the only male left in the line of possible heirs, and it was fortunate that her father's will, while singular, had left the house in her mother's name, though the upkeep was more than they could bear.

Eleanor's mother exhaled a shuddering breath. She pierced Eleanor with a serious stare. "Are you sure this is what you want to do? You might meet a gentleman yet. Have a love match as your father and I did. What Miss Pottan said at the ball—it isn't true, you know. That was three years ago now, dear." Her mother's tired blue eyes held a hint of hope.

Eleanor rose from her seat and crossed over to her mother, tugging the embroidery hoop from her grasp and crouching next to her to meet her gaze. "Oh, Mama, we simply couldn't afford a season, and I do not mourn it. How can one mourn what one never had, after all? I do, however, greatly wish that I could have married by now. Had I done so, you could have lived with me, and we would not be in the sad state that we are today. I believe, however, that the time has come for me to give up and move on. After all, the only man who has ever paid a call on me is Mr. Phips, and you know I could never marry someone so conceited as he. We are as different as a birch is to an oak. And, if I do not find a position, our finances will continue to deplete. Then where would we be? We'd have to sell this house. Our house. The place where so many memories of father have made their home."

Her father had always been by her side. Always encouraging. He had fallen ill seven years ago—before she could ever have a season—and mourning had taken much of her time. That had been the time when most of her "friends" had shown their true faces. Once they'd caught word that her family couldn't afford for her to have a season, many left. She'd seen them in public, but when she'd tried to catch their eyes, they looked pointedly away, as though they had never spoken a word to her.

The few that stuck around had always been kind, but they seemed to move forward with their lives as she remained stationary in hers. Mama had struggled too. Eleanor hadn't been oblivious to the way fans seemed to flutter when they used to go for walks about Town. It was one of the reasons Mama didn't venture out anymore.

Eleanor didn't mention the ball, though her heart fractured at the memory of it. It wasn't the time to think of it.

If only Father was by her side as he used to be, telling her about the latest events he had read of in the newspaper, smiling over his spectacles at her. He would have helped them weather the storm. He would know what to do.

Her father would've been so happy to see her with a husband and family. Now it seemed as though no one would see either—not with Eleanor's unfortunate plainness and lack of season.

Her mother lifted a wrinkled hand to Eleanor's cheek as a bittersweet look crossed her face. "Do not blame yourself, dear, for it is not your fault. It is hard to find a husband when one does not have a season, and now that you're older, even more difficult. Perhaps you will come to find love when and where you least expect it."

Eleanor swallowed the lump in her throat and tried to push the melancholy thoughts from her head, knowing her mother did not mean to injure her with the blade of false hope. She stood, her mother's hand falling from her cheek, and tried her best to smile. "It is all right, Mama. I am too old now to draw any gentleman's eye and have made my peace with being a governess. I'm determined to find a position soon, that we might no longer have to fret over paying the servants' wages and the butcher's bill."

Though she did, indeed, fret over paying the servants' wages and the butcher's bill, Eleanor was more concerned with something deeper. A fear that threatened to tear her in two. If they had to sell the house, the one remaining connection Eleanor had to her father, what would be left of him? She had a golden locket he'd given her on her twelfth birthday, a piece of jewelry she cherished, but that seemed like nothing compared to the place where he'd spent so much of his time, the place where she'd spent so much time with him.

If they sold the house...

All that she had of Papa would be gone. The memory of him would fade, as it had already started to do.

Eleanor shook those depressing thoughts from her head

and focused on the task at hand. She made her excuses and left the room, heading straight for the study and the day's newspaper.

She hurried down the hallway and thrust open the door to the study. The room was rather cramped compared to the others. A fireplace remained cold at one end of the room, and two chairs sat in front of it, their wooden arms dusty. On the opposite side stood a large bookshelf stuffed with tomes of all kinds, from agriculture to the sciences. A large desk made of cherry wood rested at the far end of the room.

A gentle light greeted her from the window near that desk, alongside the comforting smell of old books. She could almost see her father's smiling face as he peered up from his work. Eleanor crossed the room, slumped into the cracked leather chair, and bent over the newspapers, scanning the pages with intensity. Surely, someone was seeking a governess. She sent a fleeting glance to the stack of apology letters from those whose governess positions were already filled before flipping one page over. And there it was!

Seeking Governess Immediately.

Eleanor's heart jumped in her chest as a sort of desperation made the blood rush in her veins. Her gaze flitted over the rest of the advertisement.

Must be a respectable young woman who is well-versed in the usual subjects such as the French language, the playing of an instrument, etc. She must be available to begin immediately to govern a young girl of five years. Inquiries without these qualifications will be promptly discarded.

She read the address at the bottom of the paragraph and set to writing an inquiry as to the position's availability. Her shoulders tensed, and hopeful anticipation pricked at the hair on her arms.

Please…please let this be fruitful.

Eleanor attempted her very best handwriting and, after signing her name with a flourish, stuck the quill back into the ink pot. People were impressed by flourishes, were they not? She shrugged.

Eleanor sprinkled sand on the drying ink and went over the list she'd created of recommendations to her name—baron's daughter, proficient at the pianoforte, spoke French—the list went on, although Eleanor found it odd to include her accomplishments in such a way. It was too similar to boasting for her taste.

The ink was dry enough within a few minutes, and Eleanor called Crand in and sent him off with the sealed letter. With luck, her time spent at Mrs. Dorfield's school might prove to be useful.

In truth, a position as a governess might suit her very well. She'd always found enjoyment in her studies at school, and when she'd had a governess of her own—well, the sciences had always been a favorite subject of hers, not in small part due to her parents' love of native flora and fungi. Eleanor closed her eyes and prayed, hoping beyond hope she might be chosen for the position, if it were still available at all.

She rested her elbows on the old cherry desk and put her face in her hands. *Please, Lord, let the position be open!*

CHAPTER 2

*E*leanor flipped the page in a novel she was reading, absorbed in the story. Around her, the morning room with its light-green walls and antiquated furnishings seemed to dim, and she no longer sat in the cushioned space made by the oriel window, but a small cottage in the depths of the woods, surrounded by towering beech and ash trees.

It had been only a few days since she'd applied to the governess position, and she tried to keep herself from thinking of it, half eager and half dreading the prospect of it. A scratch at the door tore her from her self-made oasis, and she closed the book, using a scrap of ribbon to mark her place as she bid the person to enter.

"Good afternoon, Crand."

The butler stepped into the room, holding a silver salver. The man returned her greeting and walked closer, extending the tray to her. "A letter for you, miss."

He bowed and left as soon as he'd arrived, albeit with a few extra moments allotted for his arthritic knees. Eleanor examined the missive as she moved toward the walnut writing desk in the corner of the room. An intricate wax seal fastened it shut. Eleanor ran a finger over it, the crimson color contrasting with the creamy white paper. Hope welling in her chest, she closed her eyes for a second—only long enough to take a breath— before breaking the seal and unfolding the piece of paper.

March 24th, 1817, Oxfordshire

    Miss Clairbridge,

    His Grace, The Duke of Albemarle, accepts your application to the position of governess. His Grace wishes that you begin as soon as is convenient and requests that you send notice with the time of your estimated arrival.

    Regards,

    B. Prumb

Eleanor's heart stuttered. A duke? Never even in Eleanor's dreams had she imagined she'd be employed by a duke. She'd had little hope of her application being accepted in the first place. Her mind spun at the revelation. In small handwriting at the bottom of the letter was the address of the estate, which she glanced at before refolding the letter and heading to the sitting room to tell her mother of their new-found fortune.

Her heart lifted, and she thanked God. This was the miracle they had been praying for.

∾

*E*dmund Colhampton, the fifth Duke of Albemarle, sat in his study and ruminated over the past week. On Thursday, he had gone to London in order to attend to some business. He had also wanted to add a few books to his library, a task which he had had success in accomplishing. He didn't often go to London, as he much preferred the country with its fresh air and peaceable quiet, but sometimes he simply couldn't avoid it. The trip, overall, had been the same as any of the other trips he had taken to London, but one thing stuck in his mind. Or, rather, one person. The woman he'd met on Jermyn Street.

Her chestnut-colored locks had hung around her face in a state of disarray, and Edmund had caught the delicate scent of lavender that radiated from her as though she were the sweet flower itself. When she'd opened her eyes, he'd been frozen in place. Those eyes. They were blue like the ocean on a cloudless day, the kind of eyes a person could search in for their entire life and still never succeed in uncovering all of their hidden depths.

Remembering himself, he had been quick to release her after ensuring she was unharmed and steady on her feet. She was lovely. Her lips had slightly parted in surprise, and her cheeks had been rosy. So focused on her features was he that he had uttered the first reasonable phrase that sprang to mind. More than her pleasing features, however, was the warmth in her eyes and the kind upturn of her mouth, which only added to her vibrancy. Polite society frowned upon the possibility of exchanging any more speech—especially considering they were strangers—so he had turned and hastened away, his mind foggy.

Since that incident, Edmund had had a difficult time focusing on anything for very long before the image of her face pushed all other ideas away. The ceaseless thoughts of her, however, were more welcome than those that occupied his mind on a regular basis—those of the carriage accident that had led to Rosie being under his care. He ran a hand through his hair and sighed, backing away from that dangerous abyss and allowing his ruminations to return to the woman.

If only he could've gotten her name! There was little chance of him ever seeing her again—largely due to his infrequent trips to London. Even if he were to go into town every week, there were so many people occupying London that the search would equate to finding a single shell upon the shore or a book in a disorganized library.

Speaking of books...shelves of them and tidy stacks of papers filled the space around him. The study hardly seemed to belong to him. It still held hints of his father within the titles that lined the shelves, worn covers and all. The entire selection of the books in this room were his father's favorites. His father's pipe sat in the second drawer of the desk, exactly where he had left it on the day he had died.

He sighed again, the flames of the fire swirling around each other in a spontaneous dance of light. It wasn't as though he would court the woman, anyway. He was already struggling through the task of courting and failing miserably—or successfully, depending on how one thought of it.

He had just picked up his quill to answer some correspondence when a gentle knock came at his study door. "Enter!"

The doorknob wriggled for a moment before the door creaked open and his niece's riotous mass of blond curls bounced into view. Any melancholy that had plagued him fled. The sight of his niece could always raise his spirits.

"Uncle Edmund!" She bounded into the room and stopped before his desk, peering around with curious eyes as she always did when in his study.

He gave her a broad smile and stood from his desk. "Good evening, Rosie!"

She skipped over to him and wrapped her short arms around his waist.

Edmund returned her embrace and patted her head. "Are you excited for your governess to arrive?"

He could have guessed the answer to that question, for his

niece all but shook with excitement, a large grin upon her sweet face. The girl had always worn her emotions as a badge on a soldier's sleeve, something most six-year-olds were wont to do.

"Yes! I'm going to show her the gardens, the library, the horses, everything!" She bounced on her feet, and Edmund chuckled.

"I'm sure you will. Remember, you must be on your best behavior and give Miss Clairbridge a warm welcome. She'll need some rest after her journey here, so perhaps you might save the tour for tomorrow. Do you think you can manage that, dearest?"

Rosie nodded, her rosy cheeks glowing with excitement. "Yes! I promise."

Edmund smiled down at her. "Very good." He paused a moment before striding to the study door and checking both sides of the hallway. He glanced back to his niece and raised a questioning eyebrow. "Where's Nurse?"

Rosie wrung her skirts in her small hands, at once finding the floor very interesting.

"Rosie?"

It didn't take long for her to look up at him with a hint of guilt in her eyes. "She was tidying my room. I just wanted to see you, Uncle."

Just then, the nurse called for Rosie, likely wondering where she had run off to.

Edmund turned back toward the room—crouching so he was eye-level with his niece—and spoke in a gentle yet disapproving tone. "You mustn't run off without Nurse, Rosie. It is her job to make sure you're safe, and she can't do that if you are not with her. Understand?" She nodded and he stood, extending his hand to her. "Come, we must find her."

She held his hand in a tight grip as they exited the room.

After Rose had been deposited into the care of her grateful

nurse, Edmund returned downstairs to his study, once more sitting at his desk and sifting through correspondence. He couldn't help the somewhat wary feeling that assaulted him when he thought of his conversation with his niece. While he was excited for Rose to receive a proper education, a governess would be a new addition to the house, and Edmund very much hoped she wouldn't quash Rose's spirit. The girl only needed a gentle guiding hand, not a heavy one.

He pulled his pocket watch from his waistcoat pocket and flicked it open, glancing at the time. "Prumb!" It was half past six o'clock, the time when Miss Clairbridge had been set to arrive.

His butler entered the study and bowed. "Yes, Your Grace?" Prumb stood with confidence, and anyone could see he took great pride in his job. He was of average height yet had always seemed tall to Edmund. His dark hair was greying at the edges, and his lined face told the tale of a happy life as surely as a map told of roads traveled.

"Have you any word on the estimated arrival of the new governess?"

"There has been no word, Your Grace. Would you like me to send someone to the posting inn?" Prumb's thoughtful eyes met Edmund's.

Edmund tilted the pocket watch still in his hand toward him once more. He frowned. "Indeed. The mail coach may be running late, but it is better to make sure that she is, in fact, on her way."

"Very well, Your Grace." Prumb assented with a bow, leaving only after Edmund convinced him there was nothing else he needed.

Edmund released a slow breath as he removed Miss Clairbridge's responding letter from his bottom left desk drawer and placed it before him, the foolscap shifting with his exhale.

Hopefully, everything was as it should be, and the mail coach had simply been delayed.

He let his thoughts drift for a few moments, as they had been time and again, to the blue-eyed woman with the defeated look on her face. Why had she seemed so resigned? A look of sadness had been present in her eyes, one that was too familiar to him to miss.

CHAPTER 3

*E*leanor was lost. More than lost, although she couldn't think of a word for her current situation. Open fields surrounded her, the stone walls lining them casting eerie shadows in her path.

Where was she?

She huffed in frustration and scoured her mind for what the man at the posting inn had said. Didn't he say to take a left at the start of the hill? Or was it a right?

Eleanor had been eager to be free of the mail carriage after being cramped in it for hours with four other people. She scrunched her nose, remembering the pompous woman who had sat across from her—a Mrs. Cholert—and the way she had talked on and on about her daughter, who was to marry a wealthy baron. Once the woman had stopped her chattering in order to rest, Eleanor had been granted a pleasant respite. That, however, had not lasted long, for the woman was soon awake again and, again, looking down her nose at Eleanor and the other passengers.

The moment the carriage had stopped at the posting inn, Eleanor had hopped out, eager for peace and quiet. Though she had searched for some sort of transport sent to convey her to Ivy Grange, she hadn't been able to find one. Assuming one hadn't been sent, she began her long walk with her trunk in hand.

Botheration! The duke was expecting her at any moment, and here she was, hopelessly lost, heaven knew how far from Ivy Grange Estate!

Nearby, the tall grass rustled near the stone wall, and she dropped her trunk. Her heart raced within her chest, and she raised a hand to her mouth, stifling a scream. Yet the culprit was soon found to be a rather large mouse. It hopped through the grass, leaving her to wish she could move as quickly as it had.

Only a mouse. That was all.

Eleanor took a steadying breath. She picked up her trunk, grimacing at the twinge in her arm, and continued onward. There were no houses to be seen, only vast fields and white dots which she could only assume were flocks of grazing sheep, though they would soon plod to wherever place they had chosen to rest for the night. Her feet throbbed with every step, and before she knew it, the sun began its descent.

How was it that there were so many large fields, yet no homes to be seen?

Eleanor plunked her trunk on the side of the road and slumped onto it. She brushed at the dust and dirt on her skirts and tried to formulate a new plan of action. There were few options available to her.

~

"John told me upon his arrival that he did not see any sign of Miss Clairbridge at the posting inn. He did, however, say the owner of the inn told him that a young woman had asked for directions to Ivy

23

Grange Estate." The butler's lips were drawn downward, his hands clasped behind his back as he delivered this news. An hour had passed since he'd last been in Edmund's study.

Edmund raised his eyebrows. Could she have thought to walk? Edmund's home sat five miles from the posting inn, a large distance for a young woman on foot, unaccompanied. He ran a hand through his hair and rested his elbows on his desk, steepling his fingers in front of him.

"And John didn't pass her on the way to or from the inn?" Concern grew within him. Where could the governess have gone?

"No, Your Grace. He told me that he did not pass anyone by on the road." Prumb shook his head.

Edmund furrowed his eyebrows and glanced out of his study's window again at the sun, which descended toward the horizon in an unnerving manner. "Please have my carriage readied, Prumb. I will search the roads surrounding Ivy Grange. She must have gotten lost on her way here—assuming she decided to walk."

"Very well, Your Grace. I'll do so right away." Prumb gave a determined bow and marched out of the room.

There was no use fretting over what may be or might have been. Edmund could only hope they would find her and that she would be unharmed. Still, he lost no time making his way to the foyer to retrieve his hat and coat.

~

As the sun dipped below the horizon little by little, Eleanor began to despair of reaching Ivy Grange Estate before dark. She had determined that her best option was to continue on the road she walked on, since she was already a good distance from the posting inn. It had been about a half an hour since she had made that decision, and she still had not seen a single house or barn of any kind.

The early-spring air was cool, the evening descending like a fog around her. She shivered. Her pelisse was on its last legs—the light-green color had faded, the edges were fraying, and holes marred the thin fabric. Her mother had wanted her to buy a new one, but Eleanor had refused, insisting the money they had left was better spent on other things. She was beginning to regret that decision.

The light breeze brushing the grass in the fields and the tapping of branches coming into contact with one another filled the evening air, creating a sort of quiet melody. It was peaceful here, and she laughed inwardly at her earlier bout of nerves. She smiled to herself. The air was fresh—not thick from smoke that permeated every brick in London. The quiet allowed her to focus on what lay ahead, and she didn't have a chance of running into Miss Pottan. Eleanor grimaced at the thought of that woman but shrugged it away.

What would the duke do when she didn't show up? Would he send a footman looking for her? Would he even care? Would she be dismissed before even arriving?

She'd go around the back of the estate and enter through the servants' door. Or should she enter through the main door? Surely not. While she might not be as low as a servant in rank, she was certainly nowhere near as high in status as a duke...

Eleanor forced herself to take a deep breath.

Mrs. Brinder's letter was polite, without a haughty tone, and dukes were just people, albeit people with the power to ruin a person. And if the girl was difficult—well... she would have to be steadfast in her teachings. She could not afford to be a failure at this.

There was much at stake. Her home. Her father's memory.

As they continued to spend what little they had, her wages

would have to replenish the amount. How much did governesses make? Doubtless, not a lot. The butler had never disclosed in his letter, only writing that she would be "satisfied" with the sum.

Her shoulders hunched as the realization set in that she'd have to be a governess for the rest of her days if she wanted to keep the house—and children were not children forever. One day, she'd have to find a new position, and that was assuming she wouldn't be turned out before then.

What if she was a terrible governess?

Eleanor attempted to square her shoulders and push away her anxiety.

"Well, it's too late to go back now." She must be imagining things as well, for she almost heard the steady beat of horses' hooves somewhere in the distance. Were they growing louder? Eleanor chuckled. She was going mad.

What a predicament she had gotten herself into. The hoof beats grew in volume, as if they were approaching. Her eyes widened as a carriage rolled toward her from the north. She waved her free arm in a frantic motion. Her heart lightened with hope as the carriage rumbled closer. That hope mingled with growing embarrassment as she took in the perfect state of the conveyance. Its sleek black doors were decorated with a familiar-looking design in gold flourishes, though Eleanor couldn't distinguish where she'd seen the crest before. The driver wore fine clothing, as did the footman riding in the back.

Her mother had once told her, "The better dressed the servants are, the wealthier the employer." Considering the fine liveries the servants were wearing, Eleanor had to presume the occupant was wealthy, indeed.

Of course, the moment she was lost in the countryside, clothing wrinkled from travel, was the moment when one of the finest carriages she'd ever seen—likely containing one of the most prominent members of society—should be her only form of rescue. Would it even stop, or would it continue on past her?

It slowed as it reached her, the driver pulling the horses to a stop as Eleanor's face heated ever more. She approached the driver, struggling to carry her trunk with one hand as her palms began to sweat.

"Sir! Could you please help me? I seem to have gotten lost on my way to Ivy Grange Estate. Could yo—" The door of the carriage opened. She wheeled around and began to speak once more. "My apologies, sir. I—" Her words failed her. "You." Her breath came out all at once in that single word.

The man in front of her, the man who had just jumped out of the carriage, was none other than the one who'd caught her in London. The man with the beautiful eyes that had so captivated her thoughts ever since.

CHAPTER 4

"You." The man echoed the word, his voice but a whisper. He seemed to be just as surprised as she. It was as if his eyes peered straight through her and into her soul.

Her pulse thrummed in her veins. Eleanor shook herself out of her daze and curtsied, giving a hesitant smile. "Good evening, sir. Seeing as there is no one to introduce us, I suppose that the responsibility falls to me. I am Miss Eleanor Clairbridge. I was hoping that you might be able to point me in the direction of Ivy Grange Estate, as I have been trying to find it for the past few hours and have been very unsuccessful in my search."

The man's eyes widened as he responded to her curtsy with a bow. "You are Miss Clairbridge?" He peered at her, an uncertain look crossing his face.

Eleanor smiled in an attempt to reassure him. "Well, I should certainly hope so, sir. I've gone by no other name for the entirety of my life..." Eleanor paused before amending her words. "That is, aside from the name my father used to call me when I was a child."

The man raised his eyebrows, regarding Eleanor curiously. "I must admit that you've utterly piqued my interest, Miss Clairbridge. What name did your father used to call you?"

Eleanor shifted her grip on her trunk, the corner of her lips quirking up at the memory of her father. "Ruby." The name was as familiar on her lips as her Christian name.

"Did your father like rubies very much?"

Eleanor pulled herself back to the present and met the man's gaze once more, her cheeks heating even more at what she was about to admit. "He did—however, he did not refer to the gem when he called me that."

The man tilted his head.

"My father was something of a botanist. He studied plants and fungi when his work did not demand his attention, and he had a particular interest in mushrooms. I was a rather rosy-cheeked child, and so my father thought it fitting to call me after his favorite pink-hued mushroom—*Amanita rubescens.* Ruby." Her grip tightened on the handle of her trunk.

The man studied her, no trace of ridicule or disdain in his eyes. After a moment, he nodded. "A fitting name. It's a pleasure to make your acquaintance, Miss Clairbridge. I am Edmund Colhampton, Duke of Albemarle. I believe you are to be my niece's new governess." One side of his mouth lifted in a hint of a smile. He was quite obviously oblivious to her spiraling mind.

The man that caught her in London was the Duke of Albemarle? Eleanor had only ever met one duke, and he was on the older side. She had assumed that most dukes were and that the Duke of Albemarle would be the same. She had expected a man with wrinkles and a stern countenance, not a handsome man with an intriguing smile. This man in front of her didn't look harsh at all.

Remembering she was now speaking to a duke—and her employer—she dropped her trunk and performed the most elegant curtsy she could manage. Perhaps she could erase his memory of her previous one. Such lack of grace should be forgotten as soon as possible—for both parties' sakes.

"Y-Your Grace! My sincerest apologies. I hadn't the slightest idea—not that you do not look of noble birth. Of course, your speech is quite refined. I..." Oh dear. She was fumbling this. She tried to stand as tall as possible, her training at Mrs. Dorfield's school coming to mind. Training she had all but forgotten when faced with someone of such standing. And good looks.

Fortune smiled on her when the duke paused her rambling.

"It's quite all right, Miss Clairbridge. You had no way of knowing." He waved away her chagrin and gave her a reassuring smile, the first full smile she had seen from him. "Truly, I am not offended in the least. Are you all right? When you didn't arrive this evening, we became worried. I had sent a carriage to transport you to Ivy Grange, but as the mail carriage you took was early in its arrival, I suppose you left before it appeared. Since my butler relayed this information to me, I've been combing the surrounding area, hoping to find you before dark." He searched her face with those piercing green eyes of his.

"My feet are a bit sore, but besides that, I am fine. Thank you, Your Grace." She inwardly smacked her forehead for having spoken of her feet to a duke and attempted to keep her voice from wavering as she went on. "Had you not found me, I fear what might have happened. I have not seen a single house since leaving the posting inn, and I was unsure of what to do. I am sorry for having caused you so much trouble." She clenched her skirts in her hands and kept her eyes on the ground, feeling foolish. She expected that he'd be gazing at her with a look of disdain, but when she lifted her face, there was only understanding written in his features.

"It is a great weight off of my shoulders to hear that you are well. That is all that is important. This road in particular is seldom traveled, and these farmlands stretch on for miles. It is likely that you would not have come across a home for a while yet. Please, allow me to help you up into my carriage."

When Eleanor accepted, the duke nodded toward the footman, who loaded her trunk. The duke held out his hand. After a moment's pause, she placed her hand in his—warm through his glove. Sparks seemed to run through her fingers, traveling her arm from the touch.

Determined to ignore the odd sensation, she stepped into the carriage and slipped her hand from the duke's. She murmured a "thank you" and sat on one of the red-cushioned benches, arranging her skirts around her in order to distract herself from her scattered thoughts. The seats were covered in a soft leather, and the windows were flanked by tasseled curtains of the same red color, not a thread out of place.

After checking with the footman that her luggage was secure, the duke hopped into the carriage and sat across from her. He tapped on the roof, and the vehicle edged forward. He seemed contemplative, looking out the window at the fields passing by, brightened with only the last sliver of sunlight.

She studied his features, noticing for the first time his broad shoulders and tall height as well as his somber demeanor. She had seen a hint of it when they'd first crossed paths but had dismissed it as a trick of the light. He seemed sad, the kind of sad where one passes the days alone with their own thoughts, not daring to speak them aloud, and she had the greatest desire to lift his spirits and free him from whatever was troubling him. It was a sudden thought—one that was absurd—though Eleanor had a difficult time forgetting it.

Perhaps she could help him in some way. After all, she knew what it was like to be in pain. To be well-acquainted with lonely days. She would have to be a governess to his niece, but that didn't mean that she couldn't also seek to help him heal his wounds, whatever they might be. No one deserved to be in pain. And helping the duke would keep her mind off of her own troubles.

There were more than a few problems with this plan, however. For one, she'd not interact with him often—seeing as she'd be busy watching his niece. Then there was a good chance he'd not wish to speak to her at all. But...however much or little, she'd get to spend time with this man across from her —this man who so intrigued her!

Eleanor settled back into her seat, her pulse thrumming through her.

If she flew too close to the sun...

~

Thoughts flooded Edmund's mind. It was as if millions of raindrops were falling and joining together to form a raging river with a strong current, and if he wasn't careful, he might get swept away.

The woman across from him was at the forefront of them all, curls of her dark hair framing her face in a way that reminded him of the fine portraits at The British Museum. He still had a hard time believing Miss Clairbridge was to be his niece's governess.

When he had left London after his brief visit, he had thought that their paths would never cross again. Now she was to be living in his home, and he would see her every day. There was something about her that drew Edmund in.

He wanted to get to know her better. He wanted to know of how she came to be a governess, about her family, even her favorite books. He longed to hear her laugh. When he had handed her into the carriage, he had experienced a strange warming sensation, as though his hand had been in front of a comfortable fire. When she released his grasp, she had taken the warmth with her. And that was what worried him.

Miss Clairbridge was young for a governess, and unexpected in both looks and demeanor, but as long as she proved able to teach his niece, he would be content. While his niece would benefit from a cheerful young woman teaching her, Edmund had not prepared himself to handle the situation he was currently in.

He'd imagined the Miss Clairbridge that had answered his advertisement to be slope-backed and dour-face, perhaps with a few moles and arthritic hands. She'd smell of his grandmother's old rose perfume, and she'd still wear buckled shoes. This Miss Clairbridge, appeared quite to advantage...when he allowed himself to look at her.

He shook those troubling thoughts from his head, only for them to be replaced with even worse thoughts as the carriage hit a small divot in the road which rustled them about.

His mother and father had died in a carriage just like this one.

Edmund did not fear carriages or riding in them, but being inside of one never failed to make his heart ache. It had been five years since they had passed, and he was still troubled by thoughts of the accident daily. His mind often strayed to the tragic way they'd been taken from him—a difficult thing to combat when he'd witnessed the aftermath.

Splintered wood and broken wheels—the memories were as clear as the glass of a windowpane and just as sharp as the ridged shard of one. He bit the inside of his cheek, the tinny taste of blood there. Rose was all he had left.

As the sun finally set, leaving the fields in a veil of darkness, a silent tear rolled down his cheek. He wiped it away almost as soon as it appeared. Hopefully, in the shadows of the carriage, his new governess wouldn't discern his pain.

So enveloped in her thoughts was Eleanor that she almost didn't notice when the carriage rumbled along the drive toward Ivy Grange. As the estate came into view, she drew a quick breath. It was stunning.

The windows were aglow—the warm light coming through them contrasting the growing darkness outside. The stone facade was a pleasant sandy color, and the stairs leading to the front door were grand and wide, guiding her eyes up to towering columns that supported a carved overhang, intricate beyond belief. Elegant stone statues of what appeared to be Greek gods and goddesses lined the roof, with several of them welcoming visitors to the entrance with outstretched arms and raised hands. The carriage slowed to a stop in front of the stairs, and the footman helped Eleanor down the steps.

The duke alighted behind her and instructed the footman to take Eleanor's trunk to her room. Eleanor took in the massive building before her, wings stretching outward on her left and right. The butler opened the front doors. He was a middle-aged man of medium stature—not nearly as old as Crand—with a ruddy face and greying hair.

"Welcome home, Your Grace." The butler bowed and gave a kind smile to both the duke and Eleanor.

Her employer gestured for her to go ahead of him through the front door and followed her, pausing just inside. The entry hall was beyond anything she had ever seen. A great chandelier hung from the middle of the high ceiling, and a large staircase at the end of the foyer promised even more to see, its carved banisters resembling welcoming arms. The carpenters must have been skilled, indeed.

A dark-green rug stretched from the doors to the staircase, only half covering the gleaming cream-colored stone floor. Marble. Large alcoves lined the hall, carved from more marble and housing additional statues of ancient Greek deities, large gilded candelabras set between them. The light scents of beeswax and tea leaves greeted Eleanor's nose. Awestruck, she absorbed every detail and sensation her mind could contain. Endless exploration would be needed to truly take it all in.

"Thank you, Prumb. This is Miss Clairbridge, the new governess." He gestured toward Eleanor, who gave a bright smile to the older man.

"It's a pleasure to meet you, Prumb."

Prumb bowed and smiled. He reminded her of her own butler, and she'd liked him the instant she'd laid eyes on him. "The pleasure is mine, Miss Clairbridge."

Just then, a stout woman with full cheeks and grey hair bustled into the foyer, chest heaving. She made her way over to stand next to Prumb, bobbing a quick curtsy before looking at His Grace with wide eyes.

"John told me you'd found her, and here she is, bless her!" The woman's voice was breathless but kind. She turned warm eyes to Eleanor. "I'm Mrs. Brinder, dearie. The housekeeper." She flicked her gaze back to His Grace. "Would you like me to show her to her quarters, Your Grace? She must be quite fatigued after all that walking!"

The duke twisted his mouth to the side for a moment before nodding. "Please do, Mrs. Brinder. Would you like a dinner tray sent up to you, Miss Clairbridge?"

Eleanor gave the duke an appreciative smile. "Yes, please, Your Grace. Thank you."

"Of course. Please do not hesitate to ask should you need anything." With that, he bowed, turned on his heel, and walked down the hall away from them.

Strange that the loss of his presence should be so palpable.

Mrs. Brinder brushed her hands down her apron. "Please, come with me, miss."

Eleanor followed Mrs. Brinder as she climbed the marble staircase, admiring every painting, vase, decoration, and detail on her way. She'd have to look at the rooms in her free time. Given how opulent the halls were, Eleanor could only imagine what the rooms were like.

Mrs. Brinder led her down a long corridor, decorated with gilded landscape paintings. Eleanor wasn't sure she'd be able to find her way back to the foyer, considering how her attentions were focused so little on where she was headed. After what seemed far too long, Mrs. Brinder stopped in front of a polished wooden door, opening it for Eleanor and stepping aside. "This is your room, dearie. I will send a maid up to you with your tray. If you have any questions at any time, I'll be happy to answer them."

Eleanor stepped inside with a small gasp. She'd never seen anything so fine. There was a beautiful fireplace on one side, with a fire already warming the room. On the other side of the room sat a small bed, a comfortable-looking quilt covering it. In front of her were windows, a polished desk placed to the side. Whoever had decorated this room had done a tasteful job of it. A large wardrobe stood against the wall facing the windows, and a mirror and table sat next to the bed. A side table with legs carved in the current style held a flared candelabra, five unlit candles upon it. Eleanor's luggage was already in her room, placed at the foot of the bed.

"Thank you, Mrs. Brinder. Is the nursery next door?"

The woman nodded and smiled, eyes wrinkling at their corners as a fond expression softened her well-lined face. "Yes, and Miss Rose is very eager to meet you." The woman pointed to a door in the corner of the room Eleanor had overlooked. "This door leads directly into the nursery, and the schoolroom is right down the hall, on your left." Her tone was warm and almost grandmotherly. Obviously, Mrs. Brinder cared a lot for the duke's niece.

Eleanor couldn't help being eager to meet the girl as well. "Perfect. Thank you again, Mrs. Brinder." The woman turned to leave, but Eleanor stopped her again. "Oh, Mrs. Brinder! Had the duke mentioned what I'm to do tomorrow? Will I meet his niece in the morning?"

The housekeeper tapped her chin with a finger, propping the other hand on her hip. "He hasn't told me, dear. He wishes to remain undisturbed for the rest of this evening, but I'll send Fanny to you in the morning with word of what you're to do."

The woman curtsied and left Eleanor to unpack her trunk. The duke was so very kind and understanding. She hadn't expected to be given time to rest after her exhausting travel, but he had given it, regardless. Although Eleanor wasn't well-versed in governessing—truly, not versed at all—she'd assumed she'd have to ready the schoolroom for the next day. Perhaps she'd need to organize books and make note of what supplies were needed. It seemed that was not expected of her—not yet, anyway.

Eleanor opened her trunk—a rather small brown case with brass latches and a leather handle—and began to unpack what few items she had been able to fit inside. She dug through her shabby dresses, looking for an item in particular. When her hand met the cool greeting of the chain, she closed her fingers around it and pulled it from its confines of fabric, opening her fingers to study the golden locket that lay in her palm. It was oval-shaped, the shining face reflecting the firelight. The locket was simple in design, but Eleanor would never wear a different locket—no matter how intricate.

Before she'd left her home, she'd taken care in tucking it away to keep it safe—though she wore it every day at home. Eleanor had heard talk about highwaymen and how many of them lurked around the outskirts of London, and though the chances of the mail coach being accosted were low—given that those riding in it tended not to have much of value—she hadn't wanted to tempt fate.

She flipped the locket over and read the inscription on the

back, a mournful memory attempting to push into her mind. She brushed her thumb over the words engraved there.

> To my dearest Ruby,
> My greatest joy.
> Love, Papa

She pried it open with reverence, greeted by her parents' smiling faces painted inside. She had never been away from home as she currently was, without her family or friends to keep her company.

How she already missed home. Mama's sweet face, the house where every floorboard and every piece of wallpaper held the memory of Father.

After taking another moment to study the miniatures of her parents, she closed the locket and held the necklace to her heart.

Dear God, please grant me strength to see me through these difficult times. I must help Mama. I must remain dedicated and determined. For my sake and hers.

Eleanor raised the locket to her lips and kissed it, sealing her prayer, before slipping the fine gold chain around her neck and continuing to unpack. She hung her few worn dresses in the wardrobe and stepped to the small table with the mirror. Heavens, but she looked like a corpse risen, with those dark circles under her eyes and her unkempt hair, which stuck out in odd directions.

A light tap sounded from the door.

She turned to face it. "Come in."

A maid came bustling into the room, a tray of food in her arms.

"Good evenin', miss!" A lilting Scottish accent colored the servant's words. Her eyes were kind. "I've got yer supper here for ya. Ye're in for a real treat. Cook made roasted pheasant t'night."

The maid was younger than Eleanor, perhaps about twenty, and had a head of bright red hair. Freckles dotted her cheeks and nose, and she wore a large smile. Her gaiety was infectious, and before Eleanor knew it, she was grinning back at the girl.

"That sounds delicious. Thank you so much..." Eleanor furrowed her eyebrows as the realization came to her that she did not know the girl's name.

"Oh! Forgot me manners. Me name's Frances Guildon, but ev'ryone calls me Fanny. 'Tis a pleasure t' meet ya, miss." Fanny bobbed a quick curtsy and placed the dinner tray on Eleanor's bed.

Eleanor curtsied as well—unsure of the formalities now that she was a governess—with a smile on her face. "The pleasure is mine, Fanny. I'm Eleanor Clairbridge, the governess, but I suppose you probably already knew that. You can call me Eleanor."

Fanny scurried over to her and grabbed Eleanor's hands. "We're so glad t' have ya here, miss. Ye're all we've been able t' talk about since we's heard ye were comin'." Fanny seemed to radiate excitement, bouncing on the balls of her feet.

"I'm certainly glad to be here. I hope the staff haven't gone to too much trouble in preparing my room. I am no one special, Fanny—only the governess, after all."

Fanny shook her head. "Ya might think so, miss, but ye are part of t' household now. One of our own!"

Eleanor's heart lightened. In London, she had listened to governesses talk of being lonely—too above the servants to be accepted below stairs and too below the employers to be paid any attention. It seemed, however, as though things at Ivy Grange were different. Both her employer and the servants were welcoming.

"Thank you, Fanny. It might sound a silly thing, but I was

quite worried that I would be shut out from below stairs." Eleanor gave a small deprecating smile.

Fanny squeezed her hands in reassurance. "Ye don't have t' worry 'bout that 'ere, miss. I can already tell th't we'll be fast friends. Give me a holler if ye be needin' anythin'."

As swiftly as she came, Fanny left the room in a tornado of fiery hair.

After Eleanor had eaten supper, water was brought up for her bath. She scrubbed and soaked, then changed into a night-gown, braiding her hair and tying it off with a frayed piece of ribbon. She crawled into bed and drew the covers around her, sleep already descending like a quiet fog. As she gave in to its pull, she dreamt of her sweet parents, well-sprung carriages, and a pair of sad green eyes.

CHAPTER 5

$\mathcal{E}$leanor woke in the morning to the entrance of Fanny, who none-too-quietly carried a breakfast tray.

"Ye're up! I've brought ye some breakfast. Mrs. Brinder, tol' me t' tell ye that 'is Grace wants t' see ye in 'is study after ye've eaten." Fanny placed the tray laden with a bowl of porridge and a steaming cup of tea on the bed and grinned. "Ye must be excited for yer first day."

Eleanor yawned, accustomed to London hours as she was, and returned Fanny's smile with a half smile of her own. "Yes, I am. Thank you, Fanny." She began to eat her porridge but paused when Fanny crossed the room and threw open the curtains.

Eleanor had the perfect view of the gardens, flowers of all colors lining its stone pathways, their blooms lush and bright. She could almost smell the sweet fragrance that surely filled the outdoor air. How absolutely lovely. Perhaps she might be able to take a stroll in the gardens later.

Eleanor loved the small garden that lay hidden behind her London home. As a child, she had spent many days with her mother there, listening to her speak of the different varieties of plants as well as enjoying the occasional flitting of passing dragonflies and the soft hum of the hovering bees. The sun would warm their backs as they sat on the old stone bench with its charming mottled color.

She turned her attention to her porridge and swallowed one spoonful after another, not wanting to keep the duke waiting.

Eleanor then washed with cool water from the jug Fanny had left with her breakfast tray. The white porcelain had been painted with the image of delicate garden roses. After washing her face, she buttoned up the back of her gown with deft fingers. The fabric was a pale pink color and faded with wear. Despite this, it was among the best of what she owned.

She mustn't be late. No matter how kind the duke might be, he was still her employer and could easily turn her out. Wasting no time, she brushed and coiled her hair into a modest bun at the back of her head.

The moment she stood in front of her door, she peered down the quiet hallway on both sides. Which way to the duke's study? Had she entered her room from the right or the left?

A maid exited a nearby room, a metal bucket in her hand. Eleanor hastened over to her. The servant, a slight woman with dark hair secured in a tight knot, widened her eyes and startled.

"I'm terribly sorry. Could you perhaps tell me where the study is located?" Eleanor's nerves flared, and the prickle of tension touched her shoulders. She did not want to be late. The maid nodded and pointed to her right.

"Go down this hall, and there's a staircase on yer left." Her voice was quiet but clear. "After you go down the stairs, take another left down the hall. The study's the third door on the right."

After murmuring a breathless "thank you," Eleanor raced through the corridor. She almost tumbled down the carpeted stairs as she descended them, and when she finally stood outside the study door, she had to take a moment to compose herself.

Breathe. She inhaled a deep breath through her nose and exhaled through her mouth. She had just raised up her hand to knock when the study door swung open. The duke stood before her, eyes wide.

"Miss Clairbridge," he said in an amused tone. He stepped back into the study and held the door open for her, gesturing her inside. "Please, come in."

Eleanor curtsied, her heartbeat picking up its pace in his presence. His navy coat complemented his golden silk waistcoat, and his cravat was tied in a simple style. Though his clothing appeared neat and tidy, his coppery hair was somewhat tousled—as though he'd just run his hand through it—and Eleanor fought the unusual urge to reach out and touch it.

"Your Grace." Her eyes were eager to seek out his, but she forced them to drop to the floor as she entered the study. As she passed him by, the warm scent of spice emanating from his person grabbed hold of her senses for a moment, and she paused in her steps.

What was happening to her? She shook herself from her daze. Hopefully, he hadn't witnessed her folly.

He left the door open and moved around his desk, motioning for her to sit in one of the ornately carved chairs facing it. He waited for her to take a seat before he settled into the leather armchair behind the desk, clasping his hands and resting them on the wooden surface in front of him.

"Thank you for meeting with me, Miss Clairbridge. I wanted to speak with you of Rose's education and your expected duties as her governess."

Eleanor nodded, and the duke continued, his pleasant voice washing over her. "I would like for Rose's schooling to be daily from nine o'clock in the morning to three o'clock in the afternoon. After her lessons are finished, you may spend the rest of the day as you please."

He ran his hand through his hair, giving an explanation to its earlier mussed state and proving her guess to be right. "I would also ask that you have dinners with us in order to help Rose learn proper table manners and etiquette. It's unusual, I know, for a child to dine among adults, but Rose...well...she reminds me of her parents." He cleared his throat, abruptly changing the subject. "You will not be expected to teach on Sundays, of course, and you are welcome to join us when we go to church."

Eleanor's eyes widened. She hadn't expected to have so much time to herself. She also hadn't considered the duke would wish for her to dine with them, as she was so below him in station. She swallowed, absorbing it all.

The duke paused for a moment before releasing a long breath and rubbing a hand over his clean-shaven jaw. "Additionally, I know that it is not common for proper young ladies to learn and study particular subjects such as the sciences and mathematics, yet I would like for her to learn of them. For Rose to be knowledgeable of the world and to have a well-rounded education. I refuse to hold her back simply on the basis of her being female, and I know that her parents would be of the same opinion if they were still on this earth."

His eyes—which had drifted to the desk before him—rose again to meet Eleanor's, an almost imploring look in their depths. "Are these subjects that you would be willing to teach to her? From this list of accomplishments and your own explanation of your studies written here, it is obvious to me that you are incredibly qualified." He gestured to a few papers before him, and Eleanor recognized her own handwriting. It didn't look as neat now as it had when she'd written it, and that abominable list of accomplishment made her want to wrinkle her nose, but excitement bubbled within her at his words.

"Yes, Your Grace." Admiration for the man surged through her veins at his unexpected words. He was already proving to be unlike most men of her acquaintance. Not that there were many, but Mr. Phips was quite vocal about his beliefs.

In current society, the education of women was seen as unimportant or unnecessary—at least the subjects of the maths and sciences were—and, while Eleanor enjoyed embroidery as much as the next young lady, she'd enjoyed learning about these subjects most—particularly science. Her education in science had allowed Eleanor to be able to speak with her father of different plants and understand what he was describing when he told her of specific types of flora.

He, of course, had also taught her much of what she understood relating to science—as had her mother—but her education from her governess had helped to fill in further pieces of information.

Eleanor lifted her chin. "I would love to teach her of the subjects so often forgone in a young girl's education. I believe that everyone deserves to study what they wish, regardless of whether they are a man or woman."

The duke nodded in approval, and Eleanor could almost swear that a flicker of respect had crossed his face. "Rose may be young, but she is very intelligent and loves to learn. She especially likes nature, so perhaps you might incorporate that into your lessons. If you are in need of any supplies, please do not hesitate to ask. Do you have any questions?"

"Y-You would like me to attend church with you?" She met his eyes finally.

His Grace gave a hint of a smile. "Yes," He drummed his fingers against the desk. "I believe it would help Rose if you were there. You could explain the sermons to her and answer any questions she may have."

Eleanor dipped her chin to illustrate her understanding, bolstering her determination. "Right. Certainly, Your Grace."

The duke's gaze shifted to something behind her. She turned her head to look at what had captured his attention. A few blond ringlets peeked out from behind the door frame to the study.

"Rosie," the duke said in an amused tone. "You may come in."

A young girl—presumably Eleanor's charge—poked her head into view, looking unrepentant at having been caught eavesdropping. A broad smile stretched over her rosy cheeks, revealing two adorable dimples. She moved from her hiding spot, taking a few small steps into the room. Her dainty black slippers contrasted with her spotless white dress, and she bounced on her feet in a typical childlike fashion—all excitement.

She paused and took a moment to study Eleanor before seeming to make up her mind. The girl rushed over to her. Before Eleanor could blink an eye, Rose had wrapped her little arms around her—at least as much of her as she could reach around the chair Eleanor sat in.

Eleanor fluttered her lashes for a moment before enfolding the girl in a return embrace. She hadn't expected this warm welcome—though the servants *had* said that Rose was excited—but was glad for it.

Perhaps being a governess wouldn't be as difficult as she imagined, especially considering that she'd be teaching this little angel. As she pulled away from the embrace, Rose held onto her hand in a tight grasp.

Eleanor hazarded a glance at the duke as a grand smile brightened his face. She took in a sharp breath, having never seen him smile so before. It made him even more handsome, his eyes crinkling at the sides, and his cheek revealing a dimple of his own. The smile, however beautiful, didn't last long. It fled as if someone had blown out the flame of a candle, leaving a whisper of smoke in its wake. What could have doused it?

He cleared his throat, his expression now one of reserved politeness. "Rosie, this is Miss Clairbridge, your new governess. Miss Clairbridge, meet my niece, Rose."

Rose beamed up at Eleanor and performed a curtsy, unsteady on her feet as she did so.

"It's nice to meet you, Miss Clairbridge." The girl grinned, clearly proud of herself, and Eleanor couldn't help but laugh.

She stood and returned the curtsy. "The pleasure is all mine, Miss Rose."

The duke looked at Rose with a small smile, then turned his attention back to Eleanor. He stood and pulled her to the side of the room, leaving Rose to look at the shelf of books lining the wall near his desk.

"Miss Clairbridge," he murmured, tilting his head about an inch toward her. Her stomach fluttered at his nearness. "Rose knows much already for her age. I've taught her a bit myself through reading with her in the evenings, although there is much for her to learn yet. Fortunately, I can already tell the two of you will get along splendidly—something that greatly pleases me." He turned his head to look at his niece—the girl having moved her attention from the bookshelf to her uncle's desk—with his eyebrows furrowing in an almost unnoticeable dip. "I often worry about her, and while I attempt to devote as much of my time to her as possible, it can be difficult to do so with a growing list of tasks regarding the manor and my title, so I thank you."

"I'm sure it will be my pleasure, Your Grace. She seems like a sweet young thing."

He flicked his eyes to Eleanor once more, his expression lightening. "Your presence will provide her with an education and good company during the midday hours when the manor might otherwise be staid. Ivy Grange has been quiet since..." He paused for a moment, eyes clouding. "Since the deaths of her parents. Another person living in the manor can only bring joy. To us all."

Like the hydra in Greek myth, when Eleanor was given one answer, two more questions took its place. In this case, three. What happened to Rose's parents? Why wasn't the duke married—or perhaps he was, and his wife was away? Did he have other family?

Eleanor searched his face in the hope that something might give her answers to her abundance of questions. Alas, she could not see anything more than that same hue of sadness she'd glimpsed before. "I will do my utmost to provide good companionship. Being an only child myself, I know how necessary it is to have friends in the vicinity."

To them both. Rose wasn't the only one who needed a friend.

The duke cleared his throat. "Rosie, perhaps you might give Miss Clairbridge a tour of the estate now? I know you've been looking forward to it."

Rosie nodded with fervor and was quick to tug Eleanor from the room, leaving her barely enough time to curtsy to the duke—and certainly not enough to unravel the knot that was His Noble Enigma.

~

For the next few hours, Rose showed Eleanor the manor. All the while, the girl had a contagious grin on her face and a lightness of step. Each room seemed even grander than the last. Flowers decorated the hallways, set in beautiful vases on top of ornate tables, their legs carved in straight lines and coming to tapered ends. Luxurious furniture filled the rooms, balancing the space and providing comfortable areas to gather for both guests and family members.

Each window they passed displayed a gorgeous view of the

grounds, whether it be lush gardens or winding stone paths. There was not a speck of dust in sight, and everything was in perfect condition. The stark contrast of the place to her own house with its dusty windowsills and worn furniture made her sigh—perhaps in a more dejected manner than she'd like to admit.

Eleanor didn't have time to lament, as Rose soon dragged her outside toward what appeared to be the stables. Eleanor hadn't yet seen the outside—except for the evening when she'd first arrived—and she gazed all around, taking in the views of this heaven on earth. The large expanse of lawn had been separated into sections with rows of bushes acting as borders. In one section grew a flower garden, the plants surrounding a grand statue of a woman holding what seemed to be a bunch of wheat in her arms.

In another, there were large walls of shrubbery cut in angular shapes. A maze? A few of her friends had them at their country estates. One summer at the Witherbys', she had nearly gone into one, but she'd been too cowardly then, as she was now. Neither sister—Teresa nor Eliza—had minded, nor gone ahead to desert her. Then, she'd still had some true friends left.

After that, Eliza and Teresa had been so busy with the season's events that they'd hardly had time to call on Eleanor. She didn't blame them, for they had their own lives to attend to —and they still sent letters. The letters were infrequent, of course, but she cherished them as a miser cherished gold. Her friends had been a boon to her at that dreadful ball. She frowned.

Eleanor was brought back to the present as the distant call of a robin sounded through the air. Vibrant grass cushioned her feet in a thick carpet of green while the sun warmed her through, a light breeze playing with her hair as she followed Rose across the lawn. She hadn't known she would be going outside—Rose had said they'd be doing so rather suddenly—

and so hadn't worn a bonnet, but she took a moment to enjoy the feel of the sun on her upturned face, a luxury she granted herself as often as possible. Mama always made sure Eleanor wore a bonnet to keep freckles at bay, but Eleanor much preferred the free feeling she got when she went outside without one. As they arrived at the elongated brick building that was the stables, the sweet smell of sunbaked hay filled her nose.

"Come in with me!" Rose skipped inside, and Eleanor increased her pace, lifting her skirts as high as she could while maintaining her dignity.

She followed Rose past the line of stalls, each occupied by a different horse. The sun flooded through the windows in rays of light, illuminating the particles of dust in the air and the freshly swept floor of the building. They stopped in front of a black mare which stuck her snout out of her stall to see what the commotion was about.

Rose reached up on her tiptoes to pet the mare's muzzle, placing a small foot on one of the wooden slats of the stall in an attempt to get closer. "This is Blackberry." She spoke more quietly than before, as though in awe of the horse. "Uncle Edmund says I can ride her when I get older. She's young too."

Eleanor reached out a tentative hand and ran it down Blackberry's long mane. The horse had a tender air about her and nickered at Eleanor's touch. Then the horse in the next stall poked her head out. This mare was a light-grey color with white speckles dotting her abdomen and legs. Her muzzle was darker, reminding Eleanor of slates on a rooftop. The horse had a gentle look in her eyes, and Eleanor was immediately drawn to her.

"What's the name of this horse?"

Still caressing Blackberry, Rose turned her beribboned head toward Eleanor. "That's Snowdrop. I like her too."

Eleanor stepped closer to Snowdrop and raised her hand

toward the mare's snout. She moved in a slow fashion, not wanting to startle the sweet creature. Before she had touched Snowdrop, the horse pressed her muzzle into Eleanor's hand. Eleanor couldn't help but chuckle. What a gentle thing. She skimmed Snowdrop's mane with her hand, the hair soft beneath her palm. The horse's nostrils flared as she released a slow exhale, seeming to let the rest of her guard down as she relaxed into Eleanor's touch.

Eleanor hadn't ridden in years now. She found herself missing it. Would she be permitted to ride with Rose? With... His Grace?

CHAPTER 6

$\mathcal{A}$s Edmund's study held a view of the stables, he couldn't help but notice when Rose—and Miss Clairbridge—headed toward it. Miss Clairbridge was radiant, her face upturned toward the sun, locks of her hair coming loose from their pins and swaying in the gentle breeze.

Then there was Rose. Sweet Rose. Her blond ringlets shone like golden thread in the sunlight. She tugged on Miss Clairbridge's hand, urging her to hurry.

The indulgent Miss Clairbridge smiled and laughed, and Edmund wished he could hear it. He had been granted the chance earlier, and it had sounded like the movement of water over stones in a lively brook. A happy bubble of sound. It had washed over him like the first rays of the morning sun. He had been so relieved earlier when he'd seen how excited Grace was at meeting Miss Clairbridge—and the woman's subsequent reaction to his niece.

He'd been more carefree than he had been in some time—a long time. It hadn't been difficult to tell that the two of them would get along well, and when a strange feeling of warmth had spread throughout his chest, reality had dawned, crashing into him before tumbling to the ground, along with his smile. Edmund had known—and knew now—that whatever that feeling had been couldn't be good.

He had never experienced a feeling like it, but it was familiar to him all the same. Hours spent reading countless collections of verse now sprang to the forefront of his thoughts, memories of reading poems that included fond words and the telling of hearts entwined. A poem by Christopher Marlowe snuck past his mind's barriers.

> It lies not in our power to love or hate,
> For will in us is overruled by fate.
> When two are stripped, long ere the course
>   begin,
> We wish that one should love, the other win;
> And one especially do we affect
> Of two gold ingots, like in each respect:
> The reason no man knows; let it suffice
> What we behold is censured by our eyes.
> Where both deliberate, the love is slight:
> Who ever loved, that loved not at first sight?

Oh no. No, no, no. Edmund wouldn't allow himself to feel anything more than appreciation and respect for Miss Clairbridge. After all, they weren't well-acquainted, she was his niece's governess, and he wouldn't let himself get attached to anyone ever again. He had lost too many people in his life already to go through the torturous pain of it once more—which would be inevitable if he were to fall in love. Indeed, he'd marry Miss Pottan soon enough, and with that match, his heart would never risk being torn. After all, he'd hardly finished sewing it back together.

∽

he day flew by as a bird on wing and, before long, it was time for Edmund to ready himself for dinner. He left his study and walked toward his chambers, his mind still clouded with thoughts of his parents and the feeling he'd experienced that morning in the study—the feeling that threatened to destroy all of his meticulous plans for the future. He strode down the hallway, portraits of his ancestors and family watching him, the carpet beneath his feet muffling his footsteps. Edmund made a valiant effort to keep his thoughts off of his niece's governess.

What had Cook prepared for dinner that night? It was sure to be delicious, whatever it ended up being. Would Miss Clairbridge like it?

He paused in his steps, his brow furrowed.

She was only his employee, nothing more.

Edmund continued walking, not paying much heed to where he headed. He had to reply to Mr. Benson's letter—which he supposed he'd do after dinner—and then he'd need to open Lendin's response. Maybe then he'd be able to read in the library. The new b—

Edmund turned a corner and collided with something soft—or rather, someone. He had run straight into the person he was trying so hard not to think about—Miss Clairbridge. He grasped her arms in an attempt to steady her, her skin smooth beneath his hands. Just as he had when he had first run into her, he caught the calming scent of lavender, and his mind descended into a pleasant—yet dangerous—haze. In addition to lavender, the comforting scents of hay and sunshine clung to her. Her entire presence seemed to throw him off balance.

Shaking that thought from his mind, he focused on her wellbeing. "Miss Clairbridge, are you all right? I'm terribly sorry to have bumped into you. I fear that I was quite diverted with my thoughts."

She blew a stray strand of hair from her face and grinned, sending Edmund's heart to beating a fast-paced rhythm. "No harm done, Your Grace. I am perfectly well, just a bit surprised, is all."

Edmund was caught off guard by her sudden grin and airy demeanor, having never witnessed a proper society woman act thusly. Quite a few of the women he'd interacted with outside of his family were aloof at best and arrogant at worst. And was she not in the least discommoded at his mistake? Miss Fottan would have been. Was Miss Clairbridge singular in her behavior, or had his interactions with other women been the exceptions? Remembering himself, he quickly dropped his hands from her arms, his fingers reluctant to let go.

"Good. Very good. Good. Well...I suppose I shall see you at dinner, then." He bowed and strode down the hall with hurried steps, thoughts still disorganized. Once inside his room, the oaken door shut behind him, he exhaled.

What was he doing? Running away from Rosie's governess? She wouldn't harm a fly! At least he didn't think she would. Edmund sat in the generously cushioned chair near the fireplace and sighed, placing his elbows on his knees and his head in his hands.

Why must she always smile like that? Every time she did, he felt lightheaded. What madness had descended upon him? He didn't remember William Blake ever mentioning delirium in his love poems. It was always warmth and lightness of step that the poets mentioned—never those lesser-lauded symptoms like contracting ague. He arose from his seat, his mind a whirl, and called for his valet to help him prepare for dinner. Maybe that man could help him discern the mysterious symptoms that arose whenever Miss Clairbridge was near—or prepare a tisane.

❧

*E*leanor stood in front of the wardrobe in her room, trying to decide which of her raggedy dresses would be the best option to wear to dinner. Was she even expected to change for dinner? She shrugged to herself and picked out a light-blue gown, one of the better dresses she had brought from home.

She'd do best to err on the side of caution. She'd be sitting at a duke's table, after all. Eleanor changed out of her day dress and into the old gown, sitting herself at the table and mirror. The gown's long sleeves helped to stave off the evening's chill, and the neckline was modest, as was expected of a governess.

After pulling the pins from her hair, Eleanor brushed out any tangles it had gleaned throughout the day. She braided her hair with deft movements and twisted it into a bun, securing it with the pins she had taken out and leaving a few curls to frame her face.

"It will have to do."

Eleanor had had practice enough styling her hair when she'd been back in London—lacking a lady's maid to help her or do it for her—but was still not very skilled at the more difficult coifs. She picked up a delicate hair comb from the table and guided it into the bun at the back of her head. Her mother had given it to her before Eleanor had left home, and she now found herself drawing comfort from it. It had small metal flowers on the curve and two tiny red gems set into it. It was exquisite.

She tucked the pendant of her locket into her bodice so only the chain could be seen around her neck and, standing, she smoothed out her skirts and glanced at herself in the mirror one last time before leaving the room. As she met her own eyes in the mirror, she couldn't help being reminded of the disaster that had been her first and only ball.

Eleanor shuddered at the memory. That had been the day

when her confidence had officially fled, just as swiftly as she had fled from the ballroom at the Witherbys' townhouse. She still couldn't understand why Miss Pottan had always seemed intent on harming her, but it hadn't been the first time, nor was it the last. That woman had been one of the contributing factors in how Eleanor now viewed herself. She, among others, had convinced Eleanor she was undesirable. Someone with little worth.

Eleanor sighed. At least here, she was far away from that woman and Mr. Phips.

CHAPTER 7

$\mathcal{E}$leanor glided downstairs, knowing her way a little better now that she'd had a tour, and headed toward the drawing room. On her way down the hall, she passed Fanny, whose eyes widened.

"Oh, Ellie! Ye look so pretty!"

Eleanor smiled at the compliment. "Thank you, Fanny. However, I'm sure that I do not compare to any fresh-faced debutante."

Fanny put her hands on her hips and raised an eyebrow at Eleanor. "Why would ye want t' look like that lot? All I've seen of 'em are fake smiles and too much blinkin'. Ye have a true smile and a kind face. That's worth more than what any amount of money can buy ye."

Overcome with gratitude at Fanny's wise words, Eleanor pulled her into a tight embrace. "Thank you, Fanny. You're a veritable angel."

Fanny hugged Eleanor back with equal strength. "As are ye, Ellie. Now, don't be late to dinner on my account." Fanny grinned and shooed Eleanor toward the drawing room door, where a footman stood at attention.

He opened the door for her and gestured her inside the resplendent room, decorated with a crimson-colored carpet and drapes. Polished furniture had been placed about the room with golden-green cushions showing no signs of wear. The wallpaper was of the same color, and gilt-framed portraits hung on the walls, with some of the subjects looking similar to the duke, especially the portrait of a man with green eyes. He wore a starched cravat around his throat with a ruby stickpin, a silver waistcoat under his black coat. Who was he?

When she walked in, her employer was standing in front of the fire, his back to her. His hands were clasped behind him, and he seemed to be deep in thought. He wore a burgundy coat, his tan breeches contrasting with the dark color. A crisp white cravat encircled his throat, and his hair was styled with what Eleanor imagined had been a Herculean effort, given how meticulous it was. The duke's valet deserved his position, it seemed.

She stepped farther into the room, and the footman announced her entrance with dutiful clarity. "Your Grace." She curtsied as the door behind her closed.

He swiveled around, eyes wide, then bowed. "Miss Clairbridge."

She clasped her hands in front of her and stared at the crackling fire. She could feel his gaze on her.

"You look quite beautiful." He spoke softly—so softly that she wasn't sure she was meant to hear his words.

Eleanor tentatively raised her eyes to meet his. Was that a flicker of admiration in them? Eleanor could feel her cheeks warm, and her heart fluttered, a strange feeling—one unfamiliar, yet not unpleasant.

Perhaps she was still Ruby, after all.

"Thank you, Your Grace." She glanced around the room. What else could she say? He was dressed in quite the dashing manner himself, but it would be improper for her to say so.

Eleanor worked for him and could not risk losing her job. Too much depended on it. Eleanor's income was the sole thing keeping her mother and herself off of the streets. "Your Grace, how long has Miss Rose been under your care?"

The duke's expression changed as he turned his eyes to one of the portraits on the wall, his mind appearing to be in a faraway place. He propped one hand on his hip and brushed the other hand through his hair, sighing.

"Five years," he responded, a somber look on his face. There was something so heartbreaking in those two words—maybe it had been the way he'd said them—and Eleanor's own heart ached at the pain there. It was tangible in the space between them.

Before Eleanor could respond, the door to the drawing room was pushed open by Rose, her nurse following a few feet behind her. The nurse bobbed a deep curtsy, and Rose followed suit a moment later, skipping over to the duke and wrapping her arms around his waist in an embrace before rushing over to Eleanor to do the same. The nurse slipped from the room, having done her duties.

"Uncle Edmund! Miss Clairbridge!" Rose beamed up at them, her blond curls bouncing with her excited movements.

The duke's mournful expression disappeared as he smiled down at her, a warm look that Eleanor had seen her own father give her before he had passed replacing it. Her heart swelled at the obvious affection the duke had for his niece.

"Rosie! How are you, dearest? Did you have an enjoyable day with Miss Clairbridge?"

Eleanor grinned at the duke's words, spoken with genuine interest and attentiveness.

Rose nodded, and her large smile spread even farther across her dimpled cheeks. "I had a spel..." Rose paused, cocking her head and scrunching up her nose. "Splendid day! We looked for spiders in the grass, and I brought her to the kitchen. I even showed Miss Clairbridge the stables and Blackberry."

Eleanor nodded as her gaze flicked from Rose to the duke. "Yes, we had a wonderful day. Your horses are beautiful, Your Grace. My family once owned a few horses in the stable behind our townhome—affectionate creatures." She smiled at the memory. "I loved to ride them in Hyde Park at dawn, that magical hour when the glow of the rising sun colored the land in a golden hue. That was before..." Before she'd been unaware of her family's draining finances. They'd eventually had to sell the horses to pay the servants, back when there'd been a larger staff. Her cheeks heated. "I-I only mean to say, Your Grace, that your horses remind me of them."

He nodded, his shoulders settling. "Thank you, Miss Clairbridge. I've always had a certain fondness for the creatures—ever since I was a child. My brother and I would ride nearly every morning to the gamekeeper's cottage on the far side of the grounds."

Rose, obviously eager to be included more in the conversation, chimed in. "And she petted Snowdrop too. I think Snowdrop likes her."

The duke raised his eyebrows.

"Snowdrop?" He lifted a hand to rub his jaw. "Snowdrop doesn't warm to many people and is, in general, a shy soul. She must have seen the good in your heart to have trusted you so quickly." Once again, the duke stared at Eleanor, eyes bright and a half smile on his lips.

"'Twas nothing, Your Grace. I believe that Snowdrop was just curious about the commotion in the adjacent stall." Eleanor dipped her chin. She was tempted to measure the look on his face but forced her eyes to the floor.

"I find that doubtful, Miss Clairbridge." His voice was a pleasant rumble. "Indeed, the only other person who has had such a privilege is my good friend, Lord Lendin. The viscount visits from time to time."

"Lord Lendin?" Eleanor lifted her head and tilted it to the side. "I cannot say that I've had the pleasure in meeting the man."

The duke grinned as if to himself, seeming to remember something. "Yes, Lord Lendin is the third Viscount Harroway. He does not venture to London overly much. I've known him since we were children."

Eleanor shouldn't have been surprised, really. Of course, dukes would be and were friends with all sorts of nobility, and yet, she couldn't help but feel unimportant. After all, what was her company compared to a viscount's? She ducked her head again, unable to continue looking into the duke's piercing gaze and feeling as though every one of her thoughts was being opened and read like a letter.

"Whatever the reason for Snowdrop's taking a liking to you, please know that you are free to ride the horses and visit the stables in your spare time."

Eleanor sucked in a deep breath. "That is far too generous, Your Grace. I cannot possibly accept." Her mind reeled. He wanted to let her ride the horses? Her? A governess?

"Nonsense, Miss Clairbridge. I insist. It's obvious that you have a way with the creatures and that you like to ride. They need the exercise, anyway." He raised an eyebrow at her, waiting for an answer.

"As long as it would not be an imposition." Her stomach churned at the idea, though her pulse thrummed with anticipation.

A soft smile came over his face, and his countenance brightened. "It would not be an imposition at all, I assure you."

The door to the dining room opened, and a footman strode through, pausing and bowing before relaying his message. "Dinner is served, Your Grace."

Edmund nodded. "Thank you, William."

The footman bowed again and left the room. All of the servants seemed comfortable in his presence. Another mark in his favor, in Eleanor's mind.

"Shall we?" The duke held his arm out to Eleanor.

She froze. She had learned quite a bit at Mrs. Dorfield's school, but she was positive that she had not once been taught what to do in this situation. Never in her life had she envisioned a duke escorting her into a dining room, not even in her wildest daydreams—and she was a governess now, which added another layer of complexity to the situation.

She'd had an encounter once with an earl when she'd gone for a walk in Hyde Park with her friends, and he had been cold and harsh. They'd only been passing by, and yet he'd glared at them in such a manner that Eleanor didn't fail to shiver at the thought of the occurrence. Ever since then, she had assumed that the more noble a person was considered, the colder they were—though the duke did not fall into this pattern. Indeed, he and that earl were as different in behavior as a rabbit to a wolf.

She was nowhere near to the duke in status—being a mere baron's daughter as she was—and had never given herself the false hope of being accepted by one of so high a station, but when she glanced at him, his eyes so kind and his lips upturned into that small smile—she didn't think it possible that he'd ever been cold. He never would be.

It was the cautious smile he had so often worn, tinged with hesitation. Eleanor had the strangest feeling that the smile was held back by something, and once again, she had the urge to find out what. It was this that made her mind.

She placed her hand on his arm, and immediately, a jolt of energy rushed through her hand, so unexpected that she had to force herself to keep walking beside him with steady footfalls.

Had he experienced it too? Eleanor peeked out of the corner of her eye but couldn't tell if he had.

The duke walked with her into the dining room, and Rose followed close behind, humming to herself. As Eleanor attempted to calm her tingling nerves, she redirected her attention to the dining room, one of the many rooms she hadn't yet beheld.

A large table spanned most of the space, its walnut-colored wood reflecting the light from the candelabras set at intervals down its length. Rich red fabric with deep maroon designs of leaves and flowers covered the chairs flanking each side, contrasting the heavy-looking beige curtains which were drawn open to reveal the nearly set sun.

The duke guided her into the chair next to Rose, who had been helped into hers by a nearby footman. Rose sat at the duke's right, who himself sat at the head of the table. Eleanor clamped her hands in her lap, still disconcerted by the odd tingling sensation in her arm and her presence in a duke's dining room.

When the soup course arrived, Eleanor dipped her spoon into the white broth and tasted it, a certain sense of wistfulness falling upon her. Her family used to have fine meals together—when her father was still alive. Those times were marked by playful conversation, shared looks of affection between her parents, and a carefree atmosphere.

Now, everything had changed. Fine meals filled with gaiety had been replaced by bland meals and loneliness. Mama and Eleanor had tried to maintain the illusion that everything was the same, but in truth, nothing was. It had only gotten worse with the passage of time as the dining room walls seemed farther spread out and the company decreased in numbers.

The sound of a spoon coming into contact with a bowl drew her attention away from her melancholia. Rose was trying to eat her soup but was, instead, spilling it down the sides of the dish with her wide scooping motions. Eleanor—fighting a smile at the endearing girl's antics—managed to get her attention and show her how to eat her soup according to proper etiquette rules.

"Like this. And bring the spoon to your mouth a bit slower. It will help to keep you from spilling." Eleanor demonstrated, dipping the outer edge of her spoon into the soup and skimming it away from her body. She then brought the spoon toward her mouth in a slow motion, keeping it level to avoid spilling. Rose kept her keen eyes open wide and copied Eleanor's movements almost exactly, only spilling a very little bit this time. Eleanor beamed at her and whispered. "Very good, Miss Rose. Soon you'll be fit to have dinner with a princess."

Rose gave a toothy grin and continued eating, practicing the technique Eleanor had just shown her.

In between spoonfuls of soup, Eleanor searched for anything to keep her eyes on while her heart beat a tattoo in her chest. If the duke asked her a question or attempted conversation, she wasn't sure she'd be able to respond without making a mess of it. What could she ask him to steer the conversation into a safe topic?

"It sounded earlier as though Lord Lendin is one of your closest friends. Did you say you grew up together?"

"Yes, we did, in fact." The duke laughed. "Lendin and I were always getting into trouble in our youth. My brother, Phillip, often had to follow us to make sure we were out of harm's way."

Eleanor smiled at his expression, so clear it was that his childhood had been a happy time. "Was Phillip older?"

The duke's mouth pulled down, his shoulders straightening. "He was." A moment passed in silence before his mouth quirked up again and his tone was back to normal. "Lendin and I also went to boarding school together. Eton was a less-tolerable place in regard to mischief-making, as I was studying quite a bit in my free time—although, I also got into a few scrapes attempting to rescue Lendin from his own. He was always challenging some lord or other to a race or game of cards. I had to convince him to withdraw, one way or another. The problem was, he'd always win. It's far better to lose at a game of cards and damage one's pride than to win and make enemies of the most powerful men in England. And, at Oxford, he bet the head of the rowing team that he could make it to the bridge and back before the man did."

"And did he?" Eleanor quirked her lips in amusement.

"Not in the least," the duke replied, laughter in his voice. "He capsized his boat and had to swim to shore whilst someone's playful mastiff pulled at the fabric of his trousers. That was one challenge he was never going to win."

Eleanor couldn't stifle her laugh, and the duke joined her, his laughter warming her like a hot cup of tea on an autumn morning.

"Does he ever visit?" Eleanor tilted her head.

The duke's laughter abated, a smile still upon his face. "Indeed. He visits every now and then to discuss business and to see how we fare. I'm sure you'll meet him, one of these days."

Each dish that was served over the course of the dinner had been cooked to perfection, and Eleanor had never had a better meal. Warm bread and butter accompanied dishes of beef and asparagus, with a delicious custard for dessert. Multiple times throughout the hearty repast, she sensed the duke's eyes on her, only to look over and find his gaze elsewhere. Could she be imagining things?

Eleanor focused her attention on continuing to help Rose with her table manners—pushing her ridiculous thoughts to the back of her mind—and all too soon, the meal was over, and it was time for their little trio to part. They all stood. Rose said her goodbyes and was escorted back to her room for bed. Eleanor was about to take her leave as well when the duke's voice stopped her, an earnest expression on his face as he spoke.

"I must thank you, Miss Clairbridge, for helping Rose to learn proper table manners, and for dining with us. I know it isn't customary for a governess to dine with the family, but I believe that you will be a great help to Rose. Already, her table manners have improved, and I know many who would not be so gentle and understanding in their teaching as you have just been."

Eleanor flushed, not having expected the praise. "Thank you, Your Grace. It is my belief that children should be taught with kindness and encouragement, rather than scolding and berating."

Eleanor had seen children who were admonished and rebuked in the severest of ways, often for the smallest of mistakes, and it had always made her heart ache for them. Their governesses appeared to think that nothing less than perfection was acceptable, and in the process of being corrected so harshly, the children would retreat into themselves, so afraid were they of any repercussions they might receive for doing what was deemed the wrong thing.

One time, a married couple her parents knew had come to stay with them, bringing along their young daughter and her governess. Eleanor had only been eight and very excited to meet a potential playmate, yet when they arrived, the girl— Martha had been her name—was withdrawn, timid as a wild deer. Eleanor had understood why once she'd been in the schoolroom with the girl and her governess.

While Eleanor's governess had always been kind yet firm, Martha's governess had been cruel—and there was no other word for it. Eleanor had witnessed multiple belittling comments and harsh remarks Martha's governess bestowed on the poor girl and, even today, Eleanor shuddered at the memory. She had never heard of the girl again, so she could only hope the governess had been turned out.

The duke brought her back to their current conversation

with a light touch to her arm. "I could not agree more with your sentiment, Miss Clairbridge, and I greatly appreciate your candor. Now, I'm afraid that I've some unfinished business to attend to. Thank you, again." He bowed and left, a benevolent smile on his face as he strolled away.

She'd never dreamed she would feel so comfortable around the duke, or that he would be so welcoming and agreeable. She had been waiting with bated breath for his demeanor to change, for there was no question it would, but the truth of the matter was that the man had shattered her expectations of what he would be like in a most unexpected fashion—and now she must try to make sense of the pieces.

CHAPTER 8

The next morning, Eleanor woke at dawn and prepared herself for her first day of teaching Rose, glad for the fire that warmed her small room. Eleanor had been the student yesterday—learning where everything was located and finding out more about her little charge.

After she had donned a serviceable gray dress and pinned her hair into a bun, she ate her breakfast and then strode to the schoolroom, only a few paces down the hall from her own quarters.

Rose had breezed through this room the day before, allowing Eleanor only a brief glimpse before the girl had rushed off to another chamber. Eleanor entered and walked over to the globe near the entrance. She set it spinning with a light touch of her finger. This room must have been where the duke had been taught before he went away to school. Eleanor smiled to herself at the thought of a young duke learning Latin with a tutor and practicing arithmetic.

A small school desk and smaller wooden chair faced the windows. A larger desk for a tutor—or governess—with cylindrically carved legs faced the school desk. A clean slate and new piece of chalk rested atop the student desk. Along the wall, a sizable wooden bookshelf held tomes on every subject and topic.

Eleanor plucked one from the shelf and opened the leather cover, seeing the name *Edmund* scrawled at the top-right corner of the first page. She studied the scrawl for a moment with a light chuckle before closing it and putting it back. Just how many other books on the shelf were marked in the same way? One of the shelves was occupied not by books, but by paint brushes, embroidery hoops and floss, and sheaves of papers— all stacked beside each other in neat rows. Eleanor smiled to herself, her heart lifting in relief. Maybe this wouldn't be so difficult, after all.

She settled at the large desk and began preparing her lesson plans. She wasn't concerned about supplies, as she seemed to have everything she could possibly need—and more. Eleanor already had an idea what subjects Rose understood more or less of, and Rose herself had answered all of Eleanor's questions pertaining to her education and how she was used to learning when she had been showing Eleanor around the day before. When one combined that with the information the duke had given her, Eleanor had a good idea of where to start and what subjects to spend more time on.

Just over an hour had passed when Rose appeared in the doorway of the schoolroom, eyes wide with excitement. She skipped over to Eleanor with a bright smile on her face.

"Good morning, Miss Clairbridge." She curtsied, the little pale-blue bow in her hair fluttering with the movement.

Eleanor returned her smile. "How do you do, Rose? Are you excited for your lessons today?"

Rose's eyes seemed to sparkle with anticipation. "I am very excited, Miss Clairbridge!"

Eleanor laughed at Rose's enthusiasm. "Well, then. Let's get started right away." She gestured for Rose to take her seat at the school desk. "Today, I believe we should start with reading, then we'll practice writing, and after that, working with numbers and sums. Does that sound like a good plan?"

Rose nodded, a determined expression crossing her face.

Eleanor moved to the bookshelf and grabbed one of the reader books, its pages full of simple sentences and passages. She pulled a small wooden chair next to Rose's desk, angling herself into it before opening the book to the first page. "Let's start here." She pointed at the first sentence. "Speak with me, and we'll go from word to word."

And so began her life as a governess. It wasn't what she'd expected, but perhaps it would be even better than her expectations. Would she be able to meet the expectations of her employer?

∼

The rest of the morning passed by in a blur of numbers and letters, and when Eleanor gazed out of the window to see the afternoon sun shining high in the sky, her eyebrows flew up.

After they'd worked on Rose's reading, Eleanor had helped Rose with her writing and penmanship. The girl needed a bit more coaching in this area but was learning at a quicker pace than Eleanor had imagined.

"This way?" Rose turned her bright eyes to Eleanor, a question in them.

Eleanor—who had been watching as Rose copied the words she'd been given on the slate—smiled at the girl's desire to learn. "Exactly right, Rose. These curves look perfect."

The child grinned and continued writing, speaking the words as she did so. "Bat...mat...cat...rat...pat..."

A knock sounded at the door to the schoolroom, preceding

the entrance of Fanny, who held a rather large silver tray in her arms.

"Good afternoon, Miss Rose, Eleanor. Mrs. Brinder asked me to bring your luncheon to ye. Hope I'm nae interruptin' ye." Fanny moved farther into the room and set the tray on Eleanor's desk, granting Eleanor a view of an assortment of foods from where she sat near Rose. As if on cue, Eleanor's stomach rumbled—making Rose giggle.

Eleanor smiled at the girl's sweet laughter and rose from the tiny chair she'd been sitting in all morning. She winced a bit as she stood, her back stiff from the child-sized seat, and leaned carefully back in a subtle stretch.

"No need to worry, Fanny. You're not interrupting anything that cannot be continued later." Eleanor tilted her head to look at Rose. "I'm simply famished, Miss Rose, and I imagine that you might be as well. What say you? Should we pause our learning to enjoy a delicious meal?"

The girl bobbed her head in agreement and stood from her chair, setting her piece of chalk down on the short desk.

Fanny grinned and waved them over to the large desk. "Ye've got all sorts of good things, ye do. 'am, cheese, bread, tea, and even Cook's famous apple tarts! Once ye've eaten as much as ye can bear, just ring the bell o'er there"—Fanny pointed to a small bell on the wall at the corner of the room— "and I'll be back to collect the tray afore ye can say 'heigh, heigh, a nonny-no!'" Leaving them with this interesting phrase to mull over, Fanny made her goodbyes and scurried from the room, humming a joyful tune.

Eleanor helped Rose pull her chair to the large desk, and they both seated themselves to eat the well-timed luncheon Cook had provided. It was a pleasant affair, with Rose asking many questions about Eleanor and her life and home—which Eleanor answered as best she could.

After they had eaten, Rose's nurse arrived to collect Rose,

and they departed to her room so the girl could take a short afternoon nap before continuing with her lessons.

During Rose's absence, Eleanor tidied the schoolroom and busied herself with reading a book of poetry she'd found on the bookshelf. She had only read a few pages when a light knock sounded on the door, pulling her from images of wildflowers and fields that the poems so wonderfully described. She lifted her head from the leather-bound book and peered at the door with curiosity.

"You may enter."

The door pushed open slowly, and Eleanor was caught off guard at seeing the duke standing in the doorway, looking like the definition of nobility with his well-tailored clothing and upright stance. The black coat he wore made his gold waistcoat stand out, his white linen cravat knotted perfectly.

She stood and curtsied with frantic movements, the book still in her hand. "Y-Your Grace."

He bowed and stepped into the room, a half smile on his face. "Miss Clairbridge. I'm sorry to have interrupted you. I've only come to inquire after Rose's lessons. Are they going well? Do you have all of the supplies you need?"

Eleanor relaxed somewhat and smiled back at him, the tension in her shoulders easing. "Yes, Your Grace, all is going well. Rose is a quick learner and a pleasure to teach. Today we have worked on her reading and writing. She is currently having her midday nap."

Eleanor had imagined that the duke would leave after this short explanation but, oddly, he stayed.

"That's a great pleasure to hear. And how are you, Miss Clairbridge?"

Eleanor's eyes, which had been almost completely focused on the floor up to this point, flicked up to meet his as her brow furrowed.

She considered the short amount of time she'd spent at Ivy

Grange and the warmth of the place and those inhabiting it. Rose was an angel. Fanny was already someone whom Eleanor considered a friend, and the duke, well, he was...kind? Thoughtful? Someone who made her heart flutter whenever he walked by?

A duke. That she mustn't forget.

An image of her mother, alone in their dreary townhouse, came to mind. Guilt clawed its way into her chest. Certainly, Crand and Mary would ensure that her mother was content—or as content as she could be—but Eleanor couldn't help but fret.

"I am well, Your Grace." As well as she could be, at least. Certainly now, he would be satisfied with her answer and take his leave, but she was incorrect yet again. She must stop making assumptions, for in regard to this man, they were never on target.

A hint of concern colored his expression as he apparently waited for her to continue. She swallowed. Eleanor couldn't understand why, but she understood that she could speak to him without fear of censure. It was ridiculous. She didn't even know him! And how was it that he could see through her pretense? Those eyes really did seem to see into her soul—a thing that was as swoon-inducing as it was aggravating.

Eleanor tried in vain to resist his gentle look. She couldn't possibly confide in him. Could she? She was foolish to even consider the notion. Surely, the duke had no desire to hear what was truly running through her mind. He was just trying to be polite—that was all. Yet there was something so warm in his gaze that she couldn't help herself.

"Well, in truth...I worry for my mother. She is all alone at our townhouse, and I am a bit concerned for her wellbeing. Do not misunderstand me, Your Grace, I am so incredibly grateful to be Rose's governess. I am only...unused to being away from my home and...I...haven't quite adjusted to the change as yet."

He gave a brief, compassionate smile. "I understand completely, Miss Clairbridge. It can be difficult to leave one's home when one is unused to it." The duke tugged at his cravat, clearing his throat in the silence that followed his words. Amazingly, there was no hint of false sympathy in his expression.

"Indeed." Eleanor smoothed her skirt. "It is all the more difficult when the person you leave behind is alone. You see, my father died seven years ago now..." The duke remained silent as she paused, memories of her father flooding her mind. "He was...the greatest man I have ever known, and my mother loved him dearly, as did I. It has only been us and the servants for these long years since, and the thought of her in a silent house with only occasional company makes my heart ache."

"I'm very sorry for your loss," the duke murmured.

"Thank you," Eleanor said. "It is hard losing a parent—someone who has taught you the ways of the world, someone who has picked you up when you've fallen. No matter how long it has been, it has not become easier to bear. It does not fade away as some would like to believe."

The duke nodded, a somber expression on his face. He must have lost his father, at least, for he wouldn't be duke if the man were alive. Had he shared a close relationship with his parents? Was his mother still alive? This early in her employment, it would surely be immediate dismissal to ask.

Hopefully, in the future, he might trust her enough to keep his secrets, share in his sadnesses, rejoice with him in his successes—but for now, she would continue to share her own. One could not expect a person to confide in them without first confiding themselves.

Although...why would a duke wish to confide in a governess? The mere idea was ridiculous. Nevertheless, Eleanor was drawn to him like a hare to a garden. She mustn't get caught in the fencing.

"I appreciate your concern, Your Grace—and taking the

time to listen to a mere governess's troubles." Eleanor chuckled deprecatingly.

The duke's eyebrows furrowed, and his mouth opened, but Rose entered the room again—her nap apparently over—and beamed at her uncle's presence.

She rushed over and grasped his hand with one of her own. "Uncle Edmund! I didn't think you'd be here."

He grinned down at her. "Up already, Rosie? I just came to see how you were doing in your studies."

Rose granted Eleanor an excited smile before shifting her brown-eyed gaze back to the duke. "I'm having so much fun, Uncle! Miss Clairbridge is a nice governess. She helped me read that book"—she pointed to the volume they had been reading earlier—"and she helped me practice writing."

Rose dropped the duke's hand and dashed over to her desk, grabbing the slate they'd practiced her writing on. She clutched it with both hands and raised it in the air toward her uncle, beaming with obvious pride.

The duke studied the slate, and his eyes widened. His mouth opened in an exaggerated expression of disbelief. "You did this?" He accepted it from his niece's hands. "It can't be! It's already better than my handwriting." He touched his chin in play shock, and Rose giggled in merriment.

"I did it, Uncle! I did!"

"You magnificent girl." The duke grinned and swung Rose up into his arms, spinning a few times. She erupted into a fit of giggles before he slowed to a stop and lowered her to the floor —a smile still on his face. Rose wobbled a bit but remained on her feet, eyes bright.

Eleanor had not yet seen such a playful side to him. The duke was such a kind uncle, and Rose clearly adored him. Eleanor's heart filled with an ache of longing. This was the kind of family she wanted, yet her dreams for such a thing would never come true.

She sighed inwardly and her smile faltered. This was the closest she would come to having a family of her own. She would have to be content with these visions of happiness and store them in her mind so that she might remember them in the times spent alone, when the real thing was no longer before her.

After Eleanor's first day of lessons with Rose ended, Eleanor explored the parts of the manor Rose had left out in her tour of Ivy Grange. Eleanor first made her way down the hallway that stemmed from the one leading to the schoolroom—a corridor that was flooded with light. The hall was half windows, each casting light on the opposite wall which consisted solely of paintings. Portraits of all sizes greeted her here, but the subjects that most stood out to her were the ones in which the subjects wore styles that were more familiar to Eleanor—clothing which had been fashionable only a matter of years earlier.

Eleanor stepped toward the wall and inspected two of the portraits—one of a man and one of a woman. The man had golden hair and green eyes—the hue of them very similar to the duke's—and the woman also had golden hair, although her eyes were a dark blue.

The woman looked nothing like His Grace, with her upturned nose and pointed chin, but the man...he bore a striking resemblance to the duke, although this man's eyes were brighter—more teasing. His brother, perhaps? And who was the woman? There was a confidence in her posture and expression and something very regal about her, but also a kindness captured in her eyes. She must be the duke's sister-in-law.

Eleanor studied these portraits for a minute more until she continued walking the length of the hall, eyes flicking over large ruffs and small lips, some subjects having the milk-white skin and puffed sleeves that were so popular during Queen Elizabeth's reign. As she reached the end of this hallway, she continued onward, moving down a narrow set of stairs.

These steps—as it turned out—led to the kitchens in the depths of the manor. The sound of bubbling liquid and rhythmic tapping reached her ears as the sweet aroma of what might be cooking pears greeted her nose. As she stepped into the kitchen, a short woman came into view, an apron tied about her plump waist and a white cap upon her head.

She kneaded a large lump of dough on a table before her, humming as she did so. Her arms were thick and muscular— presumably from years doing this exact sort of activity—and she moved the dough with the ease that only practice can give. A few other women were also in the large space—some adding wood to the flames in the hearth and others slicing a variety of vegetables, fruits, and meats—and each moved with quick steps. The fire kept the room warm, and the stone floor was ungiving beneath her feet.

As Eleanor took another step into the room, the woman kneading the dough raised her head and pierced Eleanor with a stare. Eleanor froze for a second, worry creeping into her stomach, but the woman's round face broke into a large smile as she stopped her kneading and dusted the flour off of her hands.

"Ye're certainly not a kitchen maid!" She laughed heartily and moved closer, keen brown eyes inspecting Eleanor.

Eleanor returned the woman's kind smile. "I am not, no. I am Miss Rose's governess, Miss Clairbridge. Pardon me for my intrusion—I only wished to see more of the manor and hadn't the faintest idea where that staircase led." She gestured to the stairs behind her and gave a sheepish look, her cheeks heating.

"No need to worry, dearie. We don't mind a bit o' company down here—not at all. I'm Mrs. Brewer—though most here call me 'Cook.'" The woman bobbed a quick curtsy.

With the relief that came with not being an unwanted visitor, Eleanor relaxed. "It's a pleasure to meet you, Mrs. Brewer. Might I ask, what made you suspect that I am not, in fact, a kitchen maid?"

The woman lifted an eyebrow and nodded in Eleanor's direction. "Your hands, miss. They've not made their way 'round these kitchens as my maids' hands have—or mine." Mrs. Brewer raised her hand to show Eleanor what she meant, and Eleanor immediately understood. The woman's hands were rough and dappled with long-healed burn marks and old scars.

"I see." Eleanor peered at her own hand. Her hands were soft and unmarked...at the moment. Perhaps her job as a governess would change that.

Mrs. Brewer moved back to her lump of dough. As she began her kneading once more, she nodded to a plate nearby. Tarts were stacked high on the dish in a mouth-watering pyramid of pastry. "Have a pear tart if you'd like, dear. We've plenty."

Eleanor didn't need to be told twice. She moved over to the table at a pace quicker than was expected of a lady and plucked a tart from the top of the pyramid, then took an eager bite. Oh, what bliss was this? The cook at home had never made anything so delectable.

The next half hour was spent in pleasant conversation with Mrs. Brewer, and as Eleanor left the woman's company, she promised to return—Mrs. Brewer offering the additional enticement of more tarts upon Eleanor's next visit.

A kind duke, friendly maids, and a jovial cook—how different from her imagination Ivy Grange was turning out to be.

CHAPTER 9

One week passed, and Eleanor had seen little of the duke. Once or twice, she'd witnessed him in conversation with Prumb, and she sat with him at dinner and church, yet he seemed to spend most of his time in his study. She had the strange notion that he was avoiding her, but she hadn't the foggiest idea as to why he would be. Could she have been too candid when they'd had their conversation in the schoolroom? Hopefully, she hadn't made a mistake in being so honest.

She was just finishing lessons with Rose for the day. The girl had responded well to the day's outdoor lesson—perhaps the first of many. Despite this, Eleanor was having a difficult time pushing thoughts of the duke from her mind—a constant struggle in the past week. Rose twirled a small white flower between her fingers as she skipped beside Eleanor on their way through the gardens.

"Do you remember the name of that flower, Rose?" Eleanor peered down at the girl with a smile.

"Greater Sit—Stew—Stow—" Rose attempted valiantly to recall the name, eyebrows furrowing.

Eleanor smiled. "Greater Stitchwort."

They made their way toward the back entrance of the manor, the air sweet with the scents of flora as the stone steps leading to the back doors came into view.

A thoughtful expression crossed Rose's face. "Miss Clairbridge, how do you know so much about everything?"

Eleanor fought to stifle a laugh. "I had a governess like you. Her name was Miss Bly, and she thought it very important for me to be knowledgeable on all manner of things. My parents did not have any reservations about this, as they were not traditionally minded in that way, and so I came to learn of many subjects which other girls my age did not."

"And now you will pass it on to me." Rose smiled.

"And now I will pass it on to you." Eleanor matched the girl's expression.

The pair were just about to walk up the back steps when they were greeted by one of the gardeners. He was an older man, about seventy, with tanned skin and hunched shoulders which belied his long-held occupation. The hair that peeked out from beneath his cap was white, and when he smiled, his face relaxed into the well-made creases created over the years. He gave a slow bow as they moved closer.

"Hope yer walk's went well. 'Tis a fine day fer one.' He grinned, revealing a mouth full of crooked teeth. His Cornish accent was thick, with a friendly tone to his voice.

Eleanor returned his smile and nodded. "It certainly is. What better way to spend a morning than to enjoy the sun in these beautiful gardens? They're the finest I've ever seen."

She could've sworn there was a hint of a blush on the man's tawny face. "I than' ye, miss. We do our righ' bes', and keepin' i' as i' is makes 'is Grace 'appy. Ever since..." The man trailed off, a growing look of concern on his face.

What had he been about to say? Something about the duke or his family?

"Grea'er Stitchwort." He spoke with a grave edge to his words, looking intently at the flower in Rose's hand.

Eleanor's gaze flitted from the man to the flower, her brows furrowing. "Is something wrong, sir?"

The man tilted his head, flicking his eyes to the side in a plea for a private conversation.

"Wait here, please, Miss Rose." Eleanor spoke lightly, attempting to keep the confusion from her voice. She followed the man a few yards away, Rose content to stay outside as long as she could.

As soon as the man seemed sure Rose wouldn't be able to hear their discussion, he turned back to Eleanor. "I didn' wan' ta scare Miss Rose, bu' ye'd bes' be careful, miss."

Eleanor frowned. Was she being threatened? If the gardener was, indeed, trying to scare her, he wasn't doing a very good job of it. "I don't quite understand, sir."

"The Grea'er Stitchwort, miss." He grew more serious, and Eleanor grew more anxious.

"'Tis the proper'y of the piskies. When a person takes it, they ge' angry. My cousin Jowan picked a bunch once fer 'is lady. Only a week la'er, 'e fell off 'is ladder when collec'in apples," he murmured, taking his hat from his head and wringing it in his hands.

Eleanor had never been one to believe in faeries or "piskies" yet didn't want to upset the man further, so she attempted to allay his fears. "I don't think—"

"'E fell righ' off it. Jowan is sturdy, miss. 'E's never fallen off 'is ladder."

"Maybe—"

"And 'is lady burned the pasties she was makin'."

This conversation was not going well. "I think—"

"She'd never burnt 'em before."

"But—"

"I tried 'em, miss, and they was righ' scorched."

Eleanor sighed inwardly. "We'll be very careful, Mr....?"

The man grinned once more, her resigned words assurance enough. "Mr. Roskilly a' yer service, miss."

Eleanor gave a strained smile of her own. "Mr. Roskilly. Thank you for your warning. I'm Miss Clairbridge, Rose's governess, and I'll be sure we stay away from the Greater Stitchwort."

"Righ' good, miss," he replied, calmer now that the duke's niece and her governess were out of imminent danger. At least he had not been threatening her.

They made their way back to Rose, who now inspected the row of bushes lining the path, the flower still in her hand. Mr. Roskilly kindly bid them good day before returning to his work, leaving Eleanor and Rose to go back inside.

"What were you and Mr. Roskilly talking about?" Rose asked, a curious gleam in her blue eyes.

Eleanor brushed her hands down her skirt, mind spinning with possible explanations she could give. "The flowers. I wanted to know how he got them to grow so beautifully."

～

It had been ten days since the incident with the Stitchwort in the garden, and Eleanor had just finished eating a light breakfast of toast and jam that she'd learned to take on a tray in her room. It was faster than eating below stairs, and Rose ate meals with her nurse.

Eleanor was slowly acclimating herself to living in a manor, and Rose was the perfect charge. Each evening, Eleanor planned lessons, and each day, she taught—spending her free moments attempting to get to know His Grace or speaking with Fanny.

"So your cousins...they all live in Scotland?" she asked the maid.

Fanny nodded, wrapping her hands in her skirt. "Aye, except two. One worked 'ere with me, but 'e went off and got married—an interesting story too." Her eyes twinkled with merriment.

Eleanor nudged Fanny with her shoulder. "Well? Do tell it!"

Fanny chuckled. "'e fancied a lass who'd somehoo lost 'er boot in the coo pasture. He swore to 'er 'e'd retrieve it, so 'e climbed o'er the fence. Those coos were mighty temperamental. They chased 'im roond and roond." Fanny doubled over, clutching her stomach as her laughter filled the room. "When 'e climbed back o'er the fence, he was more earth than flesh, I tell ye."

"And he did all this for his lady love?" Eleanor asked in disbelief.

"Aye." Her tone was one of amusement as she sat beside Eleanor on the bed. "They married only two weeks later, so I s'pose it worked!"

Eleanor grinned, then regarded Fanny. "And are you someone's lady love?" She allowed a hint of playful teasing in her voice.

Fanny blushed to the roots of her hair. "Well—uh—I—" Eleanor waited for her to continue. "There be someone," she admitted, finally finding her voice again.

Eleanor grinned, excited for her friend. "Who is he?" She leaned closer, raising her eyebrows.

Fanny lifted a hand to her beet-red cheeks. "'E works in the stable." She took a nervous breath before releasing it in a somewhat lovesick sigh.

"And his name?"

Fanny's lips raised into a smile, a dream-like expression on her face. "Seamus. 'E's got dark brown 'air and green eyes like the grass that grows after a good rain. 'E's got soft lips too." Fanny gave a mischievous grin, and Eleanor's mouth dropped open at this last statement.

"You've kissed him?"

Fanny broke from her trance, and the girl's face went pink as a *Tremella auricula-judae* fungus, though she didn't hesitate this time to respond. "Aye, and he's a fine kisser too! It was only a quick kiss, anyway, as it wasn't long after when Mr. Prumb opened the door to the kitchen. In our 'aste to move apart, Seamus stepped into a bucket behind 'im and 'ad a right difficult time gettin' 'is foot out. Mr. Prumb 'ad to 'elp 'im get it off."

Eleanor looked at Fanny for a moment. A few moments passed before her mirth broke from its confines, and Eleanor began to laugh.

Fanny soon joined her, both women hunched over as their shoulders shook with levity. Eleanor had never been kissed, but surely, Fanny's experience was far from normal. Eleanor could only hope that her first kiss would be as memorable.

If she ever had a first kiss, that was.

The women's laughter soon abated, and once Fanny left the room to attend to her duties, Eleanor pulled open the wardrobe doors and ran her gaze over her clothing. She had risen earlier than usual that morning, and there were a few hours yet until her lessons with Rose. The issue was—what to do to fill them. She had enough energy that she wouldn't be able to focus if she read, and she preferred to be in motion. She could take a walk in the gardens, but that idea wasn't as appealing as it might have been if someone was there to keep her company.

Eleanor continued to stare blankly at her dresses until she blinked and her eyes caught on the light-purple hue of her riding habit. She took hold of the sturdy fabric, raising the outfit to get a better look. When she'd packed it, she'd planned on transforming it into a day dress—after all, what would a governess need with a riding habit?—but hadn't yet gotten around to that.

She changed into it, finding that it took longer than expected. The fit was not as it once has been. Her parents had bought the habit for her when she'd been younger, and it was now a bit tighter than she would have liked. Because it was the only riding habit she had—and not too uncomfortable—she made do with it.

Eleanor pinned her hair into a tight bun, rebel wisps defying the coaxing of her fingers. She pulled her old leather gloves over her hands—also a bit tight—and tied her bonnet onto her head. Alas, she had long ago lost her jockey bonnet.

She scurried from her room, eager for the soaring sensation she used to feel when riding. Eleanor hadn't yet availed herself of the duke's stables, though she had been there now several times. Rose had often wanted to visit Blackberry, and Eleanor used Rose's love of the place—and Blackberry—in her teaching.

As Eleanor opened the entrance to the servants' quarters and exited the manor, the fresh scent of morning dew greeted her. She strode to the stables, where workers milled about, grooming horses and sweeping the floors. Maybe one of them was Seamus. When she entered, they widened their eyes, obviously having not expected anyone to be there so early. Eleanor swallowed the lump in her throat. Would they question her presence?

An older man with greying hair—the stable manager, she imagined—strode up to her, a rag in his hand. Eleanor had seen him a few times when Rose and she had visited but had never actually spoken to the man. He bowed, a friendly smile on his weathered face that immediately eased the tension in Eleanor's shoulders. "G'mornin', miss. What can I do for ya?"

She bobbed a curtsy and gave a small smile. "Good morning, sir. I'm sorry to bother you, but His Grace said I could use the stables, and I was wondering if someone might saddle Snowdrop for me. Though, if you're busy, I can do it myself, assuming she's up for it."

The stable manager's brows rose. "Naw, miss. We wouldn't

have a lady like yerself saddle a horse. 'Tis not yer job. I'll get her saddled for ya."

He brought Snowdrop out from her stall and saddled her with a side-saddle, then looked up and grinned. "Pardon my manners, miss. I'm Mr. Haldwell, the stable manager."

"It's very nice to meet you, Mr. Haldwell. I am Miss Clairbridge, the governess."

"It's a pleasure to formally make yer acquaintance, Miss Clairbridge." He finished tightening the girth and led Snowdrop over to a mounting block. "I can get one of the stable boys to go with ya, miss. Don't want ya gettin' hurt."

She shook her head, giving an appreciative smile before mounting Snowdrop. "Thank you, Mr. Haldwell, but I'm quite all right. I've ridden before. Besides, I don't want to take away one of your workers."

He shook his head, a fatherly light in his eyes. "Ye wouldn't be, and I insist. 'Twouldn't do to have ye injured without anyone around."

While the last thing Eleanor wanted was to be a nuisance, she had to admit that Mr. Haldwell's reasoning was sound. She nodded, and he called to a nearby stable boy to get a horse named Marlow saddled.

As they set off, her attendant followed an ample distance behind.

Eleanor bent and brushed her fingers lightly behind Snowdrop's ears, then rode to the rolling fields beyond Ivy Grange, letting Snowdrop have her head. Snowdrop's muscles stretched beneath the saddle, and the wind whipped through Eleanor's hair, which was getting wilder by the minute. She glanced over her shoulder. Hopefully, the stable boy was keeping up—and not too irritated for what he might think was an attempt to lose him.

Before long, Eleanor slowed to a trot and took the time to appreciate the natural beauty surrounding her. Light glinted off the damp grass, the sky overhead was a calm shade of light blue, and aged and gnarled trees dotted the countryside. As much as she enjoyed London's architecture, it paled in comparison to this. She inhaled the intoxicating aroma of the morning air and peeked down at Snowdrop, who seemed to be enjoying herself as well.

"Good girl, Snowdrop. You're a fine horse, indeed." Eleanor whispered to the horse and patted Snowdrop's head once more before she caught sight of a pond in the distance. "What do you say to a quick ride over there?" She smiled eagerly down at those listening ears.

They perked to the side at her voice. Snowdrop nickered in response, and Eleanor grinned. She pressed her heels into the mare's sides again, and the horse galloped toward the pond. Eleanor leaned over the saddle as they flew across the land. A joyous laugh erupted from her as her heart lifted higher than it had for months. She really had missed this.

When Snowdrop lurched beneath her, her contentment dissolved into panic. Before she knew it, the mare was rearing and whinnying in fright. Her pulse raced, anxiety sending shocks through her. An overwhelming heat came over her body. What was happening?

Eleanor grasped onto the reins for dear life and leaned over Snowdrop's neck but started to slide out of the saddle. The stable boy shouted from somewhere behind her as Snowdrop pawed the air and squealed. A small shrew leapt into the air and scurried under the horse, its mousy nose pointed into the air. It bounced away before the reins slid from Eleanor's grip.

Eleanor hit the ground with a loud thump, and darkness fell over her.

~

"*Ruby*," *Eleanor's father called.*

She bounded down the stairs in her kid boots, attempting and failing to stuff her arms into the sleeves of her pink pelisse.

"Coming, Papa!" She reached the base of the steps and found her father leaning against the banister.

He greeted her with a warm smile and helped guide her arms into her sleeves. "There you are. Are you ready?"

Eleanor's twelfth birthday was in two days, and her father had informed her that he had a surprise. She grinned. "I'm ready!" She took the arm he offered, and he escorted her through the house and out the back door.

Her father's garden was an array of native plants and fungi separated into sections by old stone paths. Eleanor's father had carefully planted all of the specimens there, but it always seemed as though they had cropped up on their own.

There were many types of flora here, from wood betony to bellflowers, but her father passed them by with only a brief look of satisfaction. Instead, he led Eleanor to a small space toward the back of the garden—a shady area he reserved for cultivating fungi. This was where she often found him if he could not be found in the house. He took great pride in his fungi.

"Here we are." Father stopped, and she released his arm, her smile curious. "I said I had a surprise for you, Ruby, and so I have— but first, let me show you something." He took a step toward a cluster of familiar-looking mushrooms. "Look at these. What are they?"

Eleanor's answer was immediate. "Amanita rubescens mushrooms, of course." Her father called her after them, so she was quite familiar with the fungi.

"Ah, but they are not. You see"—he bent and carefully scratched the surface of one of the mushrooms—"they do not redden as the Amanita rubescens *do when bruised."*

Eleanor waited for a moment, but the mushroom did not blush. She turned inquisitive eyes to her father. "What are they, then?"

"They are Amanita pantherina *mushrooms. They are almost indiscernible from* Amanita rubescens*. The more the latter is bruised, the more vibrant it makes itself, while the more bruised the former becomes, the duller it appears. And so I say to you, my dear daughter—no matter how much you are bruised in this life, you must promise me to maintain your vibrancy. Be like the Ruby you are, not the* Amanita pantherina*. Do not let this life's struggles destroy your spirit."*

Eleanor frowned at the imposter mushroom before agreeing with a resolute nod. "I won't, Papa."

"Good." He reached into his waistcoat pocket and pulled out a locket. Eleanor's eyes widened at the delicate gold chain and oval-shaped pendant. He extended the necklace to her, and she took it, opening the pendant to reveal miniature portraits of her parents. She flipped the locket over in her palm and read the inscription there, eyes welling with tears.

> *To my dearest Ruby,*
> *My greatest joy.*
> *Love, Papa*

"Thank you, Papa!" She stepped toward her father and embraced him, her arms tight around his shoulders.

"I'm glad you like it, dear." He returned her embrace and helped her put the locket on. "There. Now you'll always have a piece of your mother and I with you."

CHAPTER 10

Edmund had just finished reading the morning paper in his study, a hot cup of tea at his side, when a commotion sounded down the hall. What was this? He stood from his seat behind his desk and crossed the room.

As he opened the door, a red-faced stable boy rushed down the corridor, Prumb following close behind and both with expressions of alarm on their faces. Edmund's pulse ticked up.

"Your Grace." Prumb spoke with urgency. "Miss Clairbridge was out riding this morning and has had a fall."

Edmund didn't wait to hear more, instead trailing the pair to the stables as the stable boy explained in greater detail.

"I were followin' her whilst she were ridin'—Mr. Haldwell didn't want 'er to go alone, ye see—and I sees Snowdrop rear and a shrew 'oppin between 'er legs! I rode back as fast as I could."

By the time they arrived at the stables, Edmund's horse had already been saddled, Mr. Haldwell having anticipated his arrival. Edmund thanked the man and set off, he and Mr. Haldwell accompanying the stable boy. The landscape passed by in a blur.

As the group neared where the stable boy had left Miss Clairbridge, light-purple fabric fluttering amid a section of bent grass caught Edmund's eye. His blood turned cold. He flicked the reins with fervor, urging his horse toward the area. Miss Clairbridge lay splayed on the ground, her eyes closed, her cheeks absent of color.

His heart leapt into his throat.

Edmund dismounted, fell to his knees at her side, and grabbed her wrist from the ground. His breath was stuck in his throat—caged there like a bird. He felt for a pulse beneath her soft skin and almost cried out in relief when a steady beat pushed back against his fingers. Edmund placed her arm back down with gentle movements and pressed a light hand to her shoulder, shaking it just enough to rouse her without causing further injury. She looked as though she were merely sleeping, her wild curls framing her face and her brow smooth.

Lord, let her be unharmed.

"Miss Clairbridge."

She stirred a bit.

He shook her shoulder again. Would she rouse? Though his fear had lessened when he had found her pulse, Edmund couldn't shake the anxiety that clung to him. This seemed all too familiar. "Miss Clairbridge, open your eyes. Please, open your eyes."

She groaned and furrowed her brows, mumbling something that sounded suspiciously like, "Piskies." Her eyes shifted under her eyelids for a moment before they blinked open in a squint to expose the bright blue irises that had been hidden from view. Her dark lashes fluttered as she adjusted to the bright light, and her pink lips pulled into a small frown. She flicked her gaze sideways at the grass around her.

Mr. Haldwell and the stable boy dismounted behind him, moving closer.

"Your Grace? What happened?" she murmured weakly, her voice airy.

Some of the tension in his shoulders alleviated now that she had awoken. Edmund let out the breath he was holding and scratched the back of his head, attempting to lighten the situation. "A shrew. Apparently, it wasn't very fond of you."

"Ah."

"You've fallen off of Snowdrop, Miss Clairbridge. Are you injured?"

She attempted to push herself from the ground. With measured movements, Edmund helped her stand, placing a steadying hand on her back and one on her arm. He watched her face for any sign she was in pain. She swayed on her legs and leaned heavily into his side.

He shifted one arm around her shoulders—afraid she might fall at any moment—and Mr. Haldwell moved to her other side, taking her arm and wrapping it around his own shoulders for support.

"I—I think I'm all right, though my head is aching frightfully." Miss Clairbridge grimaced and lifted a gloved hand to her head.

Edmund supported her weight as she leaned against him and attempted to take a few shaky steps forward. "Do you remember what happened?" he asked with concern.

She paused, still rocking on her feet, and tilted her head to the side, wincing again at the movement. "I only remember riding Snowdrop, then nothing after that. We were heading toward the pond. At least I think we were. She reared at something. You mentioned a shrew? Yes, I do believe it was." Her eyelids drooped, and she seemed to fight to keep them open.

Snowdrop grazed nearby, seeming to be unaffected by the incident, and the stable boy walked up to her and grasped her reins without issue.

Edmund led Miss Clairbridge to the horses with careful

steps. "I don't think you're fit for riding Snowdrop back to the manor, Miss Clairbridge. You'll have to ride with me." He might have considered returning to Ivy Grange to have a cart hitched to carry her, but he didn't want to leave her—nor did he want to risk making any injuries she might have worse by tarrying.

Eleanor gave a faint nod before he and Mr. Haldwell hoisted her into the saddle.

Edmund cautiously swung his leg over the horse's back, careful not to disturb Miss Clairbridge as he sat behind her. He wrapped his arms around her waist as he held the reins and walked his horse, ensuring she wouldn't fall on the return ride. They rode back to the manor, the stable boy leading Snowdrop by the reins.

Miss Clairbridge slumped against Edmund in the saddle, her head laying back on his chest and her hair tickling his cheek. He peeked over her shoulder.

Her eyes were closed once more. Her bonnet hung limply from her neck, apparently having come loose in the fall. As close as she was, he could smell her faint floral perfume. His heart began to beat faster as the scent overtook his senses. He shook his head. Now was not the time for such foolishness.

After maybe fifteen minutes, Ivy Grange drew near. Fighting the desire to quicken his horse's pace, he rode directly to the front door and halted the stallion, giving the reins to a footman who had awaited their approach. Mr. Haldwell and the stable boy departed to return the other horses to the stables as Edmund slid to the ground, holding a firm hand on Miss Clairbridge's arm to prevent her from tipping off of the saddle. A footman came over to help hold her on the horse, but despite their best effort, she still slumped forward onto General's neck.

Edmund and the footman lowered her down with careful movements. When she was near enough, Edmund wrapped one arm under her shoulders and another beneath her knees, making sure not to disturb her as he carried her inside.

Mrs. Brinder waited in the foyer, and upon seeing Miss Clairbridge's state, lifted her hands to cover her a gasp. "Your Grace, what's happened?" She rushed over and took a closer look at Miss Clairbridge.

"She's fallen off Snowdrop while riding. We need to get her to her room so she may rest. Please have someone send for the doctor." Anxiety colored his voice. There was no telling how bad her injuries were. Outwardly, she looked all right, but what if something was terribly wrong on the inside?

He stepped inside Miss Clairbridge's room and placed her on her bed before he turned to his housekeeper again, who'd just entered the chamber. "Please summon Fanny. She can watch Miss Clairbridge and make sure she is well and comfortable."

Mrs. Brinder bobbed a curtsy and swept from the room, wringing her hands in front of her—the jingle of the keys on her apron marking her progress down the hall.

Edmund crossed his arms in front of him and rested his head against the wall, closing his eyes tightly as a veil of darkness pressed down upon him. Images of his family strewn on the ground, bloodied and bruised, flashed through his mind. Visions he'd long tried to forget. Broken glass. Pallid faces. Lifeless bodies.

He rubbed a hand over his eyes, trying to be rid of the terrible memories. As he opened them, Fanny flew into the room with Mrs. Brinder close behind, a cloth and bowl of water in her hands.

"She fell from a horse? Oh, Ellie!" Fanny pulled a chair from in front of the fireplace to Miss Clairbridge's bedside and collapsed onto it, grabbing one of Miss Clairbridge's hands in both of her own. Fanny stared at Miss Clairbridge, tears filling her eyes and lip quivering. "Will she be a'right?" she whispered.

Edmund handed her his handkerchief, which she used to dab at her shining eyes.

"I hope so," he murmured. "She doesn't have any broken bones from what I can tell, and she even stood earlier, when she was awake."

Mrs. Brinder set the bowl of water onto the bedside table and submerged the piece of cloth into it, wringing it out and positioning it onto Miss Clairbridge's forehead. "Poor dear," she murmured.

The doctor soon arrived and bowed as he entered the room, glancing at his presumed patient and setting his black leather bag on the floor before looking to Edmund. "What has happened?"

Edmund relayed the story as best as he could, including the fact that Miss Clairbridge had moved and fallen in and out of consciousness since being put to bed. Dr. Ameson listened carefully.

When Edmund finished speaking, the physician moved over to where Miss Clairbridge lay unconscious, taking the seat that Fanny had occupied earlier. Snapping open his bag, he reached in and pulled out a small jar of leeches and a scalpel. He twisted the lid to the jar, but Edmund spoke up.

"I beg your pardon, Doctor, but are the leeches necessary?"

The doctor tilted his head, pausing in his opening of the jar. "I suppose not. It is early yet. However..." He speared Edmund with a serious look. "If I find that my patient does not wake within the next two days, they will be." He tightened the lid and set the jar on the table to his left, peering at Edmund as though waiting for him to make further protest.

Edmund—indeed, the entire room—released a collective sigh of relief at the doctor's decision.

"I'll need a lit candle," Dr. Ameson said.

Edmund motioned for his housekeeper to procure one. His blood raced more quickly through his veins with every passing second he remained uninformed as to Miss Clairbridge's condition.

Mrs. Brinder scurried out of the room and returned with a candle, a flame already lighting the wick. She handed it to the doctor, who took it and held it close to Miss Clairbridge's face, prying her eyelids open and moving the candle in front of them. The doctor nodded to himself and set the candle aside, then put the leeches and scalpel away. Thank heavens Miss Clairbridge would not be subjected to blood-letting—at least for the time being.

The physician turned to Edmund. "It is as I suspected. Miss Clairbridge has sustained a head injury from her fall. I cannot know the severity of it until she wakes, but it seems to be rather mild, considering she awoke earlier, as you said. If she wakes again, try to feed her warm broth and tea, then send for me. Your wife might yet recover, but we shall have to wait and see."

At this comment, Edmund again protested, his cheeks warming. "She's not... We're not...married. She's my niece's governess."

Dr. Ameson raised an eyebrow but said nothing more on the matter. "A comfrey poultice should be applied to her head twice daily." He peered at Mrs. Brinder. "I trust you are familiar with this poultice?" At her nod, he continued. "If she wakes and you find that she is in pain, give her a spoonful of this in her tea." Dr. Ameson brought a small bottle of laudanum from his bag. "It should help with the aches."

Edmund thanked Dr. Ameson and escorted him out, his mind spinning and fear clouding his thoughts, even more uncertain and tense now that the doctor had given his opinion.

If. The doctor had said *if*.

What if she didn't wake? His heart ached as though someone had grabbed hold of it and squeezed.

All he could do was wait and see.

He retreated to his study. Collapsing into his desk chair, he rested his elbows on the polished wood and held his head in his hands. Edmund truly didn't know much about the woman, yet he was in terrible turmoil.

He'd been avoiding her for the past two weeks in the hope of dissolving his growing affection for her, but the amount of worry pulling at his chest was much greater than one might expect a duke to have for his niece's governess.

It must be that he felt guilty. As an employee, she was under his care, and he had failed in keeping her from harm. Yes, that was what this was. Guilt. Guilt...

He had to clear his head. He could normally distract himself from his anxieties, but not with this. This, for some odd reason, was different.

~

Ten minutes later, Edmund entered the nursery. Rose sat on the floor, an impossibly small teacup in her hand and three others placed in a careful half circle in front of her. Behind one cup was a painted china doll, and behind another was a wooden horse on wheels. Behind the third sat Rose's nurse, who appeared somewhat abashed at being caught thus.

A wide grin split Rose's face as he walked in. "Uncle Edmund!" she cried, her voice filled with enthusiasm.

"Good day, Rosie."

Before he could say another word, she stood and placed her hands on her hips. "You *must* stay for tea."

Edmund mirrored her stance and raised an eyebrow in mock defiance. "Oh, I must, must I?" Both stared at the other, Rose's nurse looking on with a quivering smile. After a moment, Edmund shrugged as though relenting. "Very well."

What Rose didn't know—or perhaps did—was that Edmund had never even thought of leaving without having tea with her.

He sat on the floor of the nursery, crossing his legs in front of him. "Cream and sugar, please."

Rose sat as well, looking apologetic. "Sorry, Uncle, but Tabby ate all of the sugar cubes." She eyed the wooden horse warily, and Edmund had to force his lips into a straight line.

"Just cream, then," he replied, waiting as she poured invisible liquid from the pot into the cup and then from the creamer into the cup. He accepted it from her and stirred the contents for good measure before taking a sip. "Bit hot, that." He grimaced in an exaggerated fashion.

Rose covered her mouth and giggled. "Uncle, you're supposed to wait for it to cool!"

"My mistake." He paused a moment before taking another sip. "Much better." He nodded. "A very good blend."

Rose nodded in satisfaction, and her nurse stood, brushing off her skirt and moving to a chair in the corner of the room. It seemed she'd had enough tea, now that Edmund could take her place. Reminded of his true purpose in seeking out his niece, he set down his teacup.

"Rosie, there's something I need to tell you."

Rose placed her teacup in the saucer and rested it on the ground, eyes curious. "What, Uncle?"

"Miss Clairbridge will not be able to teach you for the next few days...perhaps, even weeks."

Rose's blond eyebrows furrowed. "Why not?"

Edmund hesitated. Should he tell Rose the truth? "She's... not feeling well. She fell off of Snowdrop this morning."

Rose's eyes widened, concern in them. "Will she get better, Uncle?"

He was quick to reassure her, although he didn't know what the outcome would be himself. "Yes, dearest. She will. For now, you will spend your days with Nurse, as you did before Miss Clairbridge's arrival." He flicked his gaze to Rose's nurse, who gave a small smile in response.

Rose didn't seem very enthusiastic about this plan, but she nodded.

Edmund patted her knee. "When Miss Clairbridge gets better, you'll begin your lessons once more. It won't be so long."

A light came into Rose's eyes. "If I draw her a picture, she'll have to get better!" She jumped up, turning the teapot on its side.

The floor now adequately covered with imaginary tea, Edmund stood and gave his niece a quick kiss on the head. "Yes, dearest. She will."

Those words were as much for his sake as for hers.

CHAPTER 11

*E*dmund was thrown from his rest as a rapid knock sounded on his study door. How long he had slept, he had no idea. His nights were often plagued with restless sleep and visions of that fateful night. Those nightmares and the subsequent tiredness—paired with the stressful events of that particular day—had exhausted him.

He raised his head from his desk and blinked the sleep from his eyes, peeling a piece of paper from his cheek where it had stuck.

After tea with Rose, he'd gone on a brief ride through the forest near Ivy Grange. When that failed to calm his thoughts, he'd enclosed himself in his study, throwing himself into any sort of correspondence and estate dealings he could to distract himself from his own fears. However, no matter how many responses to letters he'd written nor how many seals he'd pressed his signet ring into, Miss Clairbridge and the accident that had befallen her remained at the forefront of his mind.

"Enter." He practically croaked the word as he yawned.

Mrs. Brinder burst into the room, breathless. "Your Grace, she's awake!"

That exclamation dashed all of Edmund's grogginess away. He bolted out of his chair and followed Mrs. Brinder from the room and up the stairs, the evening's setting sun peeking through the windowpanes and illuminating the corridor at intervals. It was apparent Edmund had slept for a longer amount of time than he'd guessed.

When they reached Miss Clairbridge's room, they slowed, entering as though the creak of a floorboard would send her back to unconsciousness. Miss Clairbridge gave a feeble smile as they crept in. She was pale, dressed in a clean white day dress, a worn pale-blue shawl draped around her shoulders. Fanny was stationed at Miss Clairbridge's bedside, fussing over the bedcovers and making sure they were positioned around her in a comfortable cocoon. Edmund stepped over to Eleanor with all care, the tension in him fading with her weary smile.

"Miss Clairbridge." He released a breath of relief, sending his silent thanks to the heavens above. "You have no idea how happy I am that you are awake." It was as though a weight had been lifted from his shoulders, but he didn't yet know how well she actually was. He turned to Mrs. Brinder. "Has Dr. Ameson been sent for?"

Mrs. Brinder nodded, smiling down at Miss Clairbridge with a sort of maternal affection in her expression. "Yes, Your Grace. I sent for him the moment Miss Clairbridge opened her eyes."

Edmund gave her a grateful look before turning his attention back to his governess. "Miss Clairbridge, how do you feel? Are you hungry? Do you need anything?" It was a terrible thing to see her so weak, and Edmund wanted to do whatever he could to make her feel better. Miss Clairbridge gave another frail smile at his concern. How could she have the strength to smile in her state? But if anyone could, it would be her.

"I am well enough, Your Grace. I would, however, enjoy

something to eat, as I find I'm quite famished." Though her voice was soft, her reply was steadier than earlier.

Mrs. Brinder fled the room without another word, presumably to get Miss Clairbridge a bowl of broth.

Edmund wanted to say more, to converse with her further, but words often seemed to elude him when he was in her presence.

Luckily, Miss Clairbridge spoke for him. "Thank you for all of this, Your Grace. It is really too much for a simple governess like me to be receiving such attention."

He raised his eyebrows in surprise at her words and gave her his most earnest expression as he spoke. "Miss Clairbridge, it is the least I can do. You are not just 'a simple governess.' You are a valued member of this household. Rose adores you, and the rest of the staff do as well." How could the woman before him believe that the sole title she held at Ivy Grange was governess? She was so much more to Rose and the servants.

She is so much more to me.

Edmund blanched. That thought had no business being in his mind.

Miss Clairbridge lowered her eyes to her bedcovers, and Edmund could have sworn that her previously pale cheeks now had a hint of color to them. "That is very kind, Your Grace," she murmured.

Mrs. Brinder returned, holding a tray with a bowl of broth perched atop it. "Here you are, dearie." She placed the tray on Miss Clairbridge's lap and smiled at her with warmth. "My, what a lovely necklace."

Her compliment drew Edmund's attention to the chain around Miss Clairbridge's throat. He didn't remember seeing it before.

Miss Clairbridge gave her thanks, but before she could eat and before Edmund could ask about her necklace, Dr. Ameson strode into the room.

He smiled at his patient and set his bag down. "So you're finally awake! I suppose the leeches will be unnecessary, after all."

Miss Clairbridge's eyes widened.

"Forgive me, Miss Clairbridge." The older man gave a brief bow. "I'm Dr. Ameson. His Grace sent for me after you'd fallen from your horse earlier today—Snowdrop, I believe? Anyway, when I arrived, you were not awake—terribly inconsiderate of you, you must know—but I digress. How are you feeling?"

The doctor's quick speech elicited a slight wrinkle between Miss Clairbridge's brows, but she responded readily enough. "Good evening, Dr. Ameson. I'm not feeling terribly unwell, considering the circumstances. My head hurts a little, but it's not awful. Not like it was when I first awoke."

Edmund cleared his throat. "I'll—erm—step out..."

Dr. Ameson eyed him. "My examination will be basic, I assure you."

Edmund scratched the back of his head and looked to Miss Clairbridge, wishing to give her privacy if she desired it.

"You can stay, Your Grace." A pale pink hue painted her cheeks, but her eyes remained on his until the doctor procured another tool from his bag.

Dr. Ameson began his examination, once again checking Miss Clairbridge's reflexes and performing other tests. Finally, he stood straight, a mild expression on his face. Anticipation filled Edmund as he waited for the doctor to give them the news.

"She does not appear to have any severe injuries from the fall, and it is a good sign that she is awake. I believe she'll be as fit as a fiddle in a week or two," Dr. Ameson declared.

Relief surged through Edmund, making him feel momentarily weightless. Mrs. Brinder and Fanny both expressed their gladness at the good news with clapping and exclamations of joy, and Edmund grinned at Miss Clairbridge's hopeful face.

She would get better, and that was all that mattered. He moved toward the door, hoping to escape before he was noticed.

"Your Grace?" Miss Clairbridge's voice called to him from behind like a siren.

Edmund spun on his heel. "Yes, Miss Clairbridge?"

Her hands trapped themselves in the folds of her blanket. "Thank you. For finding me...and bringing me back."

His heart jumped in his chest, his ribcage smaller than it once was. He nodded, not meeting her eyes. "You're welcome."

Her words penetrated his flesh as easily as any balm. The problem was, he'd rather she were a poison.

~

*L*ater that same evening, Edmund tossed in his bed, lost in the place between sleep and wakefulness.

Prumb burst into the library. "Your Grace!"

Edmund exhaled an amused huff of breath, keeping his eyes on the pages of the collection of poems he'd been reading. "'Your Grace'? I think not, Prumb. What has your mind in such a knot?"

"Edmund," Prumb began, but a thick silence filled the room.

Edmund finally looked up at his butler's face. He set the book aside and stood, brows furrowed. "Prumb? What's wrong?"

The butler swallowed and straightened his shoulders, seeming to prepare himself for the words he was about to speak. "Your parents..."

Edmund's chest constricted. "What's happened, Prumb? Is something amiss?"

Prumb was silent, eyes mournful and red-rimmed. A tear fell down the man's cheek.

He'd never seen Prumb cry. "No...no. No—"

"No!" Edmund lurched in his bed, hair stuck to his forehead with sweat, chest heaving.

That evening, he hadn't stayed in the library, reading until the wee hours of the morning as he usually did. Reassured by

Dr. Ameson's confident prediction of Miss Clairbridge's recovery, he'd retired rather early, forgetting for a blissful moment the nightmares that always plagued him in the hours of darkness.

He buried his face in his hands, his fingers growing wet with tears. Sleep had become a curse—a curse he couldn't escape—ever since the accident that stole his family from him.

Lifting his face from his hands, he blinked his weary eyes and pushed himself back to lean against the cool, sturdy mahogany bedframe. Tilting his head backward, he stared blankly at the curtain that hung overhead—or the space where he imagined it was, as his bedroom was dark as dark could be. All was quiet. Only the sound of his breathing filled the space. Was God here at all?

He was tired of being alone. Tired of being ruled by fear—daily and nightly. His family's accident had been gruesome. It had made him wish to die, himself, but he knew—inside—that that wasn't truly what he wished for. Neither did he wish to continue to stay away from Miss Clairbridge. He wanted to know her. To befriend her.

Could he push past the darkness enough to allow himself that?

~

*E*leanor opened her eyes to behold her bedroom, the shades drawn at the windows and Fanny in a chair next to her. Eleanor sat up, covering her mouth as she attempted to stifle her yawn. "Good morning."

"Oh good, ye're awake!" Fanny set aside the stocking she had been darning and rose, a grin on her face. "Mrs. Brinder just brought in yer luncheon. I was 'opin you'd wake up to eat it."

Eleanor rubbed her eyes and blinked a few times. "Luncheon?"

Fanny picked up the tray from the side table and placed it on Eleanor's lap. "Ye slept right through the mornin', Ellie. I s'pose it's due to yer fall yesterday."

Her stomach growled as she surveyed a bowl of steaming broth, a biscuit, and a cup of tea. Skipping meals really did make one hungry.

Fanny grabbed Eleanor's shawl from the desk by the window and wrapped the worn fabric around Eleanor's shoulders with careful movements. She gave her thanks and pulled the maroon-colored garment tighter around her. Fanny sat once more, and Eleanor lifted a spoon of broth to her mouth, pausing before it reached her lips.

"Fanny?" She hesitated.

"Yes?" Fanny set the stocking in her lap.

"Have you heard of piskies?"

Fanny furrowed her red eyebrows and had just opened her mouth to respond when a light knock sounded at the door to Eleanor's room. Fanny strode to the door and swung it open, stepping to the side. The duke stood in the doorframe with a book in hand and a piece of foolscap, a hopeful expression on his face.

"Miss Clairbridge. Fanny." He bowed somewhat awkwardly. "It occurred to me that lying in bed all day is dreadfully boring —I had a bout of ague as a child and had to do the same—and so thought I might read to Miss Clairbridge—if she'll allow me, that is." The duke glanced at the book in his hands and turned it over twice whilst clearing his throat, not meeting Eleanor's gaze.

Eleanor's lips turned up in a bright smile, and she nodded, adjusting her shawl around her shoulders. Although it was dangerous to be spending time with the man—her heartbeat picked up its pace as though in agreement—she couldn't resist the endearing look of vulnerability on His Grace's face. Nor could she resist the delightfully warm feeling that filled her chest every time she was in his presence.

"I—I would love..." Eleanor tempered her enthusiasm. "I would very much enjoy that."

Fanny made the excuse that she needed to tell Mrs. Brinder something and scurried from the room before the duke could even sit down. Eleanor could've sworn there was a smile on the girl's face before she left.

The duke perched on the chair Fanny had occupied and studied Eleanor for a moment, concern in his green eyes. "How are you feeling?"

Eleanor tried her best to present the picture of health. "I'm very well, Your Grace." She grinned, although she feared it came off more like a grimace given the sluggish feeling that lingered after her injury.

The duke raised an eyebrow, an amused smile quirking up one corner of his mouth. At the realization that there were dark circles under his eyes, she fought not to raise her own eyebrows.

"Very well, you say? Pardon me if I don't exactly believe that to be true, Miss Clairbridge—though I appreciate your attempt at sparing me worry." Before Eleanor could question him, he extended the piece of paper to her. "From Rose," he explained.

She took the paper, smiling at the childish picture even as the duke's words distracted her. The girl had drawn what appeared to be herself, Eleanor, and the duke standing side by side, with Snowdrop and Blackberry off to the left.

"How lovely." She studied the picture for a moment longer before glancing back at the duke, heart light. "Since I arrived here, she has been the sweetest, most charming little girl that I have ever had the pleasure of knowing."

The duke returned her smile, albeit a tired one. "Rosie has

always been so, yet I'd be remiss not to mention that a good governess will always bring out the best in her pupils."

Heat rose to Eleanor's cheeks at his compliment.

After a quiet moment, the duke tapped the book on his knee and showed Eleanor the spine.

"Robinson Crusoe."

"Indeed. It's a story I've always enjoyed." His eyes took on a faraway look. "My father would read it to my mother in the evenings—among other books—and I would listen with all of the eager enthusiasm of a young boy. Have you read it?"

Eleanor shook her head, anticipation welling within her at the idea of listening to a new story—and in his rich baritone. "I have not. I do not believe it was in my father's library."

"Splendid." His countenance brightened, his voice eager. "We will enjoy it together."

He opened the book and was about to begin, but she couldn't let him retreat behind his mask of indomitable happiness. He did so much too often already.

"Your Grace?"

He lifted his head, a questioning expression on his face.

Eleanor continued before she lost her nerve. "Are you well?"

For a moment, they only stared at each other. There was some sort of inner conflict within him.

Finally, he shot her a grin. "Perfectly," he replied, his expression becoming guarded.

Much as she didn't believe him and couldn't help feeling a pang of disappointment that he wouldn't confide in her, she wouldn't press him. But had he made his decision because of her, or because of himself?

CHAPTER 12

*T*hree days later, Eleanor was utterly sick of being confined to her bed. The duke had continued his afternoon visits, each time reading a few more chapters of *Robinson Crusoe*, yet he had been distant ever since her question —something that affected her perhaps more than it should have.

Despite this, she never failed to become excited when his unique knock sounded on her bedchamber door. His company was...reassuring. She knew with him—somehow—that she was safe. Her only complaint was that their time spent together was so short. That, and being confined to her room.

Eleanor tired of only seeing the same four walls, day in and day out. She tired of the drapes being constantly closed, the minimal sunlight in her room, and broth for every meal. Doctor Ameson's orders were strict, and Fanny wouldn't stray from them a bit—no matter how much Eleanor begged. A pop sounded from Eleanor's back as she sat up in bed. She longed to get out and stretch her legs.

Fanny had only just left the room, going to the kitchen to retrieve Eleanor's midday meal, when a wild, likely foolhardy plan began to brew in Eleanor's mind. Ten minutes. That was enough time, surely? She'd be back in her bed before her friend was aware she'd left it. Swinging her legs out from under the covers, she set her feet on the smooth wooden floor, wrapping her shawl tighter around her shoulders.

She should have no trouble, really.

Eleanor pushed herself off of the bed, feeling only a little unsteady on her feet. Her feet carried her stealthily to the window, and she reached for one of the drapes—as excited to see the sun as a washerwoman on laundry day.

"Miss Clairbridge?"

Eleanor froze at the rich, warm-toned voice coming from behind her. She'd been caught. She turned at a glacial pace, attempting an innocent look as the duke came into view, *Robinson Crusoe* in his grasp. She moved so slowly that the skirts of her faded pink dress hardly stirred as she gripped them.

Fanny had been helping her dress every morning since Eleanor's fall. It made Eleanor feel a little less like an invalid. But her hair had long since begun to fall from the pins the maid had inserted earlier. It was difficult not to muss it when one spent one's days leaning against a bedframe.

"Your Grace." She offered a sheepish smile.

He raised an auburn eyebrow and moved into the room. "I just spoke with Fanny in the hall. She seems to think you need a few more days of rest."

"Does she?" Eleanor's voice faltered as she bit her lip.

The duke crossed his arms over his chest, a thoughtful expression on his face as he tilted his head to the side. "And I do believe Dr. Ameson said the same when he visited yesterday."

Eleanor remained where she was. "Did he?" She flicked her gaze to the floor, her cheeks heating. Silence descended. Eleanor wrung her hands behind her back, fighting the inner urging to admit defeat. After a moment, she sighed and returned her gaze to his face. One corner of his lips were pulled up in an amused half smile as he awaited her explanation. "I only wished to be out of that bed. I'm terribly tired of it, you see. I haven't even been able to look out of that window more than once per day. Dr. Ameson believes the dark will do me good." She stared at the closed drapes with longing.

"I'm familiar with your pain, Miss Clairbridge, for I suffered through a few childhood illnesses, though I'm more worried as to what Fanny will say if she sees you up."

Eleanor nodded. Talk of Fanny's scoldings had reached Eleanor from the other servants, and needless to say, she did not want to be on the receiving end of one. Odd for so sweet a girl to be so merciless in her reprimands, but the fire that warmed Fanny's lively spirit also must provide heat enough to burn.

"I guess I may bear a few more days."

"Perhaps after this." He pulled the drape back to reveal the green landscape outside, the grey clouds mottled in light and dark hues.

Releasing a contented sigh, Eleanor tried to commit the image to memory.

The duke winked. "I'll leave it open. Tell Fanny it was my doing."

He flashed her a smile, and she took a few small steps toward bed before a sudden wave of dizziness crashed into her, making her pause. The room began to spin.

The duke was at her side in a moment. "Miss Clairbridge, are you quite all right?" He placed a steadying hand on her arm, a gentle yet firm touch. Comforting. He wouldn't let her fall.

"I believe so." The room came back to a standstill. "Just a bout of dizziness—nothing more."

He led her to her bed, and she sat once more, oddly energized by his nearness. His very smile seemed to renew her.

"Thank you."

He seated himself in his usual chair.

Fanny returned, her eyes glued to the tray in her hand. "I tell ya, Ellie, Mrs. Brewer is as fine a cook as I've e'er seen, and I'll not believe anyone who says elsewise. She let me 'ave an apple tart an—Yer Grace!" Fanny glanced up and paused in her chatter, bobbing a curtsy before placing the tray on Eleanor's lap. "I thought ya might be comin' to visit Ellie when I passed ye in the hall. That Robson Crosue seems a good sort of fellow to be readin' about."

Eleanor smiled at her. "Thank you, Fanny, and yes, Robinson Crusoe is a good sort of fellow to be reading about."

Fanny blinked at Eleanor's pronunciation. "'S that 'is name? Lord above, there's more pieces to the pie than I thought. Well, I s'pose it's a bold name, anyway. Ye'd need a bold name if ye're to go on adventures and the like."

"You certainly would." Amusement twinkled in the duke's eyes.

"Oh!" Fanny shot Eleanor a sly smile. "I was s'posed to bring an extra biscuit for ye. I'll go fetch it." Fanny fled the room, an action she'd gotten in the habit of since the duke had begun his daily visits.

He focused on the book in his hand and seated himself, relaxing in the chair. "Now I believe we left off on page fifty..."

A shaft of light from the open drape fell over Eleanor, heating her skin. It was just like His Grace's presence—warm and pleasant. Could anything be better than this?

∼

*E*leanor smiled as Rose searched the colorful flower garden for a compelling object to draw. The bright sky illuminated the vibrancy of the various blooms, and the air was fresh and sweet. A pebbled path wove between daffodils and rose bushes, circling around snowdrops and crocuses before being greeted by hyacinths and tulips and at least a dozen other varieties of blooms. She'd have to make sure they didn't miss the forget-me-nots in the far back corner of the garden.

It had been almost a fortnight since Eleanor's fall, and she was no longer constrained to her room. Because of this, she could now put more energy into getting to the bottom of the duke's melancholy.

A small squeal of excitement brought Eleanor's attention to the present. Rose stared at something in the midst of a particularly round bush and seemed entranced by whatever she had found. Curiosity piqued, Eleanor stood from her place on a stone bench and made her way over to Rose. The girl almost seemed to be holding her breath.

"What have you found?" Eleanor peered over Rose's shoulder.

Rose kept her attention on the bush, or rather what was inside of it, pointing with her pencil at something.

Eleanor's gaze followed, and she gave a short exhale of surprise. A nest cradling three sparsely feathered baby birds nestled between a few branches of the bush. Their eyes were closed, and their wisp-covered heads were too large for their bodies. They must have heard movement and thought it was their parents, for their beaks were wide open, awaiting food. "How marvelous."

Rose nodded. "I think I shall draw them for Uncle Edmund," she declared in a quiet tone.

Eleanor hid her amused smile at Rose's determination and tried to straighten her face into a serious look. "A very good idea. We must make sure we don't get too close, however, as we do not want to frighten their parents when they come back with a meal."

Rose tilted her head to the side for a moment, then straightened and nodded with a resolute air. She took a few steps away from the nest and began to sketch the nest of chicks, her hand moving from one corner of the paper to the next in rapid succession.

With Rose occupied, Eleanor was free to enjoy the breathtaking gardens. Flowers of every type and color brightened the area and laced the air with a delicious scent. Birds chirruped in the surrounding foliage, and the soft beat of their wings swept against the breeze.

A particular rosebush decorated with pale yellow blooms caught her attention. She brushed the soft petals of one of them and stooped to smell its sweetness. Closing her eyes, she inhaled, the scent not overly powerful, yet intoxicating all the same. The rose was warm against her fingers, having been heated by the gentle rays of the sun.

"Beautiful, aren't they?" A voice murmured from beside her.

She startled, standing straight and dropping her hand as her head whipped around, eyes wide. The duke stood beside her, an unknown emotion in his expression. "Your Grace!"

She would have expected him to be in his study, inspecting document after document regarding tenants and crop yields, or out on his afternoon ride. Fanny had told her he was somewhat of a sportsman.

He winced in a show of contrition and took a step closer. "I'm sorry to have startled you, Miss Clairbridge." He tilted his head to examine the sky before meeting her eyes again. "It is such a pleasant day that I could not bear to be stuck inside for its entirety. I thought to take a turn about the gardens when I caught a glimpse of you and Rose here. I only hope I'm not interrupting your lessons." He scratched the back of his neck, his mouth drawn into something between a grimace and half smile. How charming was his hesitation.

She lifted the corners of her lips in a small smile, her heart beating unaccountably quickly. "Not at all, Your Grace. I just thought to smell the roses while Rose practices her drawing."

She motioned to where Rose stood, her tongue sticking out of the side of her mouth and her brow furrowed in concentration as she moved her pencil over the paper of her notebook. The duke glanced at his niece, then seemed to relax, and his arm dropped back down to his side.

He gave Eleanor a relieved grin. "Good. What is it she's drawing?"

Did Rose mean for the drawing to be a surprise? "I'm not sure that I'm at my liberty to reveal the subject, Your Grace."

A surprised chuckle escaped from the duke's throat, and the side of his mouth quirked up in that half smile which never failed to enliven the butterflies in her stomach.

"How very interesting." He rubbed his mouth, covering a hint of a smile. "I suppose I shall find out later, then?"

Eleanor returned his smile. "I do believe so, Your Grace."

The duke stared at her for a moment, his eyes softening. What was he looking for? "I would like you to call me Edmund, if you are comfortable doing so. I feel as though you are already such an important part of our household, and it seems strange to stand on such formality."

Eleanor tensed. He wanted her to call him by his Christian name? She was but his employee—a woman with neither fair face nor fortune. But then again...had she not spent many a pleasant afternoon in his company? Had she not been honest with him as she would a friend? Eleanor blinked, frantically trying to decide what to say.

"Would not that be highly improper, Your Grace? The servants would certainly talk if a governess spoke so informally to her employer—a duke, no less."

He seemed to ponder this a moment, then replied. "Perhaps you might only address me as such when we are without company. When a guest is over you may address me as 'Your Grace'—so as not to set tongues to wagging—but I do not believe it is improper in the least, and I trust my servants not to gossip. And, after all, we are also friends, no?"

Eleanor's eyes widened. She had not dared to think that the duke considered them to be friends—it was an idea too outlandish to ponder. She, herself, had considered him a friend in a sense, but the idea that he was her employer seemed to push that classification away.

Her heart desired to consider him such, but her mind would have none of it—such was the nature of the conflict that had formed within her. Perhaps it was not so improper, after all. And if she wasn't using his Christian name in company, there would be no worry for gossip.

Eleanor let a slow breath out, having come to her decision. She met his eyes. "Very well, Your Gr—Edmund. However, I will only agree to the use of your Christian name if you will use mine in return." She raised an eyebrow in mock imperiousness and awaited his response.

His Grace gifted her a winsome smile. "If you wish, Miss Clairbridge...Eleanor."

Eleanor's name had never before been spoken with such sweetness of tone, though perhaps that sweetness had naught to do with tone at all but rather who was speaking her name. That, combined with the glowing smile Edmund directed at her, made her heart pound.

How handsome the duke—Edmund—was. His tousled hair, probably mussed from having run his hand through it, reflected the noon light and appeared almost bronze in the sun's shining rays. His brilliant green eyes were light as he gazed at her—the color similar to that of the ivy vines that grew so steadfastly up buildings and structures.

Yes, Edmund cut quite the dashing figure, and Eleanor's cheeks flushed—no doubt, that time-told mushroom red. She'd been staring at him. Fortunately, it seemed Edmund had over-looked her lack of proper manners and self-control. Trying to quell the warm feeling blossoming inside of her chest, Eleanor once again touched the petals of a yellow blossom, breathing in the scent. "These roses are unlike any I have ever seen."

Edmund looked once more to the roses, a bittersweet smile on his face and, again, that sadness in his eyes. "Yes, they're rather unique. My mother planted them when she married my father. She always loved to garden, and she was constantly overseeing their care."

"Was their marriage a love match?" She was bolder now that he considered her to be a friend.

Edmund turned his sorrowful eyes to where Rose stood, still absorbed in drawing the birds. "Yes, and so was my brother's marriage." He sighed, and the weight that his exhale held was almost tangible. "They passed several years ago now."

The words hung in the air like a cloud of thick smoke, but Eleanor keenly understood his melancholy as he spoke them. "I'm sorry, Edmund. It is terrible to lose the people closest to you."

He focused on the ground, shoulders hunched. "I remember you telling me you lost your father."

"Yes." The familiar ache thumped in her chest. The pain might never go away. "He died seven years ago. Not a day passes that I do not feel the loss of his presence on this earth. That is why I'm here."

Edmund turned his eyes on her, a question in them.

Eleanor released a breath and explained. "Before my father got sick, he made investments in a few crops in the Americas. Much of our money was put toward paying the doctors' fees, and things got worse when the crops were blighted. Soon after, he died."

Edmund's gaze, which never strayed from hers, provided the strength she needed to continue.

"We had our savings, and my mother kept the ledgers from me to try to protect me. I never dreamed we were in such circumstances..." She swallowed the lump of emotion that had built in her throat. "Truthfully, I became a governess to save my home and my father's memory, and to keep myself and my mother off the streets." Eleanor blinked away tears. "I apologize. That was likely more than you wished to hear."

Edmund furrowed his brows and took a step closer. "You've no need to apologize—"

Eleanor drew in a sharp intake of breath at a sudden prick of her finger, an errant thorn being the culprit. She let her hand fall away from the rose she had been touching, then gave a light laugh at her own expense, attempting to lift the mood as she raised her hand to show him her finger. A bloom of blood expanded from where the thorn had made its mark. "'Tis only a scratch."

Eleanor thought Edmund might laugh with her, but instead, he tenderly grasped her hand and inspected the small wound. She took in a quick breath. Had he noticed her reaction?

With his head tilted toward her finger, he lifted his eyes to hers, his piercing green gaze freezing her in place. "May I?" he murmured.

Wide-eyed, Eleanor nodded, though what could he do to help?

He reached into his coat pocket and retrieved a white handkerchief.

"Edmund, it will stain! It is no matter, really." Eleanor shook her head and tried to pull her hand away, but he held it firmly in his gentle grasp and gave a half smile.

"I have many more just like it. I will gladly spare this one." He pressed the handkerchief to her bleeding finger with just enough force to stop the flow of blood. He held it there for a moment, cradling her hand in his. His hand was warm on hers.

After a few moments, he lifted the handkerchief and examined the wound once again, which had now stopped bleeding.

"Thank you." With an appreciative smile, she removed her hand from his grasp, and he placed the bloodied handkerchief back in his pocket. Her hand still tingled from his touch, and she brushed it on her skirts to try to banish the feeling.

Edmund searched her face before nodding in acknowledgement, his face unexpressive but his eyes full of emotion. "It's my pleasure," he replied before bowing and heading back toward the manor.

She was all too familiar with the pain Edmund held within —how it could eat away at a person from the inside, make them a hollow shell. After the death of her father, it had been hard for her to speak of him to anyone. When she finally did, it had lifted a weight from her shoulders.

As much as sharing his pain would also help Edmund, as much as she might long for him to confide in her, that decision could only be made by him. Time gleaned the best results.

CHAPTER 13

$\mathcal{A}$t dinner that night, Rose wiggled in her seat, her excitement palpable. Eleanor met Edmund's eyes from where he sat at the head of the table to find that he mirrored her amused expression. Things had changed between them since they'd spoken in the garden—or perhaps even earlier than that.

Rose clutched a paper, apparently trying to hide it from Edmund, as she held it beneath the table in a secretive manner and hadn't yet spoken a word of it. Eleanor couldn't help but smile, as the girl's obvious anticipation reminded her of her own childhood.

As soon as they finished the meal, they all stood from the table, and Rose jumped out of her chair. Grinning, she skipped a few steps over to Edmund, her curls bouncing. She peered up into his amused face and thrust forward the wrinkled paper. "Uncle Edmund, I have a gift for you."

Edmund accepted the page with care, a doting smile on his face. "How very thoughtful of you, dearest. Thank you." He met Eleanor's gaze before he examined the drawing. After a moment, he puffed out his chest and stood tall, his chin raised ever so slightly. A resolute expression came over his face. "I declare, this is the most magnificent piece of artistry I have ever beheld. I assume that the London museum has been notified of this masterpiece, as they will surely wish to view it and meet the most talented artist."

Rose giggled, and Edmund grinned down at her, breaking character. "It's a drawing I made of a bird's nest that Miss Clairbridge and I found outside. Do you like it?"

Edmund knelt on one knee so that he was at eye level with her. You've done a wonderful job, dearest. I love it. Thank you, Rosie."

The skin around Rose's eyes crinkled in delight, and she rushed forward to hug him. Eleanor's heart swelled in admiration for the kindhearted man in front of her. He would make a great father one day, and he was as good as a father to Rose already.

At the idea of watching Edmund marry some upper-crust lady and having children, Eleanor's thoughts strayed down a gloomy path. Would she still be there then? Perhaps so. Edmund was of the age when most men were already looking for a wife. Perhaps she'd even be the governess to his children.

Edmund deserved a kind and loving wife. Someone who would make him happy and who would never take him for granted. Her heart seemed to shrink in her chest, and a small frown settled on her face.

As Edmund rose after embracing Rose, he turned to Eleanor and, always observant, seemed to note her expression. "Miss Clairbridge, are you all right?"

Eleanor tried her best to smile convincingly. Hopefully, it didn't look as false as she imagined. "Yes, Your Grace. Thank you."

His mouth pulled into a straight line.

Before he could reply, Rose's nurse appeared in the doorway. Edmund touched his niece's shoulder. "You should be off to bed, Rosie. I'm sure Miss Clairbridge has many interesting lessons planned for tomorrow, and you wouldn't want to sleep through them."

Rose yawned, then smiled with half-closed eyes at Edmund. She stepped over to Eleanor to give her a quick hug before wishing them both goodnight.

As Rose left on the heels of her nurse, Edmund called after her, "Sweet dreams, dearest."

The cherubic girl peeked over her shoulder at them and gave a toothy grin, yawning again before exiting the room. Edmund and Eleanor were now alone, save the footman stationed at the wall.

She cleared her throat. "I believe I shall head to bed as well, Your Grace. I wish you a pleasant rest of your evening." She hurried from the room.

As much as she wished to stay and speak with him more, it was imperative that she leave for her chamber to preserve some formality between them—and distance, if she wished for her heart to remain unattached.

～

*L*ater that evening, Edmund sat reclined in the library reading a book by the dying fire. Late-spring nights were typically warmer, but tonight brought a chill. He sipped a cup of tepid tea and set it back upon the tray which Mrs. Brinder had brought him before she had retired for the night. She had even included a plate of his favorite biscuits. What a thoughtful woman she was.

Edmund settled deeper into his leather chair and flipped another page in *The Complete Poetical Works of Robert Burns*. All was quiet except for the sound of the smoldering coals in the fireplace and the steady tick of the grandfather clock, its hour hand pointing at the space only a few ticks before two, its pendulum reflecting the small amount of light the dying fire provided. Because of the hour, the sound of shuffling books from what seemed to be the opposite side of the room brought him immediately upright. His shoulders tensed.

As a light humming reached his ears, he peeked around the back of his chair. Eleanor, in her dressing robe, candle in hand, balanced on her tiptoes to reach a book high on a shelf.

He averted his eyes, his face flushing with warmth. Edmund tossed his book aside and stood, intending a quick escape, but his movement caught Eleanor's attention. She froze, her mouth open and her arm still in the air. After a moment, she dropped her arm and frantically tried to pull her dressing gown around her, a blush stealing across her cheeks. Her hair hung in a long braid over her shoulder, a ribbon securing it.

"I'm sorry, Your Gr—Edmund. I—I had no idea that anyone else was awake."

Edmund forced himself to look anywhere but at her and clasped his hands behind his back in a tight grip. "There is no need to apologize—my chair shielded me from view. Of course, everyone is free to use this library, at any time." Now that she was sufficiently covered, Edmund walked over to her, his feet seeming to move of their own accord. He took the small amount of time these steps afforded to breathe in what air he had lost upon seeing her. "Do you need help in reaching a book?" He did his utmost to mask the waver in his voice caused by her state of undress.

She nodded as she gazed up at the shelf. "I was trying to reach that book up there." She tilted her head back. "The collection of poems." She pointed to a dark-green book with a worn cover.

"Wordsworth. A fine collection, indeed—I've read it many times myself." He reached up and slid the book from its place on the shelf before holding it out to her.

Eleanor's eyebrows raised as she took the volume from his

hand. "You're fond of Wordsworth? Not many of my acquaintances enjoy poetry, though I always have."

Edmund's lips curved into a warm smile at her admission. "He's one of my favorite poets," he replied, taking a step forward.

Eleanor hugged the book to her chest and returned his grin. "Mine as well." The words were a murmur on her lips as she half leaned against the shelf.

Edmund's smile turned thoughtful as he recited a favorite poem from his memory.

> "I wandered lonely as a cloud
> That floats on high o'er vales and hills,
> When all at once I saw a crowd,
> A host, of golden daffodils,"

Eleanor spoke the next lines without hesitation. The words flowed like honey from her lips as she painted the poem's picture.

> "Beside the lake, beneath the trees,
> Fluttering and dancing in the breeze."

Their eyes locked, and the air between them filled with energy. How long did they stand like that? Perhaps mere seconds...or minutes. The faint firelight reflected in her eyes and gave a sort of golden glow to her face. She looked just like an angel, or what he presumed them to look like. Her skin appeared so soft and her hair so silken.

Edmund forced his hands to remain at his sides, to not reach out to her. Despite this, he found his face nearing hers ever so slowly. He was entranced by her—his mind in a sweet fog whenever she was near.

Eleanor's chin tilted up, and wisps of hair that had come

free from her braid grazed her cheeks. She appeared to be leaning closer as well.

Their lips were mere inches away from each other when a light howling of wind rattled the windowpanes and broke the reverie. Edmund blinked as though he'd just woken from a pleasant dream—something he never experienced anymore. It was why he was in the library in the first place.

"Thank you." She murmured the words, then turned and fled, her braid coming loose ever more with the movement. She left the room, her white dressing gown flowing in her wake.

As though an apparition, she leaves as quickly as she arrives. Something on the floor caught his attention, and he bent down to examine it. The ribbon from her hair.

Picking it up, Edmund brushed the blue silk between his fingers before pocketing it and moving back over to his chair by the fireplace. His tea now chilled, he once again settled himself and opened the book he'd been reading before his interaction with Eleanor. Edmund tried to continue to read, though his attempts were in vain, for he could not focus on the words written on the pages when his mind was filled only with thoughts of that beautiful angel and her light-filled eyes.

But she would not be his. Not with her spirit or kindness or smile or beauty. He would love her too much, and he could never bear losing her.

CHAPTER 14

The next morning, Eleanor woke, groggy from her lack of sleep. The night before, after she had left the library, her mind had been a whirlwind of conflicting emotions. A part of her was drawn to the duke, yet another piece of her reminded her of her true purpose in becoming a governess.

Almost kissing her employer was not a part of that plan!

Indeed, she hadn't been able to sleep very well once she'd returned to her room—tossing and turning in her bed throughout the night and admonishing herself at intervals—and truly, it was a wonder she'd slept at all.

Rubbing her eyes, she yawned, then threw the bedcovers off of her, swinging her legs over the side of the cozy mattress.

Fanny bustled into the room with a breakfast tray in hand, humming a cheerful tune, although she stopped in her tracks when she caught sight of Eleanor. "My!" She placed the tray on the bedside table. "Ye look as though ye haven't got a wink o' sleep!"

Eleanor gave a wry smile. "Thank you, Fanny."

Fanny giggled and sat on the bed next to her, grasping one

of her hands. "Oh, come now, Ellie. Ye know I don't mean a thing by it. I'm right concerned, is all."

Eleanor squeezed her hand and gave an affectionate smile to her companion. "I know, Fanny—and I'm exhausted. I scarcely slept at all last night."

Fanny jumped from the bed and handed Eleanor the tray of delicious-smelling foods, a steaming cup of tea tickling Eleanor's nose as she picked it up and brought it close to her mouth.

"Maybe a good meal will help ye. I always feel better after I eat." Fanny was about to leave when she paused, looking over her shoulder at Eleanor. "Oh! I meant to tell ye, His Grace asked to speak to ye in his study."

Eleanor half choked on her tea, and her pulse began to race, but Fanny was gone.

She walked over to the dressing table, her breakfast forgotten, and glanced at her drawn face in the mirror. Dark circles had made their home beneath her eyes, and her hair had come out of its braid—now a tangled mess of knots and wisps. Fanny was right. Eleanor didn't look like she'd slept at all.

"Oh, heavens."

She could only imagine the forthcoming conversation—and the possibility that she would be packing her trunk following it. She'd been dreadfully close to kissing Edmund the previous night—abominably, terribly, awfully close—although she hadn't stuck around long enough to see his reaction. Perhaps he'd been about to dismiss her, and her fleeing had only served to prolong the inevitable.

～

"Thank you for meeting me, Eleanor." Edmund loosely clasped his hands on the wooden desk in front of him, though he released one to stifle a yawn. His hair was even more mussed than usual, although his green eyes were bright. He had shaved, however tired he might be. Eleanor could smell the soap's refreshing bergamot fragrance. He also wore fine clothes, as he did every day. Today, a dark-brown waistcoat and blue tailcoat, though his cravat was tied somewhat haphazardly around his throat.

Angry moths fluttered in her midsection. She'd fixed her appearance as best she could, but the circles under her eyes had proved more difficult to make disappear. Even her most presentable lilac gown likely wasn't distracting from them. Was she about to be thrown out without a letter of reference because of their near-kiss?

A small smile graced Edmund's lip. "I called you here because—well—I pay my employees their wages on a monthly basis, and as you've now been Rose's governess for a month, it is time for you to receive yours." He pulled open a drawer on the right side of his desk.

Eleanor nearly sighed in relief as he lifted a small brown purse from it and placed it on the desk in front of her. Her body relaxed as the tension left her shoulders, and she was, once more, able to breathe properly—or somewhat properly, given the duke's inconvenient effect on her heartbeat and lungs.

Excitement was quick to steal the place that nervousness had left as she imagined how this money could help her mother and go toward the upkeep of their townhouse in London. She tempered her smile at Edmund, attempting to keep herself in her seat as that smile threatened to break into a grin.

"Thank you." She'd send it off to her mother just as soon as she had a spare moment. The clouds were clearing for Eleanor, and she couldn't wait to face the sun again.

Her brain urged her to get up and leave, but her body wished for her to remain seated. She tapped her fingers along the edge of the chair. "Erm...how are you?"

His eyebrows raised. His shoulders sunk, his head tilted. "I suppose I'm as well as can be, thank you." He sounded resigned.

Eleanor eyed him. His lips had pulled into a small frown. Something was bothering him. It was clear. Perhaps she could help him. "You look rather tired, if you don't mind my saying so. Is something troubling you?"

Edmund gave a smile, but it appeared forced. "Nothing I have not dealt with before."

Eleanor rose from her chair, the small purse in hand. She could not help him if he was silent. "Well, I thank you again, Edmund."

As she left the room, Eleanor's heart deflated at the lonely image he presented in his study. If only he would open up.

⌒

"Are you going to marry Uncle Edmund?" Rose asked.

Even had Eleanor slept well the night before, she probably would not have been prepared for Rose's question. Though her fatigue had abated when she'd received her first wages, the event had also served to distract her, making her even less prepared for this inquiry.

Eleanor choked on her bite of a particularly delicious cucumber sandwich and coughed a few times before clearing her throat with a sip of tea. The two of them had just paused in Rose's lessons to enjoy the luncheon Fanny had brought to the schoolroom from the kitchens.

"What a funny thing to suggest, Rose." Eleanor smiled indulgently. "You must finish your lunch, for we still have much to do this afternoon, and I cannot have your stomach growling throughout our reading."

"Oh, please marry Uncle Edmund, Miss Clairbridge! He likes you!"

Eleanor's stomach plummeted. "W-What makes you think that?" Her voice quavered.

Rose tilted her head before answering. "Well, he always looks at you. I think he tries to keep it a secret, but I notice. He didn't smile much before you got here. Now he does all the time! And you smile at him too. Your cheeks turn red when he talks to you." Rose grinned and clapped her hands together in glee. "I think you'd be a good aunt! We could play outside and pick flowers...and we could visit Blackberry... and..."

Her cheeks must be flaming—right now. Were her feelings so obvious? She'd simply have to try harder to mask her emotions. But even if Edmund did feel that way about her, he would never even think to marry a governess...Would he?

She shook the thoughts from her head and turned back to Rose, who was patiently waiting for a response. What could she say, not only to avoid hurting the girl now, but to make sure she didn't suffer from greater disappointment later on, when she found that Eleanor was not to be her aunt?

"Well..." Eleanor attempted to form her words in a careful manner. "Though I'd love to be your aunt, I'm afraid your uncle will not want to marry me. As the duke, he's expected to have a wife who comes from a well-known family and who has connections. I'm sure whoever he marries will love you just as much as I do."

Rose pouted, a glum look on her face. "But I want you to be my aunt. And you're well-known. I know you! So does Mrs. Brinder and Fanny. Is that enough?" The girl lifted hopeful eyes to Eleanor's, and Eleanor gave a watery chuckle. She would, one day, have to leave this wonderful girl.

"I wish it were, Rosie. That's simply not how our society works. Even though the people at Ivy Grange know me, that is not the same as being well-known—and even if it were, I have no connections to speak of." Eleanor patted Rose's back, but

Rose continued to look up at Eleanor, tears filling her eyes. Eleanor's brittle heart broke at the sight.

"But I love you," Rose whispered.

Eleanor wrapped the sweet girl in a tight embrace, her own tears threatening to spill. "I love you, too, dearest, and I always will." She rested her chin against the top of Rose's head. She had grown immensely fond of Rose in her time as the girl's governess, and she wished with all of her heart that she'd never have to leave.

"Miss?" Rose's soft-spoken nurse stood with wide eyes at the door to the room, looking as though she might turn right around and leave at any moment.

Eleanor wiped Rose's tears—and more than a few of her own—before standing and handing the girl off to the woman. Though Rose seemed reluctant to leave Eleanor's side, she did so without complaint.

"I'll see you after your nap."

The poor girl only nodded and sniffled before leaving on her nurse's heels.

Eleanor cleared their plates from her desk and brought them back to the kitchen, her heart heavy.

Cook smiled at her when she arrived and wiped her hands on her apron. "Miss Clairbridge! I could have sent up one of the maids to retrieve those."

Eleanor quirked her lips at the kindly woman with a white cap upon her head and smile lines decorating her soft cheeks. Ever since she'd set eyes on the woman, she'd liked her. "I know, but I thought I'd spare them the trouble. Or rather, I didn't want to bother Fanny. She's been a bit preoccupied, as of late."

Cook rolled her eyes. "It's that stable hand, ma'am. He's been crowin' to the under gardeners that Fanny'll walk out with him. Oh, she likes him well enough but can't seem to make up her mind."

"She told you all this?"

"She didn't have to. I've got eyes and ears everywhere." Cook grinned, then sobered when Eleanor only gave a half-hearted smile in return. "Something troubling you, miss?" She raised a questioning eyebrow as she kneaded a large lump of dough, looking exactly as she had when Eleanor had first met her.

Eleanor sighed, knowing she couldn't fool the woman who did, indeed, seem to notice everything, from the smallest gossip to the largest mistake. "Truthfully, I have been a bit worried about His Grace..." Indeed, this was still the truth, even though it hadn't been at the forefront of her mind lately.

Cook nodded, a sad look crossing her face. "'Tis a sad thing. Since losing his family, His Grace has not been the same. And who could blame him? I've noticed a shift in him recently, however. Seems he's been happier since your arrival." She gave a knowing half smile.

"I doubt that my arrival has anything to do with His Grace's mood." Eleanor raised her hands.

Cook *tsk*ed and shook her head but didn't reply.

"How did his family pass, anyway? Does he have other relatives?" Maybe this was finally her chance to get some answers.

Cook gave an apologetic smile. "Sorry, dearie, but I think you'd be better off learning from His Grace. It's his tragedy to speak of. All's I can say is that it was a right terrible thing. Just terrible." Cook focused on her kneading, and Eleanor nodded in understanding.

Perhaps she'd speak to Edmund after dinner and learn more about the circumstances. Eleanor had been putting it off —worried as she was at offending him—but resolved to do so and stop her fretting.

She walked back up the stairs to the schoolroom and plucked a book of poetry from the shelf—a rather small book entitled *Poetical Sketches* by W.B. As she settled herself in the cushioned chair, she flipped open the cover and turned the first page, beholding the verse in a sort of reverence that came with such perfect weaving of words.

Before long, she had read the first section of poems—those that focused more on the seasons and nature—and had moved on to the songs. Eleanor read one about the passing of true love and the coming of despair. There were little notes written beside the text—comments on the meaning of the poems and fixes for grammatical errors, but written by whom? She flipped the page and began another. As her eyes flitted over the third song, she whispered the words to herself.

> "Love and harmony combine,
> And round our souls entwine
> While thy branches mix with mine,
> And our roots together join."

The words reminded Eleanor of the love her parents had shared. She couldn't remember a day in which they hadn't shared a warm look or gentle smile. How absolutely beautiful. It must be wonderful to have a love like this bloom in one's heart.

Eleanor allowed herself to imagine herself as a wife—in a marriage like theirs for a moment. A loving partnership. The partner in her mind looked suspiciously like Edmund, and one of the children had Rose's laugh, but she didn't pay much mind to these similarities. It was a lovely blur of her hopes and dreams. She read on.

> "Joys upon our branches sit,
> Chirping loud and singing sweet;
> Like gentle streams beneath our feet
> Innocence and virtue meet.

Thou the golden fruit dost bear,
I am clad in flowers fair;
Thy sweet boughs perfume the air,
And the turtle buildeth there."

As she continued to read the poem, her vision clouded. Tears fell from her eyes, for she knew in her heart that she'd never feel a love like this with anyone—not a requited love, anyway.

Teardrops of longing and desire for a love of her own streaked down her face. Droplets fell upon the page before her and soaked into the paper. With a heavy exhale, Eleanor shoved the book away from her and wiped the moisture from her eyes. Her face must now look red and splotchy. W.B., whoever they were, was certainly skilled at drawing emotion out of his or her readers—that, or Eleanor was more of a watering pot than she'd previously thought.

Rose returned from her nap, a refreshed look on her face and a bright grin to match. However, when she caught sight of her governess's red-rimmed eyes and tear-stained face, she ran over as quickly as her little legs could take her. "Miss Clairbridge? Why are you crying?" she asked in a concerned tone.

Eleanor tried her best to smile, but it wavered as her lip quivered in a most ungoverness-like fashion. She brushed away the last of her tears and grabbed Rose's hands in her own. Eleanor spoke in the most assuring tone she could muster. "It is nothing, Rose. Everything is well."

Rose didn't seem in the least convinced, but thankfully, she let the matter drop without further questioning. The rest of their lessons passed with ease, though Rose would, on occasion, throw a worried glance in Eleanor's direction.

"Miss, are yer lessons finished?"

Eleanor tore her eyes from the slate Rose held to the nurse

at the door. She summoned a smile and nodded, spinning back to Rose. "These words are perfect, Rose. Very good work."

The girl gave an uncertain smile and erased the slate before handing it off to Eleanor. "I'll see you at dinner, Miss Clairbridge." Though the sentence was a statement, her words sounded more like a question.

Eleanor straightened her shoulders and gave Rose a reassuring smile. "You will."

And she had better check her appearance in the mirror before facing the duke, who was even more discerning than his niece.

~

*E*leanor scurried to her room whilst attempting to maintain proper decorum, a wave of dismay building in the space behind her ribcage. Flinging open the door, she strode into the now-familiar space before shutting it behind her with a muted thud. She leaned back against the thick wood and covered her face, tears pricking the backs of her eyes.

Although she'd worn a mask for the remainder of Rose's lessons and had done a rather good job at acting undisturbed —at least, she hoped she had—Eleanor could not uphold the pretense while alone.

What a ninny! Letting a simple poem work her up like this! Yet within her heart, she knew it was not solely the poem that had upset her. The poem had reminded her of that dreadful ball and the cruelty she'd suffered. Was it truly cruelty, or simply truth?

Miss Pottan's words rang through her mind, making their way into each crevice. *I do not have to be a judge to see that Miss Clairbridge is lacking.*

Eleanor walked the few steps over to her bed and flung herself onto it, burying her face into her pillow. Her old "friends" had found her lacking, certainly. Perhaps Miss Pottan had been the only person of her acquaintance to have had the nerve to speak what everyone was thinking—to Eleanor's face. Silent sobs wracked her body, and the cold grip of sadness encased her.

It was as though the poem had been the straw that broke the camel's back. All of the despair and sorrow she'd been trying to keep buried within herself for so long was breaking free from its confines. All of the emotions she had been trying to push away since her father's death were now drowning her. The loss of her dear papa, her great worry for her mama, her friends abandoning her, her disappointment at her lack of suitors—her confusing feelings for Edmund. All threatened to break her now. Eleanor's prayers flowed past her lips in shuddering exhales as she asked God for peace and guidance. He had never left her side, although she was finding it difficult to feel His presence now. Where was He when she needed Him most?

She gripped her locket, her fingernails digging into her palm, and let herself drift off to sleep—only somewhat comforted that she and her mother would be able to keep their home.

$\mathcal{E}$dmund had been walking down the hallway toward his study when Rose descended the grand staircase, an open green book pressed to her chest. He stopped in his tracks and propped his hands on his hips, waiting for her to reach the bottom. When she finally did, he dropped his arms back to his sides and strode over to her.

"Rosie, do you remember what I said about not going anywhere without Nurse?"

Rose nodded her head up and down in quick succession, eyes wide. "Yes, Uncle Edmund, but I didn't! Nurse was following me." She glanced over her shoulder at the staircase.

As though they had willed her to appear, Rose's nurse came into view, scrambling down the steps. When she reached the bottom, she moved to stand behind Rose and bobbed a frantic curtsy. She was out of breath, hands clasped behind her back and lips frowning slightly in consternation at Rose.

Edmund nodded to her in greeting and tried to hide his smile. He turned his attention back to Rose as her foot gave a little tap. She thrust the open book she was holding toward him, and he took it from her, his eyebrows furrowing in confusion. His father's handwriting crowded the margins of the pages in a familiar scrawl, seeming to remedy the minor grammatical errors in the poems there. It had been a long while since Edmund had beheld this book.

Rose was quick to explain. "Miss Clairbridge was crying today. I think this book made her sad." Her expression was the same as when she'd eaten something she didn't like, and Edmund had to stifle his smile once again. Any humorous thoughts fled him, however, as he took in what Rose had said.

"She was crying?" His shoulders tensed as Rose confirmed her statement.

"Yes, while she was reading this book. I think we should get rid of it." Rose crossed her arms and frowned at the volume.

"I'm not so sure that the book is what made her cry, but I will keep it in my study for now. Thank you for telling me, Rosie."

Rose left with her nurse, a satisfied look on her face.

Once more, Edmund glanced at the book in his hands and continued toward his study, using his thumb as a placeholder between the pages.

He entered and closed the door behind him, striding to the chair behind his desk and slumping into it. He examined the volume more closely. It made sense that Eleanor would be reading poems—she had mentioned her love of poetry when they'd met in the library. He scanned the poem on the pages before him, and his lips turned downward. A love poem? Why would this have made her cry? Did she have some sort of beau in London that she was missing?

Just thinking of Eleanor crying created an almost physical pain in his limbs and chest. Imagining her with a beau stirred a discomfort in his stomach. Had this truly been what had upset Eleanor, or was a piece of the puzzle lost in the book's changing of hands? He stood from his chair—the wooden legs emitting a scuffing sound as they slid across the floor—and dropped the volume on his desk, determined to find her.

~

Two hours after her fully clothed stumble into bed, a loud rapping sound woke Eleanor from her fitful slumber. She lifted her head from her pillow, a painful headache making her wince as she did so. The noise sounded again. Someone at the door.

She freed herself from her tangled bedcovers and stepped onto the floor, trying to avoid bumping into her side table as she stumbled. She moved to her door and opened it wide, expecting Fanny. It was not Fanny—nor was it anyone else she would have expected.

Edmund stood in her doorframe, his lifted eyebrows set above anxious eyes.

Eleanor stifled a gasp. Her hand flew up to smooth out her hair, most of which had come traitorously loose from its pins. "Your Grace! Edmund!"

He made no move to enter her bedchamber. Instead, he waved a hand—forgoing formalities—and took a few steps back, farther into the hallway. "I'm here because..." Edmund paused and stared past her shoulder and into her room, seeming to look for an explanation.

While he sorted his thoughts, Eleanor popped her head out of her door and peered down the long hallway, relieved to see it empty. The last thing she needed was to be the subject of gossip below stairs—although Cook would likely put a stop to it, were it to arise. She pulled her head back in and glanced once more at Edmund, who met her gaze with a determined expression. Why had he searched for her? They were friends, as he'd said, but never before had he sought her out so directly.

Thoughts of their meeting in the garden flickered in her

mind. Well...perhaps he had. Certainly, that had been for Rose's benefit, not for her own. And Eleanor couldn't help but remember his daily reading to her after her head injury. That had been quite direct. She shook away this irrelevant thought and focused on the present—which was when her own anxiety increased. There were only so many reasons for him to have sought her out as he had.

"Why *are* you here, Edmund?" There was definitely worry in his expression. She hesitated. "Is Rose unwell? Has something happened?" Eleanor clenched her skirts as she imagined the possibilities.

Edmund swallowed and ran a hand through his hair. "Pardon my interruption, I...well..." He gave a huff of frustration. "Rose told me that you were crying—earlier in the schoolroom. I was worried. Is something amiss?"

Her face must be bright as a beet. The heat veritably attacked her cheeks from within. She tried to summon a smile—but alas, it refused to follow her orders. As her cheeks would be of no help to her in convincing him nothing was amiss, she called upon her voice. "I'm quite well, Your Grace," she managed to murmur.

She could not tell him she'd somehow been broken by a poem. She could not tell him that she grieved her father and despaired of ever having a future family of her own. She could not tell him he made her feel like laughing and crying at the same time, or that he disoriented her like nothing and no one had before.

Edmund leaned against the wall facing her door and crossed his arms in front of his chest. He studied her face. What could he be looking for?

She stepped out of her room and closed the door behind her, unsure of what to do with her hands. Hopefully, her short reply had been convincing enough despite her feeble response and how her outward appearance contradicted her statement.

Edmund finally dropped his eyes for a moment before uncrossing his arms, moving one hand to his hip and the other hand to hold his chin in a contemplative pose. He maintained this pose for a moment, gripping his jaw before he let both arms fall back to his sides with a sigh.

"I'm not sure why you feel the need to keep your troubles to yourself, but you have not pressed me to speak of mine, and I cannot—in good conscience—press you to speak of what I, myself, have not. I only hope you will remember that you can be honest with me and that I will always listen to what you have to say." Edmund reached forward and took her hand in his own, gently squeezing her fingers as he pierced her with a stare of unmatched earnestness. "I truly hope you are well, Eleanor."

Edmund bowed and turned around, taking a step forward to leave.

"Wait." Eleanor reached a hand out to grasp the air, anxiety piercing her chest. What was she doing? He turned back to face her, brows raised. While she couldn't possibly tell the whole truth, a half truth would suffice. She leaned against the doorframe with an exhale, shoulders slumping. She would not look at him. "I do want to be able to tell you my troubles, and for you to tell me of yours. I...I was simply reminded of an interaction I had with someone a few years ago. I'm sure you understand the effect that words can have on a person."

He resumed his place at the wall opposite her and nodded, waiting for her to continue.

Eleanor clasped her hands at her waist, grip tight as she thought back to the awful night that had so altered her idea of herself.

"It was three years ago, at a ball. My mother's friend, Mrs. Witherby, was hosting it. We—Mama and I—were both invited, even though I'd never had a season, and I was so excited to go. I'd never been to a ball before. I was close friends with Mrs. Witherby's daughters, Teresa and Eliza, and I thought the evening would be everything I dreamed it would be. We'd grown up together and had spent summers at each other's homes. When we arrived, everything was beautiful—the candles, the chalked ballroom floor, the colorful gowns. Nothing could be grander. I was making simple conversation with a gentleman when a certain woman—I'll not name her—intervened."

Edmund's mouth pulled into a frown. "Intervened how?"

Eleanor swallowed. "The man had complimented me on something. I can't remember now what it was. Before I could respond, she said to him, 'It is good of you to pay her a compliment, sir. It will certainly be one of very few she receives in her lifetime.'"

Edmund's brows furrowed, and he crossed his arms again. "What a cruel thing to say."

Eleanor nodded. "My friends attempted to defend me, asking her who she was to be such a judge of others." She paused before speaking aloud the words that had earlier played through her mind. "She only said, 'I do not have to be a judge to see that Miss Clairbridge is lacking.'"

Edmund scoffed in disbelief, but Eleanor wasn't finished. "Later on, when I was dancing in the line with that same gentleman, the woman even stepped on the hem of my gown, tearing it. That was the end for me. I could take no more of her barbs nor cruelty. I went home with Mama after that, leaving my confidence behind. Since then, I have wondered if—if she's right. Perhaps I am lacking. Perhaps I'm just as plain as she believes."

Edmund uncrossed his arms and stepped toward her, grasping her shoulders in his warm hands. His eyes were all honesty as he stared her down, mouth in a firm line. "You are not lacking, Eleanor. Do not believe that woman, whoever she is. She is wrong. I do not know why she felt the need to slander you as she did, but she had no right nor reason to do so. It sounds to me as though she had her own problems to contend with and was unleashing her anger onto others in order to cope with them. Do not believe her, Eleanor, for you are magnificent."

Magnificent? Eleanor's heart leapt and she blinked. *Magnificent.* She'd never been called that before. Did he normally call people in his employ magnificent?

As much as Eleanor wanted to believe Edmund's words, she couldn't take them to heart. Her pain had been sitting in her heart for too long, and she had more evidence to support his words than Miss Pottan's.

If only she could find a way to be free from the sting of inferiority. She could not believe a man like Edmund would truly admire her until she could.

~

One week later, Eleanor sat in the library, flipping through another book of poetry. Hopefully, this one wouldn't send her to tears as the one before. Edmund's library was vast, and shelves upon shelves of books lined the walls. Eleanor had seen various authors and texts, foreign titles, and those written in places nearby. She often found herself marveling at the variety and size of the collection, being a lover of reading as she was. The warm sun bathed her in its pleasant light whilst she reclined in a cushioned chair by the windows, the scent of books, old and new, making her drowsy in a most pleasant way.

Her day's lessons with Rose had ended about an hour earlier, and now she was relaxing and trying to occupy her time. Her feet were tucked beneath her, and the soft fabric of the chair made her feel as though a cloud surrounded her. Eleanor was so comfortable that she was reminded of her home in London. She never would have imagined she would feel so at ease in any home aside from her own, yet she did. Pausing in her reading, she grasped the warm metal locket around her neck, closing her eyes for a moment in a reverie.

There had been a day much like this one, sunny and bright without a cloud in the sky. Her father had been the one to introduce her to poetry, smiling as he read aloud. She had sat on his knee as he had pointed his favorite poems out to her and told her what he thought their meaning was. Eleanor was Rose's age at the time. She had been so amazed at how simple words could be used to create a scene, story, an idea.

Then, when he had been sick, it was no longer him who read to her—but rather the opposite. She had spent entire days in a chair by his bedside, simply reading to him. He had had a weak smile at the end, but such fondness in his eyes. Her Papa.

Eleanor broke from her daydream as the steady sound of footsteps reached her ears. Her eyes fluttered open to see Edmund enter the library in a fine green waistcoat and dark-brown coat. He stopped when he spotted her, eyes widening.

Eleanor stood up from her seat and curtsied, giving a gentle smile. "Edmund."

He bowed and gave a half smile in return. "Eleanor." All of a sudden, his eyebrow raised. "What is that you're holding around your neck?"

Her cheeks warmed as she gripped the locket tighter in her fist. She'd forgotten to hide it beneath the fabric of her bodice. "Oh...this...is a locket that my father gave me. Before he passed away. I always wear it. It makes me feel closer to him."

Edmund nodded in understanding, a thoughtful look crossing his face. She unclasped the locket and opened it, walking closer to show him the two miniature portraits of her parents inside.

Edmund peered down at them, and his eyes softened. "A handsome couple, to be sure. They look very pleasant," he murmured.

Eleanor nodded and closed the locket once more, clasping it around her neck again. "They are—or, at least—my mother is. My father was, as well, when he still lived. He never spoke ill of anyone, and Mama is so very kind."

"My parents were the same," he commented. "Some parents of those in the peerage are distant from their children—cold, even. Mine never were."

A conflict arose within Eleanor. Should she take the risk of furthering this branch of conversation? It might put his words to an end, but it also had the potential to provide answers and —dare she say—peace for Edmund. She took the chance.

"You don't speak of them often."

Edmund tensed almost imperceptibly, his expression becoming closed. "It...pains me to do so. Forgive me. I've some business to attend to."

And with that, he was gone, leaving Eleanor to reprimand herself for mentioning them at all.

CHAPTER 16

"Mr. Phips, Your Grace." Prumb handed a calling card to Edmund, waiting beside the study's desk.

A few days had passed since he'd fled Eleanor in the library, and Edmund had come to regret that decision.

Now he examined the card. *Mr. Phips?* Edmund couldn't remember ever meeting the man. Intrigued, he set aside his correspondence and bid Prumb escort him in. His butler did so, and soon, a man of medium height stepped through the study door, his dark eyes scrutinizing his surroundings with a look of disdain. Among the looks and expressions Edmund had received in his lifetime, he couldn't recall a time when disdain had been in any one of them. Edmund stood from his desk.

"You're the Duke of Albemarle, I presume." The man looked him up and down, then gave a short bow, the action seeming like an afterthought.

Edmund had never been so quickly irritated in his life. He did not deign to bow in return.

"And you're Mr. Phips, *I* presume." Edmund lifted the man's calling card between his middle and forefinger, showing the pompous man his own name.

The man sat in the brown leather chair across from the desk, crossing one leg over the other and looking for all the world as if this was his home.

Edmund clenched his jaw and sat himself. "What is it that brings you here, Mr. Phips?" He remained unsmiling.

Mr. Phips sighed and met Edmund's eyes. "You see, Your Grace, I've spent the last month on a wild goose chase, attempting to track my betrothed. Her mother gave no hints as to her location and neither could her friends. Finally, Mrs. Floret spoke to me of a woman resembling her—"

"And what does any of this have to do with me?" What a self-important man. Edmund drummed his fingers on the desk in a steady rhythm.

"It seems my betrothed is in your employ. Your governess."

~

*E*leanor headed down the corridor leading to Edmund's study. The spring air made the manor warm, but this unexplained summons made her even warmer. It was odd to meet there again, so soon after their previous exchange in the same room. Her palms were sweating, and she wiped them on her skirts. *Breathe, Eleanor.* It would be nothing. A quick meeting and nothing more. She needn't worry about a thing. Still, why did he wish to speak with her again already?

Prumb stood outside the study door, a hard-to-read expression on his face. He examined her for a moment, an unknown question in his gaze, before opening the door to the study and announcing her. "Miss Clairbridge, Your Grace."

She entered the room, and Prumb moved back into the hall without a word, closing the door behind him. Eleanor was not prepared for what she saw.

"Mr. Phips?" She blurted out the man's name.

Edmund appeared grave. Miserable, even. But why? At her

entrance, both men had stood, Mr. Phips with a self-satisfied smile on his face.

"Eleanor," Mr. Phips practically purred. "How glad I am to see you."

Why was he present? She flicked her gaze from Edmund to Mr. Phips, receiving no answers. "I—well... This is quite the surprise. Might I ask what business you have here, sir?" What business could Mr. Phips possibly have with Edmund?

"I'm here to bring my betrothed back to London," he explained with an air of haughtiness.

Eleanor lifted an eyebrow. "And who might your betrothed be?"

Mr. Phips laughed as though Eleanor had said something humorous. He moved closer to her, a smug smile on his lips. "Why, *you*, my dear," he said, no doubt in his tone.

Eleanor's jaw slackened at such boldness. "I beg your pardon?"

Edmund's mouth twisted to the side. His nostrils flared. "Mr. Phips claims that you are his betrothed, Miss Clairbridge. He says he's been looking for you for a month."

Eleanor furrowed her brows as she glanced at Mr. Phips, anger welling in her breast at his utter lack of shame and over-abundance of presumption. Before she could sharpen her tongue and lash him with it, he moved ever closer, grabbing her arm. She tried to pull away. "Sir, you are much too—"

"Eleanor, we are to be married." Again, that firmness.

She yanked her arm from him. "No, sir, we—"

Before she had time to finish what she was saying, Mr. Phips leaned over and pressed his lips to her cheek.

A loud smack rang out in the room as Eleanor's palm connected with the man's cheek.

He pulled away, his expression turning from one of stupor to outrage. "Why, you worthless little—"

Edmund was next to the man in a second, grabbing him by

the cravat and pulling him away from Eleanor. His eyes flashed with fury.

"You, *sir*, are a contemptible coward and utter cad." Edmund's voice was calm and full of steel. "If there's even one ounce of good sense in that pomade-slathered skull of yours, it will now be telling you to leave. Else, face the further consequences of your actions."

Eleanor tried to wipe away the memory of Mr. Phips's lips on her skin, rubbing her fingers on her cheek where he'd placed them. She couldn't regret slapping him. Not even a little.

The man scrambled away from Edmund as he released his shirt, fairly falling out of the door that Prumb had swung open in anticipation.

"Please escort this rogue out, Prumb," Edmund snapped. "He has quite overstayed his welcome."

Prumb nodded and grasped Mr. Phips by the arm, pulling him down the corridor.

The man didn't struggle but made his grievances known. "I've never been so mistreated in my life! You don't realize how poor a decision you have made! I—"

Once he was no longer in sight, Eleanor leaned against the frame of the study's door, covering her eyes with her hand. No duke wanted a governess who brought scandal into his home, whether it be from her own choices or not. She'd be dismissed.

～

*E*dmund berated himself for letting that blackguard into his home. He should have sent him away sooner. Blood boiling, he ran a hand through his hair as the man disappeared down the hall. Prumb would ensure the man understood he was not to return. Edmund turned on his heel and faced the study. Eleanor slumped in the doorframe.

"Eleanor." He murmured her name, stepping closer to her. His inner anger vanished as his concern for her replaced it. She remained silent, her eyes covered by her fingers and her bottom lip trembling. "Eleanor?" His tone held a hint of pleading this time.

Finally, she dropped her hand, revealing red-rimmed eyes and a sorrowful expression.

He took a step forward. His heart ached at the distressing sight she made. "I am so sorry for ever allowing that man into this house. Rest assured, it will never happen again. Had I known... No one will harm you here, Eleanor. I'll make sure of that."

Her watery eyes pierced him as her brows furrowed. She hesitated before speaking. "You aren't dismissing me?"

Edmund reared his head back. "Dismiss you? Why—"

"I'm what led Mr. Phips here. If I hadn't been here, no scandal would have ensued."

Edmund rubbed his jaw. "Scandal? I trust my servants—no one will speak of it. This is no London ballroom. Besides, the man accosted you. It's not as though you ran off to Gretna Green. You're not at fault. I do wonder, however, how you came to be acquainted with Mr. Phips in the first place."

Eleanor crossed her arms over her chest and bit her lip in a most bewitching way. He forced himself to focus on her words.

"I met him at a friend's home while in the country. My friend's mother is quite close with his mother, and so we became acquainted. He's always seemed to take a liking to me —though heaven knows why. I never reciprocated his attentions. We are *certainly* not betrothed, nor shall we ever be, if I have any say in the matter. His presence here was unexpected, to say the least. He's never been so...brazen." She shuddered, and Edmund had to stop himself from wrapping his arms around her.

"He won't come near you again—I promise. You are safe here."

"What if he should decide to retaliate for you throwing him from the manor?" Eleanor frowned, turning her eyes to the floor.

"I'm a duke, Eleanor. One of the recommendations to the title is that there are few with the power to sully my name." It was odd to think about, but his words were true, nevertheless.

Eleanor only nodded her head, a desolate look on her face.

What could he do to make her feel better? To convince her he would do all in his power to keep her safe?

The carriage accident flashed through his mind. Eleanor had shared her own story with him. If he could share his with her, then she'd know she could place her trust in him.

Could he muster the strength to put to words the horrors of his past? Could he dig up the bones he'd sworn light would never again touch?

~

*A*fter dinner that evening, Eleanor acquiesced to Edmund's request to speak with him. Though wary of spending more time with him, knowing he could unearth her thoughts and emotions with a few simple words and that merely being in his presence would further warm her heart to him, she followed him into the library. The room was lit with candles. Fanny had told Eleanor that Edmund read there every evening after dinner.

He gestured toward a leather chair for her to take a seat, which she hesitantly did, before he walked toward the empty hearth and leaned against the shining marble mantel. He faced it for a moment and took a few breaths before turning and clasping his hands behind his back, pinning her in place with his green eyes and sorrowful expression.

"I'm certain that there are many questions which have sprouted in your mind since your arrival at Ivy Grange, specifically concerning my family. While I do not wish to hide from any of my staff or friends, this is a topic I have a hard time speaking of to anyone. In fact, I've only spoken of this to Prumb and Lord Lendin."

Eleanor started to understand where this conversation was going. "Edmund, you really do not ha—"

He began to shake his head with a sad half smile, pausing her words. "I thank you, but I believe it is time I confide in someone. Who better than a friend? You've trusted me enough to speak of your own hardships, after all. I trust you enough to do the same."

At this, Eleanor quieted, gratitude swelling in her breast.

"Five years ago, my...family went to a ball. My mother, father, brother, and sister-in-law all traveled together. I had opted to remain home. At one-and-twenty, marriage was not yet on my mind. We only shared a few short moments together before they left. They were late, you see. I told them to take the lesser-traveled road. It would be quicker. Little did I know it would be the very thing to seal their fate."

Pain evident in his expression, Edmund seated himself in the chair adjacent to hers, both facing the cold hearth. "I received word that the..." He stopped and took a steadying breath, his exhale shaky. "The carriage my family had been traveling in crashed. The road had been muddied from the previous day's rain. When my family met a particularly rough area..." He squeezed his eyes shut, his mouth twisting.

Eleanor gasped, raising a hand to her mouth.

"I—I immediately set out on my horse to find them, having known the way to the manor they were heading for. When I came across the wreckage—" Edmund's voice broke, and he took a shuddering breath, leaning his elbow on the chair's arm and propping his chin on his fist before continuing to tell the story, eyes taking on a faraway look. "Their carriage had been on a road that wound atop a hill. One of the carriage's wheels broke, and the carriage had tipped, rolling off the road and down the side of the hill."

Edmund's eyes glistened with tears, and Eleanor's heart broke for him, cracking into little pieces that spread throughout her chest. She seemed to hold her breath as he continued, a part of her hoping the story would somehow end well, even whilst already knowing the conclusion. "There...amongst the wood...and...glass was my family. My brother, Phillip, had been thrown from the carriage when it tumbled. His body was in the grass beside it."

Eleanor's eyes began to water, and she tried to blink back the tears.

"My sister-in-law and parents were within, their bodies strewn about. They were all so pale. The blood..." He broke off for a moment, moving his hand to cover his eyes. "I died that day along with them." Raw pain splintered his voice.

Eleanor could not keep herself still. She stood from her seat and crossed over to his, placing a light hand on his shoulder.

He tensed for a moment before relaxing under her touch. With her other hand, she tenderly withdrew his hand from his eyes. When he looked up at her, his green irises gleamed with the tears which also wet his cheeks. She squeezed his hand. "You need not go on, Edmund."

He rose and peered into her eyes. He was so close that if she leaned forward, she could rest her head against his shoulder.

"I have begun, and so I should end," he replied with determination. "Never again would I experience moments in the drawing room with my family. Phillip would never tease Anne again. My mother would never again ask me if I wanted to go to a ball—or anywhere, for that matter. I would never again get the chance to look my father in the eye. As you might imagine, the grief was unbearable."

He rubbed a hand down his jaw. "Rose was the only family I had left. The only family I'd ever have. I became her guardian then—a guardian to a girl of one year old. She was too young to understand death, to understand that her parents would not come back, to understand why they no longer smiled down at her when she woke up from her slumber."

He turned his head toward the windows looking out into the gardens, the moon shining brightly from the heavens and combating the shadows on the earth. "I promised then that I would always protect her. Promised to my brother and sister in heaven that I would take care of her."

"Edmund, I'm...so sorry." She knew too well that her words could not change what had happened. They were inadequate for the amount of pain he'd had to endure.

He turned his head to her again, face pale. His eyes were dark and anguished, brows drawn low, his lips pulled into a thin line.

Her heart tore at the sight, and she couldn't resist. Eleanor wrapped her arms around his waist in a tight embrace, pressing her head against his chest and trying to infuse the action with all the warmth she possibly could. He stiffened for a moment but was quick to ease and return her embrace, his arms coming around her and pulling her close.

Eleanor closed her eyes and let herself enjoy this moment. She could hear his heart beating in his chest and could feel his every inhale and exhale. His scent of spices enveloped her in a blanket of comfort. In his arms, she was protected and safe. His soft dinner jacket was smooth beneath her fingertips, and she was ....at home. They remained like that for an indeterminable amount of time before she slowly released him from her grasp and peered up into his face, her hands grasping his in between them.

His gaze was intense, many emotions filling his eyes. A few she could not identify, but one she could. Gratitude.

"Edmund...you are...everything that Rose could wish for in a guardian. You are everything your parents could wish for in a son. You are everything..." *To me.* She wished to say the words, but they wouldn't form on her tongue.

His gaze on her at dinners, his smiles at church, his warm words, they all told of something. Some sort of admiration. Eleanor was unused to any man harboring warm feelings toward her and could not be sure, but she had to be cautious if her suspicions proved true. While he might hold some affection for her, she could not allow herself to return it in any way. She wouldn't. Any admiration he had for her was likely due to his own pain, and that alone, so she would keep her feelings to herself.

"Thank you, Eleanor," he whispered. "It is difficult to tell anyone that I am the reason my family is dead. It is difficult to face the fact myself."

Eleanor shook her head. "Do not say that, for you aren't. You have held onto this guilt for too long, and for naught. It isn't your fault they are gone."

Edmund's shoulders drooped. "But it is. I am the one who told them to take the lesser-used road. If they hadn't, they would still be here. Rose would still have parents, and so would I."

"You cannot know that, Edmund." Eleanor squeezed his hands. "It is not for you to take the blame." She straightened her shoulders. "You must release this guilt into God's hands. Allow Him to take it from your shoulders. Allow Him to free you from these chains that you have wrapped yourself in. This might have happened whether you made the suggestion or not. Your family, after all, could've decided to take the regular route, couldn't they have?"

Edmund sighed, the sound seeming to come deep from his chest. "Yes."

Eleanor's voice was soft. "Do not blame yourself any longer."

Edmund nodded, closing his eyes. His head tilted forward, and he pressed his forehead against her shoulder.

She forced herself to remain composed. "I'm honored you would share this with me. I promise you that I will never tell another soul of it."

Edmund leaned back. He released one of her hands and raised the other to his lips. He bent over it for a moment before placing a soft kiss on its back, a gesture that sent sparks shooting up her arms and into her chest. As he released her hand, it tingled where his lips had been, as though he'd left a permanent mark.

"Eleanor? How do you manage to be so happy when your father has passed? Don't you ever worry about the pain you'll experience when you lose your mother?" He hesitated, an uncertain expression on his face. "Why love at all when it can only end in pain?"

Eleanor exhaled. "When my father died, a piece of myself was gone. It was difficult to go on with my daily activities, but I knew my father would want me to live. He would want me to continue on in my life and to be happy. Though I do worry for my mother sometimes, I know that loss is a part of life. Yes, she will leave me eventually, as all parents do, but I cannot allow myself to live in fear of the pain I'm sure to experience when that happens. Everyone dies eventually, but that does not mean we should not enjoy the time we have left with the people we love most. No one can predict the future, but we can alter the present. The happiness of time spent with loved ones outweighs the pain of living without them, don't you agree?"

Edmund quirked his lips to one side, deep in thought, before he replied. "Yes, I suppose it does."

Eleanor's lips rose into a bittersweet smile. If only it could always be like this...if things were different. But she could not allow her affection for him to grow—not when they had no future together.

"I'll retire for the night, Edmund. I've lessons to plan. Thank you again for trusting me enough to confide in me." She murmured the words, leaving the room with even greater conflict in her heart than before.

CHAPTER 17

As Eleanor swept from the room, Edmund had to force himself to stay put. He slumped into one of the leather chairs with a sigh, feeling lighter than he had in years. Few people had been made aware of the details of that day, yet he had just revealed them to Eleanor. Sweet Eleanor. He had been surprised when she'd embraced him, but she had fit so right in his arms. It was as if she was meant to be there. With her embrace, she had melted away his pain, the pain which had kept his heart frozen in its icy grasp for so long.

Edmund had never imagined that speaking of the tragedy would feel so freeing. He had only wished to be open and to make her understand that she could be open with *him*. She should know the information, especially given it regarded Rose, as well. He had the strongest urge to tell her everything. Anything. His triumphs, his defeats... There was no one he trusted more than her, and in so short a time. Had he gained her trust too?

Edmund could still see her warm eyes in his mind, eyes that found their way straight into his soul. He had been broken for a long time, but now she was sewing him back together. Every word she spoke was a stitch in his soul. Everything about Eleanor was angelic. Her chestnut hair curled perfectly to frame her face, her cheeks were the color of roses, her skin smooth and soft, and her lips were a delicate pink. She was the epitome of loveliness, both inside and outside. His heart was beating quicker at just the thought of her. He was warm as though the sun's rays were shining on him.

Edmund sat bolt upright in his seat.

He loved Elea—

No, no. No. He could not. For goodness' sake, he'd just spoken of the deaths of his family members! That was the entire reason he'd vowed to never marry in the first place. He could not stand to face more loss. And yet...

Eleanor's words rang through his mind.

The happiness of time spent with loved ones outweighs the pain of living without them, don't you agree?

Edmund left the library, his mind in a whirlwind of conflict. Eleanor had spoken of her father's death and, in doing so, had altered his view of his own life. The columns of reason that had supported his argument for remaining a bachelor were crumbling like pillars of sand. His own mental storm threatened to demolish them entirely.

How had his grief blinded him so? He'd thought for so long that if he were to lose another loved one, he would perish from sorrow, but that thinking was flawed.

He paused and rested against the wall of the corridor, placing a hand over his eyes. When relationships were formed, memories and fond moments were created which acted as the bandages to those wounds caused by grief. Though the scars might remain, the wounds were healed by lasting love and the remembrance of every smile, conversation, and interaction. His brother and sister-in-law had always shared intimate smiles when they'd thought no one was looking. They'd been happy —blissful, even. That much had been apparent.

Ever since their deaths, he'd refrained from forming close attachments. He'd let fear rule his life, but no longer. Eleanor was right. They could not predict what would happen in life, only hope and pray for a good outcome.

As Edmund strode outside to the gardens to further clear his mind, he nodded his head resolutely. He would live in fear no more. For his family. For Rose. For Eleanor. It was what his parents and brother would have wished.

Edmund walked down the main garden path, letting the evening air heal him. It was dark, but he didn't mind. The moon cast shadows across the area. It was a beautiful work of art. He wandered over to the yellow roses that his mother had planted and inhaled their fresh scent, remembering his interaction with Eleanor in this exact spot.

He still ached from the loss of his family, but the ache had dulled from what it used to be. A small smile graced his lips as he imagined his emotional wounds healing and scarring over.

And so I let go of this weight that has half drowned me for years. What freedom it is to release my fears for the future

A new feeling began to fill Edmund's chest. Acceptance.

A soft light glowed from Eleanor's bedchamber. He stopped in his steps, his eyes following the flicker of brightness. Like the candle that lit up her window, she was the flame that was lighting up his life and brightening his days.

Now he only needed to make her see that.

～

*L*ord Lendin stepped into Edmund's study, a grin on his face. He was dressed in a maroon silk waistcoat and black jacket, a bright white cravat tied around his neck in a fashionable knot.

"Good afternoon, old friend!" Lendin's enthusiasm was contagious.

Edmund stood and shook hands with Lendin, a smile flashing across his own face in return. He gestured the man into the chair opposite his desk before seating himself behind it. "You seem quite the chipper fellow today, Lendin. What has you in such a mood?"

Lendin sat in the chair facing Edmund, the grin still on his face. "No reason needed, old fellow, yet I've just had the honor of running into your intriguing governess. I never knew that you employed one, and you never spoke of her in your letters. She seems very pleasant." He shot Edmund a knowing look. "And perhaps she's what...Rose...needs."

Edmund avoided his friend's gaze, clearing his throat. "Yes, I hired Miss Clairbridge a few months ago. Rose is very fond of her."

The viscount brightened. "Then I suppose she'll be here for some time?" His brown eyes missed nothing in Edmund's countenance.

"I...believe so..." Edmund's gut tightened. Why did Lendin want to know? "How was your trip? I hope rather uneventful." He furrowed his brow. "Weren't you meant to return next week?"

Lendin sighed, crossing one leg over the other. "Indeed, I could stand it no longer. The return trip was worse. My mother has been pressuring me lately to find a wife. As you well know, I'm not very fond of the simpering misses that flood the ballrooms in London."

The unwelcome image of Lendin and Eleanor arm in arm entered Edmund's brain. He pushed down the swelling discomfort in his stomach.

"I even ran into Miss Pottan and her mother." He shivered. "Dreadful occurrence, that. I still cannot believe you're contemplating tying yourself to that woman. Word is, she's returned from Town." He wrinkled his nose in distaste.

Edmund straightened his shoulders and gave his friend an

amused smile. "You'll be glad to know that I no longer wish to do so. I've lately realized the error in my wishing for a marriage without love. You know my reasons for having done so, yet I've been reminded of Lord Tennyson's great wisdom—'Tis *better to have loved and lost than never to have loved at all.'"*

Lendin grinned and relaxed into his chair. "I'd hoped you'd come around. You certainly made slow work of it."

Edmund glanced at his friend with a half smile. "And you certainly pestered me throughout the process."

Lendin's eyes grew wide. "I was worried you might go through with the whole thing, and that would be a disaster if I've ever heard of one. She's never cared for you, only your title. Don't you remember when she tricked your brother into dancing three times with her at the Meltons' ball? My mother told me Anne had a horrible time that night. The poor girl was convinced she'd been spurned! And once you were the duke, you were the new prize to be won."

Edmund had, actually, completely forgotten that occurrence. Miss Pottan was the eldest daughter of a wealthy merchant, and her father had always given her whatever she wanted. "I've never been under the assumption that she cared for me. In fact, that is what made her the perfect candidate. If neither of us cared for the other, then there would be no pain in the end when we parted."

Lendin shrugged, raising an eyebrow in Edmund's direction. "Not your best idea, in my opinion, but I digress. You know Miss Pottan won't make this easy," Lendin warned him. "In London, it seemed the only thing the woman spoke of was your courtship and how she was bound to be a duchess."

Edmund sighed. They'd spent but a few hours in each other's company when the other family had been at their country estate, which bordered his to the south. He'd only taken Miss Pottan on two outings before she'd last left for London.

"I'll simply tell her I wish for our courtship to come to an end. There have been no declarations, and her reputation will remain intact. Perhaps if she plays it right, the association might increase the number of suitors who come to call on her."

"That may be, but it's well known she's looking for a man with both a title and deep pockets."

"There are others who fit her qualifications." And yet... unease grew within him at her possible reaction.

～

The next afternoon, Edmund was in the library, the early sun casting rays upon the carpet, when Prumb entered with a bow. "Sir, a Mrs. and Miss Pottan have come to call. I have settled them in the sitting room. Shall I send for tea?"

Edmund inwardly groaned and closed the book he had been reading with a resigned thump. He'd been dreading this meeting ever since the day before when he'd spoken with Lendin. Realizing that Prumb still awaited his answer, he replied, "Yes, please, Prumb. Hopefully, their visit will be short."

His butler bowed again and strode from the room, leaving Edmund to make his way to the sitting room. The footman beside the door bowed, waiting for Edmund's signal to open it. Edmund shuddered and took a moment to prepare himself before nodding to the servant, who swung open the door and announced him.

Edmund all but trudged into the room. Mrs. Pottan and her daughter rose and curtsied, and he bowed in return, Miss Pottan taking the opportunity to move closer to him. She was a tall woman with golden hair, not unpleasant-looking, yet generally unpleasant to speak to. She was dressed in a coral-colored dress with an abundance of ruffles.

"Your Grace! How lovely to see you. We were missing your

company terribly." Miss Pottan tittered and placed her hand on his arm with familiarity. Edmund fought the grimace that threatened to cross his face. "Mama and I have been so very busy, you see. I needed an entirely new wardrobe, so we had to visit Madame Chauncelier. She's simply the best with fabrics. Then, of course, that horrid Miss Waterton came to stay for weeks! How she manages to keep the attention of Sir Roland, I'll never know."

Edmund tried to distract himself from her incessant chattering and rude remarks to no avail. Her voice was shrill and nasal, the kind that grated against a person's ears. She would've been perfect as a wife if his never being able to fall in love with her remained his sole qualification. Now that didn't matter.

Mrs. Pottan sat on the chaise, and Miss Pottan sat on the settee, leaving Edmund no choice but to sit next to her or be intentionally rude. Mrs. Brinder was a blessing, for Miss Pottan's chatter paused when the housekeeper walked into the room, tea tray in hand, and placed it on the table with a curtsy. The blessing was short-lived, however. She poured each person a cup and fled from the room. If only he could do the same.

Miss Pottan raised the teacup to her lips and took the smallest sip of tea that Edmund had ever seen. Had she drunk any at all? She placed her cup back in its saucer and set both items back on the table with a small clatter, then turned her calculating eyes to Edmund. Why had he ever thought a marriage to her would be tolerable? She seemed so disingenuous. Meanwhile, he never doubted a thing that came from Eleanor's mouth, nor her behavior.

"And how is that darling niece of yours? We've been beside ourselves with curiosity. Haven't we, Mama?" Miss Pottan glanced at her mother, who nodded with an overeager smile on her face.

"Yes! Beside ourselves." The stout woman usually let her

daughter do the talking. However, she also had that calculating look in her eyes that made him uneasy.

Irritating, how he had to examine his every word before he spoke in order to make sure his sentences couldn't be twisted or interpreted incorrectly. He had experience with other misses like Miss Pottan. They were both so scheming that would latch on to any words or phrases they could use to pull unintended meanings from their victims.

"She's well." He shifted in his seat. "But there's som—"

"Might we visit her?" Miss Pottan gave a cat-like grin, her lips pulling up into a tight smile. "We've been so wishing to see how she's grown."

Edmund fought back a sigh. Perhaps if he agreed, she might be more amenable to his ending of their courtship. "I shall inquire if her lessons are over." He nodded to one of the footmen. The footman bowed and flew from the room.

Perhaps Eleanor's presence could help alleviate some of his discomfort. She'd certainly be a comfort to Rose as the poor girl was forced to endure the company of these women.

~

*E*leanor's nerves fluttered as she walked down the stairs with Rose. The footman who'd asked her to bring Rose to the sitting room had not mentioned who the guests were that wanted to see the girl. Would she know them? Eleanor chuckled to herself. Likely not, considering how far above her in society Edmund was.

She grabbed Rose's hand in her own, and, together, they followed the footman to the sitting room. Eleanor glanced down at Rose, who nibbled at her bottom lip, gripping her skirts with her small hands.

"Are you well, Rose?" Eleanor whispered to her charge.

Rose peered up at her and frowned. "I think I know who is visiting." Her foreboding tone raised Eleanor's anxiety.

Before Eleanor could ask any more, they were at the drawing room door. She squeezed the girl's hand to ease her worries. The footman waited for Eleanor's signal, then opened the door and announced Rose. As a baron's daughter, Eleanor had grown up with such formalities, but they were no longer necessary given her reduced status. It seemed unusual for Eleanor to not be announced, all the same.

She urged Rose in front of her as they stepped into the room, given she was the one the visitors wished to see, but Rose didn't let go of her hand. Edmund sat on the settee next to a blond woman, and another lady sat across from them on the chaise, but they all stood expectantly when Eleanor and Rose walked in. Eleanor kept her lashes lowered, almost hoping she would be invisible.

Rose also stared at the floor and dipped into a curtsy, the poor thing looking for all the world as though she'd rather be anywhere else. A few steps behind her, Eleanor did likewise. Edmund bowed, and the women curtsied as well, though only directed at Rose. They would doubtless think it beneath them to curtsy to a mere governess, after all. One of the women gasped, and Eleanor flicked her eyes up in surprise.

Her blood turned to ice.

Edward was speaking. "Miss Clairbridge, thank you for bringing Rose. This is Mrs. Pottan and Miss Pottan. I hope I haven't interrupted your lessons."

She met Edmund's gaze, warm and comforting—the complete opposite from the smug look of triumph on Miss Pottan's face.

Breathe. "We had just finished for the day when we received your request, Your Grace."

Edmund nodded, and Miss Pottan took the opportunity to speak.

"Why, Miss Clairbridge! A governess, after all. Perhaps you heeded my words, then."

Eleanor fought against the tense sensation in her chest. This was the last person she wished to see—aside from Mr. Phips. She forced a smile to her lips and bobbed a curtsy. "Mrs. Pottan, Miss Pottan. How do you do?"

Edmund's eyebrows furrowed as he glanced at Miss Pottan. "You know Miss Clairbridge?"

Miss Pottan smirked, eyeing the faded skirt of Eleanor's gown. "We met about five years ago, I believe. She hasn't changed since last we crossed paths."

Eleanor inwardly winced at the subtle barb.

The woman turned her attention on Rose, stepping forward with a sickly sweet smile pasted onto her face. "How nice to see you, Rose," she crooned.

Rose shifted under the woman's attention and remained silent.

Miss Pottan tilted her head. "I remember my days in the schoolroom. I always loved to practice etiquette. What have you been learning?"

Rose seemed to warm a bit at this question, a small smile coming to her face. "Miss Clairbridge has been teaching me all sorts of things. I really like when she teaches me mathematics and I get to solve sums. I also like when she takes me outside and I get to learn the sciences."

Miss Pottan's eyes widened to an almost impossible degree. Then she directed her steely gaze at Eleanor. "Mathematics?" Distaste practically dripped from the word, and she wrinkled her nose. She glanced back to Rose with a reproachful expression. "You won't need those to be a proper lady. Proper ladies such as myself"—she emphasized with a directed stare at Eleanor—"focus on necessary skills such as dancing, painting, and singing. To learn about science and mathematics is, quite simply, very foolish."

Rose's smile disappeared as soon as it had appeared. Given how much the girl enjoyed those subjects, Eleanor frowned. Irritation bubbled within her at the cold woman's words. It was one thing to insult Eleanor, but to be so unkind to Rose?

Edmund's countenance darkened, and a look of vexation flashed across his face. "It is at my request that Miss Clairbridge teaches Rose the subjects of mathematics and the sciences. I believe that 'proper ladies,' as you say, can benefit from learning these subjects. They are certainly ones Rose will use in the future."

Miss Pottan pouted, now acting as though Rose and Eleanor were no longer in attendance. She looked away from them and retook her seat on the settee. "I'm sure Miss Clairbridge would encourage you to think so. No doubt, she is relying upon this employment since she's clearly not marriage material. The last I heard, she was attempting to save her little house. I do hope that disaster has been diverted." The woman glanced at Eleanor, a glimmer of triumph in her eyes.

Through the tears filling Eleanor's eyes, she noted Edmund's muscles tensing. Miss Pottan's words had made their mark. Her cheeks warmed, but Miss Pottan wasn't finished.

"I know a friend in need of a scullery maid, Your Grace. Perhaps Miss Clairbridge would do well in that position. Rose might do better if she learns of more useful things, fitting to her station—"

"Enough!" Fire practically shot from Edmund's eyes. "Your cruel remarks about Miss Clairbridge will not be tolerated, Miss Pottan. I suggest you keep them to yourself."

Eleanor's heart warmed at Edmund's defense of her.

Then Rose, the dear girl, piped up as well. "Miss Clairbridge is a fine teacher, Miss Pottan. She's the smartest woman I know." Concern was plainly written on her face.

Eleanor sent a shaky smile her way.

Miss Pottan ignored Edmund's words and waved a dismissive hand at Rose. She stared at Eleanor. "You only think she's a fine teacher because you haven't had a proper model of one." She eyed Rose and put on her mask of friendliness again. "But I'd be more than happy to visit and instruct you how to be a proper lady. It is clear that you do not have anyone to teach you that here. How will you find a husband if you don't have a skilled teacher?"

Edmund crossed his arms over his chest. "I won't tell you again, Miss Pottan."

Rose's brow furrowed, a confused scowl upon her face. "I'm only six."

Eleanor's chest tightened at the insults, and she desperately wanted to escape to her room. It wasn't just that Miss Pottan had insulted her, but that she spoke of things that Eleanor had questioned herself. Eleanor tried to blink away the rising tears in her eyes, but one leaked out and rolled down her cheek.

Miss Pottan pouted and raised an eyebrow. "I know, child, but I'm to be your mother soon, anyway. You must get used to listening to me."

Eleanor's stomach dropped to her feet. "W-What?"

Miss Pottan stared at her, false pity on her face. "You haven't heard? His Grace is courting me."

Eleanor whipped her head toward Edmund, his irate expression shifting to an apologetic one. He wasn't denying it. She couldn't breathe. "Uh... I... Excuse me." She fled from the room. Her fears had just become a reality.

CHAPTER 18

*E*dmund's hands tightened into fists as his anger grew, jaw clenching. What a mess this had become. He couldn't remain quiet. He rang for Rose's nurse to collect her—with a whispered promise to the girl that he'd speak with her later—before facing the Pottan women once more.

"Miss Clairbridge is an exemplary governess to Rose. She is the finest example of a proper lady that I have ever witnessed, and if she can pass on to Rose even an ounce of her vast knowledge, I will know that Rose is well-prepared for the future."

Miss Pottan raised her eyebrows, her mouth open in shock. "But Your Gr—"

Edmund held up a hand to stop her. He wasn't finished. "And I wish to put an end to our courtship."

At this, the woman's face blanched.

Her mother began to protest, coming to stand next to her. "You took Arabella on three outings—"

"Two, yet I have never once made a declaration of any kind."

"What of my reputation?" Miss Pottan cried in an exaggerated fashion. "I'll be ruined!" She lifted a gloved hand to her forehead and closed her eyes. "I feel faint, Mama. Do you have your smelling salts?" Her mother fished them out from her reticule as her daughter continued. "You would really have this on your conscience, Your Grace? To think of for the rest of your life?"

Edmund crossed his arms in front of his chest, his irritation growing. Lendin had been right—she wasn't making this easy. "You will not be ruined, Miss Pottan—far from it—and do not attempt to guilt me into continuing our courtship. There will be other suitors, I'm sure."

Miss Pottan put an end to her act, instead glaring at him with cold eyes. "There are few dukes to be had," she replied, her tone as sharp and cool as a shard of ice.

"I believe Duke Kershop is searching for a wife," her mother murmured, holding out the smelling salts to her daughter.

Miss Pottan turned her head toward her mother and scowled, stomping her foot. "He's eighty, Mama!"

Edmund sighed inwardly. It was unlikely he would be able to change her mind on the subject, but fortunately, he didn't need her to agree with him. "I believe it time you leave, Mrs. Pottan, Miss Pottan. Please do not call again."

With that, Edmund had the footmen escort them out. On their way to the front entrance, the pair kept whispering back and forth.

Miss Pottan abruptly turned. "Is this about Miss Clairbridge? She'll never be your equal. All of society will look down on you!"

Edmund remained silent, not willing to say anything that could be gossiped about and not willing to do damage to Miss Clairbridge's good name.

Miss Pottan grumbled to herself and turned back toward the door.

A few snippets of conversation reached his ears as they exited.

"Thinks she's good enough to..."

"And tried to entrap Mr. Phips..."

"Can't see she's lacking..."

Their voices faded, and Edmund was finally able to relax as Prumb closed the door behind them.

But wait...lacking. *Lacking.* The puzzle pieces began to fit together in Edmund's mind. *I do not have to be a judge to see that Miss Clairbridge is lacking.*

Miss Pottan was the woman who had so cruelly treated Eleanor at the ball three years ago.

~

A sob escaped Eleanor as she crumpled onto her bed. She covered her face with her hands and attempted to choke them back, her shoulders shaking with her shuddering breaths. Her face was hot with humiliation, and she wanted to curl into a ball, away from the cruel words that had been spoken to her.

Miss Pottan had said Eleanor was plain, that she had no redeeming qualities. Perhaps she was right, after all. What she had said at the ball... Eleanor never did have any suitors.

She had no fancy clothing like Miss Pottan either. Her gown had appeared to be incredibly fine, indeed. Eleanor examined her own well-worn dress and ran her finger along the fabric. She frowned.

Eleanor touched her own hands—still soft, but now a bit more worn. These were no longer the hands of a proper lady, but rather, those of a person who worked to earn a living. She'd been so foolish to let herself get ideas of marriage. But more than the insults, it had been Miss Pottan's last statement that had pierced Eleanor to the core of her very being.

His Grace is courting me.

Eleanor stifled a sob with her hand.

Though she had tried to tamp down her growing affection for Edmund in the past months, she couldn't lie to herself. She had let herself dream of a happy future. The kind of future she had always imagined. One with beautiful children, a loving husband, a happy life. How stupid of her. Though she had little chance of marriage before becoming a governess, no gentleman wanted to marry a woman who worked. Especially one that was as plain and poor as herself.

Teardrops slid down her face and dropped to the covers. Her eyelashes were wet with the moisture, and a headache was coming on.

Even if he cared for her, Edmund was raised to think like a member of the peerage. Didn't his courtship of Miss Pottan illustrate that? He would never marry Eleanor. No one would. She would forever remain a spinster. A woman on the shelf.

$\sim$

*E*dmund sat on the chaise in the library, elbows on his knees and face in his hands. That was an absolute disaster. A surge of anger burned within him as the cruel words that Miss Pottan had said about Eleanor rang through his mind.

The nerve of that woman. Only the pain of Eleanor's obvious hurt and sadness overshadowed his anger. She had appeared so broken. So hopeless. So small.

While Edmund wanted to console her, Eleanor had shut herself up in her room. Mrs. Brinder had informed him that Eleanor had requested to have a tray brought for her evening meal. Though the potential lasting effect of Miss Pottan's words concerned him, he hesitated to go to Eleanor now. She needed rest.

Edmund raised his face from his hands and scanned the shelves of books surrounding him, unseeing. He clasped his hands in front of him, deep in thought. Miss Pottan's words had not only been cruel, but false as well.

Eleanor truly was the greatest woman he had ever met. She was so intelligent and so good with Rose. She was compassionate and kind, caring and gentle. She was beautiful, inside and out.

And she was in pain. He must talk to her—first thing the next morning. His heart squeezed in his chest. He could not be comfortable until she was happy and at peace again.

~

Seated at the small desk in her room that night, Eleanor tightened her grip on her fork and took another bite of the delicious meal Cook had prepared, the taste wasted on her.

When Miss Pottan had revealed that Edmund was courting her, Eleanor's mind had crashed in upon itself. It was something that had shaken her and strengthened her resolve to steel her heart—because Eleanor loved Edmund. She didn't know when her growing affections had solidified into love, but she must try to make peace with her unrequited feelings.

If she could hide her emotions, perhaps with time they would fade. Should Edmund learn she was in love with him, Eleanor didn't think she could bear to continue on there as a governess. All their interactions would turn awkward; they would avoid conversations, and he would pity her.

No. He could never know how she felt.

Eleanor chewed and swallowed, the bite of chicken descending down her esophagus like a lump of lead. She wasn't hungry but forced herself to eat, for if she did not, Fanny would be concerned when she returned to take the dinner tray away.

When Eleanor laid in her bed after she'd eaten, she tried to close her eyes and block any infiltrating thoughts.

She pulled her covers tighter around herself, the soft sheets bringing a small amount of comfort to her heart, a heart that was being crushed in her chest. The day had been emotionally exhausting, and Eleanor was very much ready to let sweet oblivion claim her. But her dreams were more akin to nightmares.

～

Eleanor walked through the house, excitement bubbling inside her. She had worn her best dress tonight, the pale blue silk with the embroidered flowers at the hem. She pictured Edmund in his fine clothing and smiled. As she moved through the quiet and empty hallways toward the library, the distant ring of laughter bounced off the walls. Her heart swelled with love. She seemed to bounce with each step, anticipation making her as light as the feathers in her hair.

Even the portraits on the walls seemed to smile down at her. As she moved closer to the library, the peals of laughter beckoned. She couldn't wait to see Edmund and Rose. She stepped up to the doors and grasped the handle of one, turning it slowly and pushing the door open, a wide grin on her face. Then her grin fell away.

Edmund was conversing with Miss Pottan, both of them smiling. He grasped her hands in his, affection in his eyes. Rose stood near, watching the interaction with joy in her countenance. They all turned toward her. Edmund still held onto Miss Pottan, and Rose pierced Eleanor with a frown. Edmund's expression was one of mocking, and Miss Pottan's matched it.

Eleanor's fingers fell away from the door handle. Her heartbeat slammed in her chest, each beat more painful than the last.

"Look at what she's wearing!" Miss Pottan exclaimed with a cruel

smile on her face. She turned to Edmund, and they laughed together at Eleanor's expense.

Eleanor's heart felt as though it had been torn into pieces and tossed into the hearth. The room's walls moved closer. But she could not flee without an explanation. "I thought—"

"You thought what?" Edmund cut her off, eyes bright with derision. "That I'd love a governess like you? What nonsense! Look at yourself." He sneered.

Eleanor examined her dress. Just moments before, it had been so lovely. Now it seemed as though she were wearing a frayed piece of fabric. Tears welled in her eyes. She shifted her attention to Rose, but her face was contorted into an expression of disdain.

"Rose?" Eleanor begged with her eyes for Rose to say something. The girl always had something nice to say. But she remained silent.

Eleanor's legs wobbled beneath her. She might just as well be falling from a great height, her limbs dangling and nothing to support her but air.

"Why did you even hire her in the first place, Edmund?" Miss Pottan asked Edmund.

He shrugged indifferently. "I can't remember, but it's clear that it was a mistake."

Miss Pottan's lip curled up as she snickered. "That's an understatement."

"You're dismissed, Miss Clairbridge."

Eleanor couldn't tell who had said it, but she was sick all the same. The people she had come to love hadn't shown even the slightest bit of warmth. They had insulted her. Made fun of her. Crushed her.

She bolted from the doorway and ran down the hallway toward her room. Her legs were liable to buckle beneath her at any moment. But each hallway she moved down only seemed to lead to another. Where was she to go from here?

～

*E*leanor heaved into a sitting position in her bed, hot tears gliding down her face. Her heart hammered, pounding frantically against her ribs. She swiped at the hair stuck to her face with a sheen of sweat and took deep breaths to calm her nerves.

She threw back the covers of the bed and tiptoed to the window, searching the stars for peace. The moon hung full in the great expanse of sky, its light a gleaming beam of hope in the dark. Twinkling stars dotted the blackness. Eleanor let out a long breath. It was only a nightmare. Everything was all right.

Then she stiffened, for it was not all right. Edmund was going to marry Miss Pottan.

Two days after Miss Pottan called, the morning light was bright in Edmund's room. He jumped out of bed, determined to talk to Eleanor today. She had been avoidant yesterday, hiding away so that he had been unable to speak to her. According to Mrs. Brinder, Eleanor had taken Rose into the estate's apple orchard to examine the buds on the branches. Wherever she'd been, Edmund hadn't found her.

In the morning room, he nearly scalded his tongue with tea and almost choked on his toast, so unwavering was his desire to seek her out. After he had finished a rudimentary breakfast, Edmund pulled his gold timepiece from his waistcoat pocket and flicked it open with his thumb, inspecting its face.

She would be in the schoolroom with Rose by now. Perfect. He placed his watch back into its designated pocket and stood from the breakfast table, pushing back his chair and bending to take one more sip of tea before heading for the schoolroom.

The maroon carpet lining the hallway muffled Edmund's purposeful footsteps. When he finally reached the schoolroom door, he knocked and waited for an answer. Eleanor's sweet voice called from the other side to enter.

When he set foot in the room, Rose, who was seated in her school desk, brightened. "Uncle Edmund!" She leapt from her chair, rushing toward him with her arms outstretched and a wide smile on her face.

He grinned and crouched to give her a tight hug. "Good morning, Rosie." He shot a glance over to Eleanor. A strong emotion—pain?—flashed across her face. It seemed as though the moment it appeared, the expression was gone, replaced by politeness. Edmund released Rose and straightened, meeting Eleanor's eyes with concern.

The look of deference remained on her face. "Greetings, Your Grace. I was just having Rose practice her reading. To what do we owe the pleasure of your visit?"

Edmund raised one eyebrow. "I hoped I might speak with you, Miss Clairbridge. If you have a moment, that is."

Her mouth twisted to the side before she instructed Rose to continue her reading. "I'll be back in a moment, Rose. See if you can sound out those words you were having difficulty with."

Rose turned her attention back to her book as Edmund gestured for Eleanor to follow him from the room. She closed the door behind her as she stepped out into the hallway, seeming to look anywhere other than at him. "What is it you wish to speak with me about, Your Grace?"

Edmund's brows tugged down. Your Grace? And why the timidity? He cleared his throat and ran a hand through his hair, tousling it for the first time that day. His valet knew by now that Edmund's hair did not stay the way he had styled it for long.

"I wished to speak with you about yesterday, Eleanor. After Mrs. and Miss Pottan's visit, I know that you were left in pain. I realize now that she is the one who treated you so unfairly at the ball you spoke of. Am I correct?"

Eleanor nodded, her gaze on the floor.

Unable to prevent himself from doing so, he began to pace back and forth in front of her. "Ms. Pottan's words were unbearably cruel, and when you left the room afterward…Well, suffice it to say, I set her straight on the matter. She won't be seen around here in the future." He stopped pacing and heaved a great sigh. What a relief to be free of that woman's machinations. "Pray, tell me how I can help you." Edmund took a step closer, forcing his hands to remain at his sides—hands that were aching to grasp hers.

Eleanor stared at the ground. "I am well, Your Grace. There is nothing for you to help with. No issue at all." she replied in an unconvincing tone.

He ran a hand through his hair again and took another step closer to her. "I don't believe you, Eleanor."

Surprise crossed her face before her features shifted back into an impassive look. She clasped her hands in front of her, and he finally caught her gaze. Her blue eyes, normally sparkling with joy in their depths and gleaming with life, now appeared dull and empty. She tilted her head down once again and shuffled her feet. "I assure you, Your Grace, I am perfectly content."

He released a breath in frustration and crossed his arms. "You may always speak to me, and I will always listen to what you have to say. It pains me to see you acting so differently than your normal joyful self."

Eleanor tilted her head almost imperceptibly.

Why wouldn't she speak to him? After all, he'd told her about the misunderstanding with Miss Pottan. If only he could help Eleanor. She need only tell him what to do, and he wouldn't hesitate. It seemed as though he would not be getting answers from her today, however.

Edmund dropped his arms to his sides, disappointment aching in his chest. "Very well, then. I suppose I shall take my leave of you and let you get back to your lessons. I thank you for your time." When she did not protest, he turned away, albeit reluctantly.

Feeling the need for fresh air, Edmund pushed himself to go for a brisk ride on General. He donned his riding boots, gloves, and hat and made his way to the stables. The morning was overcast, typical for an English day, but the grass was shining and the flowers were in bloom. He sighed.

If only he could be as content as the day seemed to be. As he strolled into the stable, the stable hands on duty bowed and waited for Edmund to make a request. Before he could ask for his horse to be saddled, Mr. Haldwell, the stable manager, stepped out from the nearby tack room. He gave a paternal smile, his wrinkled face forming a pleasant expression. He took a few steps toward Edmund and bowed low.

"Yer Grace, what ken I do for ya?"

Edmund returned Mr. Haldwell's smile, hoping it was convincing enough. "Good day, Mr. Haldwell. I wish to ride General. Could you please have someone saddle him for me?"

"Certainly, Yer Grace." The man signaled to one of the stable hands to saddle General.

"How is your family, Mr. Haldwell?" Edmund ran a hand down General's side as his horse was brought from his stall, stepping back when the stable hand moved forward with the saddle.

Mr. Haldwell grinned and scratched his chin. "They've been good. Thomas's wife is expectin', and Fred's little boys are a han'ful." Mr. Haldwell chuckled. "Now they can see what me and their poor mother had t' go through! They always were causin' trouble. And dear Lucy's t' be married! My little gal, all grown up." He paused, a nostalgic look on his face. "Mary's been knittin' up a storm. I can't find one chair in my house that isn't occupied by some small babe's hat or gown." He chuckled.

Hearing about the old man's family lifted Edmund's spirits and proved to be a welcome distraction from his troublesome thoughts. Mr. Haldwell seemed lost in his own musings, a proud tilt to his mouth. After a moment, he snapped himself from them and turned his attention back to Edmund.

"How've ya been lately, Yer Grace? Ya haven't been fer a ride in a long while." Mr. Haldwell raised an eyebrow at Edmund, waiting for his response.

Edmund shrugged. "I suppose I've been busy as of late. A lot has been on my mind." He kept his answer vague, aware of how talented Mr. Haldwell was at pulling information from him.

Mr. Haldwell crossed his arms and quirked his lips in a knowing smile. "Has a certain someone been occupyin' yer thoughts? 'Haps that Miss Clairbridge of yours?"

Edmund's cheeks heated as he shifted on his feet, though he was—for the most part—unbothered by the question as he'd known the man since he was a child. And now saw him almost daily when he went for a ride. He was somewhat used to Mr. Haldwell's direct manner of speaking.

Edmund cleared his throat. "She has been one of the many things, Mr. Haldwell."

The man continued to stare at him with a question in his eyes, apparently dissatisfied with Edmund's answer.

A few seconds passed in unbearable silence before Edmund could take it no longer. He tugged at his cravat and spoke. "To be honest, she has been at the forefront of my every thought."

Mr. Haldwell leaned against the side of a stall and gestured for Edmund to continue, an intrigued look on his face. "Go on, then."

Edmund continued, feeling the relief of speaking to a trusted friend of what he had been keeping inside. "It seems that I cannot make a decision without thinking of how it might affect her. When she's upset, I only consider how I might ease her mind. When she leaves a room, it feels as though she has taken a piece of me with her." He pulled the hat from his head and ran a hand through his hair before setting his hat back in place. "I have never met a woman like her. She is kind, intelligent, beautiful, caring..." Words simply could not do her justice.

"I see." Mr. Haldwell rubbed a hand over his chin and waited, rightly guessing that Edmund was not finished.

Shaking his head, he released a sigh. "I have tried to guard my heart from her, but her whole being has managed to break my defenses. She captivates me to the greatest extent. I have tried not to but, I..." Edmund paused to take a deep breath. "I love her." He exhaled.

Mr. Haldwell raised his eyebrows. "There's no question about that, Yer Grace, but does she return yer feelings?"

Edmund ruminated over all of their encounters since he had first run into Eleanor on that busy street in London. Mr. Haldwell waited a few minutes for him to answer.

Edmund's lips pulled down. "I haven't the slightest idea. Sometimes she smiles at me with such warmth, yet at others, she acts as though I'm the last person she wishes to be in company with."

Mr. Haldwell nodded in understanding.

Before he could respond, a question struck Edmund. "How did you know I would fall in love with Ele—Miss Clairbridge?" Somehow, the stable master hadn't seemed the least bit surprised that Edmund had developed feelings for Rose's governess.

Mr. Haldwell's eyes gleamed with mirth as he replied. "The day Miss Clairbrige fell from Snowdrop, ye came in ' ere lookin' half wild with worry. Then off ya went to find 'er. Ya didn't hesitate at all. I knew then that ya were through."

Edmund placed a hand on his chin, remembering that day vividly. He had been so overcome with fear that something had happened to Miss Clairbridge. Even now, he didn't quite remember traveling to the stables on the day of the accident.

He had been so focused on finding Eleanor that he didn't think much of his surroundings. "I never did stand a chance, did I?"

The horse in the stall nearest to him stuck its head out as if curious. It was none other than Snowdrop herself.

A deep rumble of laughter sounded from Mr. Haldwell. "It's as if she knows we're talkin' of 'er!" He grinned, a sparkle of humor in his eyes.

A smile formed on Edmund's face, and he placed a gentle hand on Snowdrop's muzzle, the hairs soft beneath his fingertips. Snowdrop nudged his palm in greeting and let out a slow breath. Would Eleanor ride again, or had her accident made her wary of it? Maybe he could help her if she was. If she'd let him. As things between them stood now, he wasn't sure she would. He gave Snowdrop another pat before nodding farewell to Mr. Haldwell and mounting General.

Together they flew across the open fields, the wind breezing through his hair. His talk with Mr. Haldwell had served to make his thoughts even more muddled. His mind surely resembled a piece of string, knotted and tangled. He was now trying to find the end of it to untie the knots. Edmund eased General into a walk, only halfway seeing the wide green land around them.

Did Eleanor love him as he loved her? When he had wrapped his handkerchief around Eleanor's pricked finger in the gardens, his hands had tingled as he held hers. But had she experienced the same sensation? Edmund frowned as he tried to recall. Yes. She had blushed. He was sure of it. But was it out of embarrassment, or something more?

In the library late that night, they had spoken of poetry, even quoting Wordsworth. Did she feel the connection he did? He'd had a hard time taking his eyes from hers. Though these interactions had been pleasant, Edmund could not be sure she'd experienced the same attraction he had. Perhaps before... but now, Eleanor wouldn't even look at him.

He huffed a breath of frustration, and General nickered, seeming to ask what was wrong.

"I'm just a tad aggravated, old boy. I wish Eleanor would talk to me. I wish I knew if she returned my feelings." He leaned over in the saddle and petted General's shoulder. "Don't worry. It's nothing for you to concern yourself with."

He pressed his riding boots into General's sides and urged him into a trot, then a gallop. Though he was surrounded by beauty, he focused instead on the puzzle that was the woman he loved.

And he spoke aloud his dreadful conclusion. "Alas, I fear she does not feel the same."

❧

When Edmund returned from his ride, he changed from his riding clothing and went to his study, having business to see to. As he settled himself into the comfortable leather chair behind his desk, he picked up a stack of correspondence, left there by the ever-prompt Prumb. Edmund sifted through the letters, scanning the writing on them.

Mr. Benson again, an invitation from the Feldings, a letter from Mr. Kently... Edmund paused as he read the name written on a letter and grinned. Lord Lendin. He broke the wax seal on the paper and unfolded it, reading the messily written words.

Colhampton,

How've you been, old friend? How did Miss Pottan take your decision? Rather rough business, that. I've been well myself. I'm currently attempting to read Byron's work for the fifth time. You know how well the first four went. No matter how hard I try, I cannot find it in me to like it. I will gladly read Robert Southey on any day, and Byron on none of them.

Edmund paused in his reading and snorted in amusement.

How's Rose? Is she well? And how's that governess of yours? Upon speaking with you, it became evident to me that an affection for her had already begun in you. You seemed happier, brightened whilst talking about her... Needless to say, a person would have to be quite daft to miss the signs, and I am not a daft person. Well, not typically, though I will agree that I can be at times. The point is, do not let your fears muddle your affection for her.

There is a good woman nearby, and you would be remiss to let her go. Pray for me, that I might find a good woman for myself someday soon. This estate seems to get lonelier by the minute.

Ever your faithful friend,

Lendin

Edmund finished the letter, his mind clearer now than it had been before he'd opened it. He inhaled a deep breath and released it, feeling a bit lighter. He chuckled to himself, rereading his friend's words. Lendin had always been too observant for his own good.

He hoped his friend did, in fact, find a woman to wed soon. Lendin was one of the best men of Edmund's acquaintance, as well as one of his closest friends, and deserved to find a love of his own. Preferably one that loved him back.

Edmund dropped the letter back onto his desk and ran a hand through his hair, his current fears creeping back up on him. He lifted his eyes toward a portrait of his father he'd had placed over the fireplace after his death, seeking an answer.

Father, what should I do? Your marriage to Mother was the perfect example of a love match. Do I tell her how I feel? Or do I keep silent on the matter? Does she even feel the same? Should I seek her out, or let her come to me?

Just then, a knock on his door sounded, and he bid the person enter. Of all things, the person who wished to see him was Eleanor herself. She kept her eyes on the floor as Edmund stood from his desk, nearly knocking his chair over in his haste. "Eleanor."

Hope rose within him that she had finally come to talk to him of what had been troubling her. He longed for answers regarding her unusual demeanor as of late. There seemed to be more to it than Miss Pottan's cruel words.

"Your Grace," she replied, voice hesitant.

He gestured for her to sit in the chair across from his desk, which she did, albeit a bit reluctantly. He seated himself back in his own chair and stared at her, waiting for her to begin the conversation. Perhaps she would finally confide in him. She straightened out her skirts and clasped her hands in her lap before meeting his eyes. He had lately been gifted fewer glances of their brilliant hue and found himself missing their warmth.

After a moment of silence, Eleanor spoke. "I have come to ask that I might visit my mother for a few days. I wish to make sure she is well. I will not be long, of course."

Any hope that had risen in Edmund's chest crumbled. He fully understood her desire to visit her mother, but his disappointment didn't wane. "Of course, Eleanor. When would you like to visit her?"

Eleanor tightened her hands in her lap, knuckles white. "As soon as possible. Perhaps in two day's time?"

So soon? It seemed too close to the Pottans' visit to be a coincidence. Edmund leaned back in his chair. "Certainly. I'll let the footmen know to ready one of the carriages when you wish to leave."

Eleanor stood and gave her thanks before leaving the room. Having risen when she took her leave, Edmund resumed his seat and ran a hand through his hair.

This latest interaction only strengthened his theory that Eleanor did not return his feelings. Edmund glanced over to the small table in the corner of the room that held a decanter and glasses, looking at them for a moment before shaking his head. That would do nothing.

The book of poetry still sat on his desk from when he had taken it from Rose, who had been under the impression that it had upset her governess. He picked it up and studied the worn cover before opening a drawer and shoving it inside.

He'd been foolish to let her into his heart. He should not have let his hopes run rampant, dreaming of her as his wife. Dreaming of a family. Of picnics in the fields, children playing in the gardens, joyful days spent together. The woman he loved did not love him, and yet he couldn't imagine loving anyone else.

~

*E*leanor was curled up on one of the stone benches in the garden, listening to the birdsong and quiet breeze. The roses blushed around her in thorny masses.

"A letter for you, Miss Clairbridge." The footman, John, was coming towards her, a letter in hand. "'Twas delivered by a man on horseback who's just ridden here from London."

Eleanor thanked him and took the letter, worry creeping into her heart. She eyed the writing on the front, but it was unfamiliar to her. "Is the man still here?" She examined the wax seal. Perhaps she'd seen it before?

"He is in the kitchens awaiting your response."

She grasped the envelope with both hands and broke the gold wax seal with her thumb.

Dear Miss Clairbridge,

Your mother is unwell. I beg you to come at once. She is very frail. Please hurry.

Phyllida G. Witherby

Eleanor must have gasped, for John, who still stood there, took a step closer. "Are you all right, miss?" he asked, concern lacing his words.

Eleanor reread the letter and covered her mouth with her hand, her heart beating at a race horse's pace. "Tell the man, today." Her breath came out in heavy exhales. "I'll arrive today."

With that, John was off, and Eleanor was rushing inside. She nearly ran to Edmund's study. Arriving at the heavy wooden door, she rapped on it.

Edmund was there almost as soon as her third knock made contact, swinging open the door with lowered eyebrows. His expression changed to one of concern. "Eleanor?"

She couldn't speak, worry silencing her, so she extended the letter to him. He took it, an uncertain expression on his face. It only took him seconds to read.

"You must go at once, Eleanor. See your mother." He looked worried, but it didn't compare to the sea of emotions and thoughts tumbling in her mind. She was drowning. He didn't know the state Eleanor had left her mother in, her gowns hanging around her like loose Holland covers hiding furniture.

"I'm aware I planned to go two days hence—"

"It matters not, truly. See to your mother."

She'd have to pack immediately, only a few things, and— "What about Rose?"

Edmund put a gentle hand on her arm. "Rose will be well. You must only worry about your mother. I will see to the rest."

Eleanor trembled at the thought of her mother in a simple wooden box—one only as large as her small frame. She'd have no one. Edmund's hand left her arm, taking the warmth with him. As long as he continued to court Miss Pottan, she could expect no security with him either.

She would be alone. Who would save her then?

CHAPTER 20

*E*leanor awoke a few hours later when the carriage rolled to a stop, the sun a bit lower in the sky. She peeked out the window, and her eyes widened. The carriage had stopped in front of her familiar London townhome.

How did she manage to sleep through the busy London roads? She must have been tired, indeed. She clutched her carpet bag's handles as the footman that had accompanied her on her journey stepped toward the carriage door and opened it, letting the stairs down.

He offered his hand, which she took, and he helped her down the steps. The townhouse door opened, revealing Crand with a grave look on his face.

"Good day, miss." He held open the door for her, and she walked up the steps and inside the foyer. Eleanor set her carpet bag down on the floor beside her, and Crand immediately reached for it.

Eleanor stopped him with a gentle hand and smile. "Thank you, Crand, but I will take my bag to my room."

His lips pulled into a stern line, but he refrained from protest.

Eleanor did hand him her traveling bonnet, however. "Where is Mama? Is Mrs. Witherby here?"

"They are in your mother's chambers, miss."

"How is she faring?" Eleanor's chest constricted.

Crand tucked his chin. "I cannot say exactly, miss, for the doctor left recently. Would you like me to send up tea?"

Eleanor blinked, her eyes stinging. She nodded and gave her thanks to Crand before rushing up the stairs and down the corridor to her mother's room. Her home appeared unchanged—shabby as ever. The carpets were threadbare, the wallpaper was peeling, and the windows were dirty and smudged. There was simply too much work for the limited number of servants. The money she sent didn't seem to have made much of a difference in fixing what needed to be fixed, or replacing what needed to be replaced. Perhaps the funds had been used for something else.

In front of her mother's chamber door, she took a steadying breath, attempting to prepare herself for what she might see. Footsteps sounded beyond the door before it opened, revealing Mrs. Witherby's ashen face.

"Miss Clairbridge, thank goodness you're here." She opened the door wider and ushered Eleanor into the room, unbearably hot with a fire blazing in the hearth. "The doctor left not long ago. He determined your mother's illness to be scarlet fever. He said we should keep the room very warm so as to let the illness out through perspiration."

No amount of steady breathing could have prepared Eleanor for the sight of her mother propped up on her bed pillows, fragile-looking as a piece of crystal from a chandelier. Blankets were wrapped around her torso and legs, her thin arms laid on top.

"Mama!" She flung herself to the side of the bed and grabbed her mother's warm hand.

She turned sunken, red, tired eyes to Eleanor and gave a weak smile. "Do not fret, dear. I am well enough." Though her voice came out raspy. And surely, her mother said this in an attempt to comfort her. Even when she was so sick, she only thought of others.

"But, Mama…"

Mama patted Eleanor's hand. "Hush, dear. There's no need to worry."

Eleanor's mother was as stubborn as ever. Eleanor turned her somber gaze to Mrs. Witherby once more, the dear woman wringing her hands as one might wring a poor chicken's neck. "What else did the doctor say? When will she get better?" Her eyes stung, and her chest ached.

Mrs. Witherby hesitated before answering. "He isn't quite sure. Due to your mother's frailty before she became ill, it is hard to say how she will weather this. He thinks, perhaps, a few weeks, assuming she will get past the worst of it."

A few weeks? And…*assuming*? She couldn't bear to consider the alternative. Her mother had once been a hale and hearty woman. Now she had been reduced to…a cream-colored shawl one might throw over their shoulder before they go out—and just as light as one. Would she be just as lifeless soon?

"I *will* get past the worst of it, of course." Mama's voice was small but insistent. "I'm not so terribly ill, after all. Your father always said I had the strongest constitution of anyone he knew."

"Miss Clairbridge, might I speak to you in the hall for a moment?" Mrs. Witherby asked, still wringing her hands.

Eleanor nodded and gave her mother's hand a squeeze before standing and following the woman from the room.

Once outside, Mrs. Witherby grasped both of Eleanor's hands in her own. "Dear, she is not well…the doctor is unsure if she's strong enough to fight the illness. She'll need medicines, as well. Dr. Glimble wrote a list of herbs you might wish to get from the druggist down the street."

Eleanor trembled. "And the doctor's fees?"

"Fifteen pounds."

Eleanor's head spun. What might have once been seen as a small sum was now insurmountable. As a governess, Eleanor only received forty-eight pounds per annum, and she'd only received eight pounds of that, given she'd worked but two months under Edmund's employ. Now she'd be forced to spend all of it, as well as more of their savings. Her eyes watered as the reality of their circumstances set in.

"Oh, dear." Mrs. Witherby pulled Eleanor into a tight embrace. "It'll all be put right, my dear. Just you see."

Eleanor wanted to believe the woman, yet couldn't. Edmund was to marry Miss Pottan, her mother was ill, and their finances were no better than they were before Eleanor had left—in fact, they would be worse.

How had everything declined so quickly?

∼

Thirty minutes later, Eleanor moved with purpose down the cobbled street toward the druggist's shop, the doctor's list in hand.

Contrayerva
Oxymel of Squill
Elderberry Tea

The list went on.

Eleanor had volunteered to go to the druggist, hoping the fresh air and familiar surroundings might calm her nerves. In fact, this was the same street she'd walked that fateful day she'd met Edmund. Many times, she'd passed the same druggist's shop that she headed to now. When her father had fallen ill, servants had been sent to collect any medicines he had needed. She had been separated from his illness. However, the fact that she was retrieving them at this point in time, and for her *mother*, only reminded her of their drastic change in circumstances. Things were even bleaker now than they had been then.

Eleanor entered the shop and was greeted by an elderly man with large round-rimmed spectacles and a whiskered smile. "Welcome, miss. What can I do for ye?"

She attempted to return his smile. "Good day. I have a list of herbs from the doctor to procure." She placed the paper on the front counter, and the man reached for it, lifting it close to his face to read what the doctor had written.

"Contrayerva, eh?" He furrowed his eyebrows. "Well, I'm a bit low in supply of that, but I'll give ye what I can." He moved around behind the counter, pulling jars of varying sizes from different shelves. He filled smaller jars and bags with a variety of dark-colored liquids and crushed flora. When he was finished preparing the items, he stuffed them into a bag and handed it to her.

She took it with equal care and paid the man, murmuring her thanks before leaving the shop. Eleanor plodded home, legs heavy with the despair that coursed through her. They would lose their home.

And it was her fault. Had she been married, they would not be in their situation. At the very least, she should've begun the search for employment earlier.

Father had been ill and he...

And now Mama...

Eleanor couldn't bear to think of the possibility of her mother not being able to get better. She'd have nothing left of her family. They'd be gone. Her home would be gone. She'd be utterly alone, and with not a penny to her name.

~

*M*ama's fever had spiked. It had only been a few hours since Eleanor's trip to the druggist, yet her mother had taken a turn for the worse. She'd been peacefully sleeping when Eleanor had returned home, but now a red rash flamed on her face and speckled down her neck and arms in a peppering of angry dots. A pale ring circled her mouth, and the flesh around her throat was slightly swollen.

Eleanor leaned over her, holding her shoulders down as the woman thrashed in her bed as though she'd disturbed a hive of angry bees. Mary was holding her mother's legs, but only so much could be done.

"Fetch more water, please, Mary. The water we have has grown too warm."

As Mama gave another soft cry of anguish, Mary fled the room with the bowl of water in hand.

Eleanor shook her head, tears streaming down her face. "Mama, it is only I. Please, Mama. We are here to help you." Her mother seemed to calm at the sound of Eleanor's voice and the soothing tone she used, so Eleanor continued, settling in the chair she'd placed next to the bed. "You are safe, Mama. You are only ill. We will help you get better."

Mary reentered the room with the requested water and a small towel. "Here, miss." She set them on the bedside table.

Eleanor dipped the towel into the water and began to wash her mother's forehead, cooling the skin there. Was her mother getting any relief?

Eleanor picked up the now-tepid cup of elderberry tea from the side table—she'd had Mary bring it up before the thrashing had started—and lowered it to her mother's chapped lips. "Drink, Mama. You must be parched, surely."

Mama did not open her eyes but swallowed as the liquid was poured into her mouth. Not a minute later, she was casting it up into the chamber pot, her wretches loud in the quiet room.

Eleanor covered her mouth as her mother slumped against the headboard in exhaustion. Her already frail body was growing weaker. Eleanor took her mother's limp hand. Mama was unconscious again.

Eleanor knelt at her bedside and closed her eyes. Why must everything be happening at once? Why must all of her problems be falling upon her as heavy and unbearable as a bag of bricks?

God, I beg You. Take these worries—these problems—away. Take them into Your hands. I cannot bear these burdens on my own. Let my mother be healthy again, please. Guide me, Lord. Do not leave me when I most need You.

Eleanor opened her eyes. The steady flame of the candle on Mama's bedside table glowed in the evening light, illuminating the darkness around it.

An unseen weight lifted off her shoulders. The Lord was with her. He would not leave, no matter what happened. He would always take care of her, no matter where she was, for He was as steady as the flame of that candle. He was the light in the darkness. He was the hope when all seemed lost.

Eleanor lifted her mother's hand to her lips and kissed it. The Lord would help them through.

～

*E*leanor's mother slept for the next day—and even the day after that—but, after several treatments of herbal compresses and tisanes, she finally seemed to be getting better.

Eleanor stayed with her mother throughout the evenings and ensured that her fever broke by the second morning, regularly bathing her forehead with the damp cloth. Now that the woman was awake again, she seemed eager to share with Eleanor all of the news she had been storing over the weeks, even if she was still in no fit state to do so.

"You must be so tired from your travels and then from nursing me, dear. How was the carriage ride here?" her mother asked after Eleanor had coaxed her to eat a piece of toast.

The evening sun was sinking low on the horizon, casting shadows about her mother's room like reaching arms. The candle on the bedside table fought them.

Eleanor moved closer to the bed, patting her mother's hand before replying. "It wasn't such a way, Mama. You shouldn't add worry for me to your list of concerns."

Her mother lifted her eyebrows. "Mrs. Witherby was telling me of her daughters when she was here."

"I've missed them." A hint of dejection colored Eleanor's voice. They sent letters occasionally, but with how busy their lives were, not as much as she wished they could.

Her mother seemed not to notice. "Mrs. Witherby received a letter the other day from Eliza, and apparently, she is with child! Isn't it exciting?"

A pang of sadness reverberated around Eleanor's chest, but she nodded and tried her best to look as pleased as her mother was. She lifted an oddly smelling cup of tea from the bedside table and handed it to her mother. Their cook had steeped the herbs Eleanor had bought. "Please drink, Mama."

Mama did as bid, wincing as she swallowed. When Eleanor furrowed her eyebrows, her mother was quick to explain. "'Tis my throat, dear. It is terribly sore, but nothing I cannot weather."

Eleanor bit her lip, heart aching that she could do no more

for her mother. "And how's Teresa? I remember she married Mr. Wicker a few years ago."

Her mother took another sip of tea. "According to Mrs. Witherby, Teresa has been kept busy with her little ones. Her daughter is but one and her son, three. I remember vividly when you were around that age. You were quite the wild one yourself, you know," Mama replied with a loving smile.

At the thought of her dear friends with children, Eleanor's melancholy grew heavier. Her own hopes for such a future had withered on the stem. "How quickly time has passed." Though she tried to maintain a facade of contentedness, her lips pulled into frown of their own accord.

Unlike before, Mama took notice and frowned. "What's wrong, dear? Has something I've said upset you?" Concern laced her words.

Eleanor had tried to hold in her despairing emotions, but she was tired of doing so. She needed to speak of her feelings to someone, and who better than her mother?

Eleanor's shoulders slumped. Who was she to vent her woes when her mother was in such a state?

She breathed in deeply and exhaled with a sigh, her whole being wilting with the pain of the past weeks. "I—It is nothing."

Her mother raised an eyebrow and waited for Eleanor to speak what she was keeping hidden.

Eleanor bolstered her courage before sitting in the chair beside the bed. At last, she told the entire story, from the moment Edmund had caught her when she'd tripped on the London street to the present. Her mother remained quiet, giving Eleanor her full attention.

"After Miss Pottan revealed what she did, I realized I had been incredibly foolish. Edmund will never love me the way that I love him. I thought—well, it is of no consequence what I thought. I am only the governess to his niece, a sort of friend, and nothing more. How could I have been such a ninny as to allow him into my heart? I should have known things could ever only end this way."

"My poor girl…"

Eleanor leaned back into her seat, raising a hand to cover her eyes in shame. "Oh, Mama, what am I to do? I can't let him know that I love him, but I can't bear to watch as he marries some titled woman and then try to govern their beautiful children. He is so kind. He even chided Miss Pottan for her rudeness! He made me aware that she would not disturb the schoolroom after her last visit, which is a relief, but I cannot bear to see them together. And yet…" Her voice wavered. "I cannot leave my position. We need the money."

Her mother sat forward and gently pulled Eleanor's hand from her face before wiping away her tears. She hadn't even known she'd been crying. Her mother searched her face with knowing eyes. "I wondered if you might have been falling in love when I received your last letter. You mentioned the duke quite a few times."

Eleanor opened her mouth to speak, but her mother pinned her with a look, signaling that she wasn't finished.

"It seems to me, dear, you are jumping to conclusions and letting your own insecurities get the better of you. How do you know for certain that he doesn't love you? From what you have been telling me, he sounds like a man very much in love."

Eleanor replayed their pivotal interactions in her mind, her heart beating ever faster as the memories flashed through her mind. "He…couldn't possibly love me, Mama. He's a duke, for goodness' sake. And courting Miss Pottan," she added to further make her point.

Her mother spoke again, slowly and with understanding filling her voice. "Are those the only reasons for your disbelief?"

Eleanor wrung her hands in her lap and turned her eyes to the wall across from her, avoiding her mother's gaze. "I…" She swallowed the emotion building in her throat. "At the ball, Miss Pottan said—"

Her mother waved her hand. "I know very well what Miss Pottan said to you, but why should one woman's words crush your worth?"

Eleanor's face heated. "But maybe she was right, Mama. After all, I've never been courted by any man, nor has anyone ever shown more than a passing interest in me."

"And this lack of suitors determines how much value you hold?"

"Well..." Wasn't that the way of society? A woman was only as valuable as her accomplishments, dowry, and outward appearance made her. By those standards, Eleanor had very little to recommend her.

Her mother sighed. "Society can be cruel, my dear, as you have come to learn over the years. But just because you've had little attention from gentlemen does not mean that you have little worth. Bright and colorful jewels may be displayed at the front of the box for all to see, but the truly beautiful and precious ones are hidden away where no trouble may befall them. You have been hidden, my dear, and perhaps the duke is the one who has found you."

Eleanor stopped her wringing hands, eyebrows furrowed in thought. "Though you may be correct, what about our disparate standings in society? Edm—His Grace cannot possibly marry me. It is too much to hope for."

"It is rare...but not unheard of." Mama smiled weakly. "Love does not follow social rules or strictures, dear. Love knows no bounds. It springs up in the most unusual places, even the places with the harshest of environments. Love may come when and where you least expect it, and though you might find it hard to believe, there is a very real possibility that the duke loves you just as much as you love him."

Eleanor's mind was reeling. Could he truly love her?

"And do not bear any mind to those horrid women who seek to see you fall. No one can tell you your own worth or value. There will always be those who wish to tear you down in life, and you mustn't let them. You must rise above their words and continue on. Eleanor..." Her mother took one of her hands and squeezed it. "You are so much more than you think. You are incredibly kind and good, very intelligent, and not the least bit plain. You are not only a governess, but a woman who has the intelligence to teach and the fortitude to continue on through troubled times. Do not ever forget that."

Eleanor's heart swelled, and she embraced her mother with care, Mama's frail body small in her arms. "Thank you." Pulling back and wiping her eyes, she gestured to the teapot on the nearby table. "Would you care for some more tea, Mama?"

"I would, thank you." Her mother leaned forward as Eleanor poured, arranging the covers around herself. Her face was much less flushed than two days ago.

Eleanor set the teapot aside and seated herself again. Perhaps her mother was right. Maybe she was simply letting Miss Pottan's words get the better of her. She'd certainly struck a chord within Eleanor when she'd spewed them. Eleanor must let go of her insults and banish them from her mind. They had no place there. Her mother believed in her, and it was time Eleanor started doing the same.

With that promise to herself, Eleanor lifted her lips in an appreciative, albeit strained, smile. "I hear the wisdom in your words, Mama, but I believe my relationship with the duke is the least of our troubles at the moment."

Her mother's eyelids drooped as fatigue began to set in. "That is not for us to worry about today, but tomorrow."

Though her mother no doubt meant to ease her troubled mind, Eleanor could not push her problems away, hoping tomorrow might bring an answer.

Her mother's sleepy voice drew her attention once more.

"I'll always listen to you, dear. I do wonder what you'll do when you go back to Ivy Grange, however."

What would she do? She could not go on without knowing Edmund's feelings.

"I'll just have to tell him how I feel and pray that he feels the same." She spoke with a bit of uncertainty tinting her words. If Edmund didn't, in fact, feel the same, there was a good chance she would be dismissed. He was courting Miss Pottan, for goodness' sake! Would Eleanor's admission of love matter, and was telling him worth the risk of losing her employment?

CHAPTER 21

*E*leanor awoke with a crick in her neck, the chair beside her mother's bed being the culprit and Eleanor the accomplice for having allowed herself to rest there. She glanced around her mother's room, the fire still blazing in the hearth. Mary was an angel. Everything now was as it had been when Eleanor had gone to sleep, only, there was sunlight peeking through the drapes.

It had been one week since she'd had the conversation about Edmund with her mother, and while she had reached a resolve concerning her feelings for him, she still hadn't a single idea as to how she would better the state of their finances. Mama continued to get better with every passing day, yet the doctor's fees were quickly eating away at what little money they had left.

If Edmund allowed her to remain after she declared her feelings—even if he didn't feel the same—perhaps she could work in the hours after Rose's lessons had finished. She knew how to sew, and maybe a seamstress in the village near Ivy Grange would like another set of hands in her shop. If he returned her feelings and wished to marry, however, there would be no reason for her to work...

Her mother's voice startled her. "You needn't have slept in that chair, dear. I'm perfectly well on my own."

Eleanor tilted toward her mother and gave a small smile. "It is true that you are getting better, but I don't believe it is a bad thing to be available to you should your illness give us one last struggle."

Her mother huffed playfully and adjusted her blankets.

Eleanor stood and stretched before moving to the bell pull and ringing for Mary. She had a few minutes before the girl would arrive. "Mama..."

Her mother flicked her gaze up to Eleanor's, causing her to pause. Mama waited patiently, giving Eleanor a moment to collect her thoughts.

"Our finances...the doctor...I fear it's not long until we must dismiss the servants." Eleanor's vision clouded as tears welled in her eyes, threatening to spill at any moment. Crand...Mary... Cook... Eleanor couldn't bear the thought of parting with them. They were family. Crand had always been like a grandfather to her. Mary—she'd grown up alongside Mary! Cook had been serving her family for as long as she could remember.

"Darling, do not cry. We will think of something."

Eleanor sank back into her chair. "What if there is no other option?"

Her mother was quiet for a moment, a moment Eleanor used to wipe away her leaking tears. "Would it be so terrible to sell this house?"

Eleanor's eyes widened, her breath leaving her lungs in one fell swoop. "What?" She could not believe what her mother was saying.

Mama rushed to explain. "We have no need for a house this spacious, and Mary and Crand are being run thin with all of the work that has been thrust upon their shoulders. It is too much for so few people to shoulder, my dear."

Eleanor brushed her hands over her skirt in an attempt to soothe her shrieking mind. "W-What about father? We cannot leave him behind—"

"We will not be," her mother insisted.

"This is where he is. If we leave—"

A knock sounded at the door, and Mary scurried in, a breakfast tray in hand. She bobbed a curtsy and gently placed it on Mama's lap, giving a small smile before turning to Eleanor. "Will ye be eating in the morning room, miss?"

Eleanor shook her head, somber. "Thank you, Mary, but I'm not hungry."

The maid bobbed another curtsy before fleeing just as quick as she'd come and closing the door behind her.

"Your father does not inhabit this home."

Eleanor searched her mother's face as her heart fell into her abdomen in absolute misery. "How can you say that? Fath—"

"Eleanor," her mother interrupted, expression unwavering, yet soft. "Your father does not inhabit this home," she repeated, lowering her gaze to Eleanor's neck. "Where is your locket, dear?"

Eleanor's hand flew to grasp the metal there, warm from her skin, only to find it wasn't there at all. Her gaze dropped to the floor, searching all around for a hint of gold. There was none. "It was—I just—but—"

She stepped to the looking glass at the far side of the room, near the washbasin. Her own visage greeted her, circles under her eyes and pale throat bare. It was gone. She brought her hand up to cover her mouth, lungs no longer working. Eleanor made not a sound. She could only stare in disbelief at the place where her dearest possession had once been.

Again, Mama's gentle voice chided her. "Your father lies not in our possessions, dear, but in our memories and our hearts."

Eleanor turned from the looking glass, feeling hopeless. "I am not so sure as you are, Mama."

Her mother beckoned to Eleanor, gesturing for her to come closer. Eleanor did as she was bid and rested on the old cushioned seat once more. If only she could sink into the ground and disappear as the rain did on a stormy day.

"You are not wearing your locket. I suppose you cannot feel his presence, then?"

Eleanor furrowed her brows, not quite understanding what her mother was trying to tell her. "I—"

"Do you remember how he loves you?" Her mother went on. "His smile? His name for you? Ruby?"

Eleanor had no trouble picturing these things, regardless of whether she'd lost her locket. "I—I can."

Her mother smiled and patted Eleanor's hand, a loving gleam in her eyes. "Ah, you see? He is with us, always. We do not need this house to be close to him. We made fond memories here, but it is not what connects us to him. He is in our every action, thought, and word, no matter where we may go."

Eleanor settled back into her chair. A spike of electricity shot through her spine, then a warm feeling filled her, from the tips of her toes to the top of her head to the pads of her fingers. A realization. What her mother said was true. The townhouse was only a place where Eleanor's father had once been. His memory, however, remained with her even if she was elsewhere.

Eleanor blinked. "How do we go about selling it?"

≈

As the footman who accompanied her on her journey stored her carpetbag in the carriage, Eleanor turned in the doorway to look at her mother with a smile. It had been two weeks since her arrival at her London townhouse, and

Eleanor's mother was well enough that Eleanor felt comfortable returning to Ivy Grange.

"I'll be sure to write when I get back, Mama. Thank you for helping me. With everything."

Her mother dabbed at her eyes with an embroidered handkerchief before pulling Eleanor into a tight embrace. "Do not forget what I told you, dear, and do not lose hope." Her mother released her, and Eleanor nodded, resolute.

Eleanor kissed her mother on the cheek before turning around and walking down the front steps, determinedly stepping to the awaiting carriage. The footman held the carriage door open for her and helped her inside.

As he closed the door, her mother called from the doorway. "Safe travels, dear! I love you!"

Eleanor grinned and opened the window to call back to her. "I love you, too, Mama!"

The carriage rolled forward. Her crumbling townhome and smiling mother faded from view as they made their way along the busy London street. She leaned her head back against the cushioned seats and released a contented sigh. She had arrived with her mind full of turmoil and conflict but left with a spark of determination within her chest, at peace with her decision to tell Edmund of her feelings and with her mother's suggestion of selling the townhouse. She didn't even mind the idea of leaving their home anymore.

It was odd. Odd in the way that emotions are when one feels so strongly against something, only for the strength of such opposition to fade, and yet, she was glad for it. Where she once floated as a paper boat in a babbling stream, she'd now reached the calm pond where the stream deposited, and the reflection there was clear. Eleanor was aware of what had to be done.

As the carriage swayed along, she gazed out the window. They were just moving out of London, the countryside becoming wider and less populated. Sheep grazed in faraway fields, farmers tended their crops, and the morning sun seemed to shine upon her. She was filled with a lightness she hadn't experienced in weeks now.

The carriage trundled on for some time before entering Woodstock, a village near Ivy Grange. Shops began to pass on either side of the road, workers and customers bustling about. Couples strolled arm in arm, groups of ladies balanced multitudes of boxes, and unamused mothers chased their frisky children. A small bakery came into view, and Eleanor was struck with an idea. Rose would appreciate something sweet from the village. She tapped on the roof, and the carriage slowed to a stop.

Eleanor poked her head out the window and called to the driver. "Could we please stop here for a moment? I would like to buy something from the bakery."

The driver peered over his shoulder at her and nodded, an amiable smile on his face. She smiled back and thanked him before being assisted down the carriage steps by the footman.

As she entered the shop, the sweet aroma of baked goods assaulted her senses in a most pleasant way. The inside of the shop was small and cramped, but the stout woman at the counter had a smile on her face.

"What ken I help ye with, miss?" she asked, dusting her flour-covered hands on her apron.

What would Rose like best? Eleanor spotted a plate of delicious-looking cakes on the counter and grinned. "I would like three Shrewsbury cakes, please."

The woman placed the cakes in a bag, and Eleanor handed her a few coins from her reticule.

She took hold of the parcel and smiled once more. "Thank you."

She hurried back out and immediately collided with an entering patron. Eleanor managed to catch herself before she careened out onto the street. With all her stumbles lately, at last, her limbs seemed to be learning.

"Pardon me." A deep voice spoke as Eleanor righted herself.

She kept her eyes down, brushing her skirt with one hand, the other clutching the bag of cakes for dear life. "It was my fault. I was far too hasty—"

"Miss Clairbridge?"

She glanced up at her name—far up in order to see past the brim of her bonnet. Lord Lendin stood before her in a gold waistcoat and black trousers, his brown eyes kind. She stepped back into the shop—allowing him to do the same—before bobbing a curtsy, lashes lowered and cheeks heating. Of course, of all people, she would run into Edmund's best friend.

"My lord." She murmured the words, inwardly cursing herself for her clumsiness.

"How fortuitous!" he exclaimed in good humor, causing Eleanor to lift her gaze with eyebrows furrowed in confusion. Lord Lendin grinned, looking altogether pleased with himself.

"My lord?"

He gave her an apologetic look before reaching into his waistcoat pocket and retrieving a piece of paper, carefully folded with her name on it. "My apologies, Miss Clairbridge. I only meant that our meeting is fortuitous as I happen to have an invitation to give to you."

He extended it toward her, and she took it, her confusion mounting. An invitation? Why should Lord Lendin wish to give her an invitation? Her hesitation must have been evident, for he further explained.

"My mother is hosting a ball, you see, and has asked that I invite those persons I wish to see present. Considering you are Rose's beloved governess and Edmund's friend, we'd like the opportunity to become better acquainted with you." Eleanor was about to protest, but he continued speaking. "I make frequent visits to Ivy Grange when I am available to do so, and it seems only reasonable to get to know someone who I will cross paths with so often."

At this, Eleanor could not protest, for Lord Lendin's reasoning was sound. After all, she would like to get to know him as well, as he was Edmund's closest friend.

"Edmund will be there, of course. He's already promised me that. I need all of the help that I can receive when faced with the countless guests my mother invites." He leaned in closer as though imparting a secret, lowering his voice to a murmur. "She means well, to be certain, yet has the tendency to invite quite a few unmarried ladies and their eager mothers."

Eleanor fought the urge to laugh at the exaggerated grimace he gave. "Thank you, my lord. I shall certainly...attempt...to be there, however...do you not think my presence might offend your other guests?" She bit her lip.

Lord Lendin only gave a reassuring smile as he clasped his hands behind his back. "If any of the other guests are offended by your presence, then they were not worth inviting and their presence at the next event my mother hosts will not be required."

"I'm not quite sure how I'd get there, my lord—what with His Grace escorting Miss Pottan."

"Escorting Miss Pottan?" Lord Lendin's brows shot up. "I believe they are no longer courting, though I'm not sure that two outings suffice as a courtship. In any case, I do not see why he would do so."

Eleanor froze, eyes widening. "They aren't? But she visited the other day."

"I assure you, Miss Clairbridge, that even if my friend was 'courting' Miss Pottan then, he certainly isn't now." He flashed Eleanor a grin. "I congratulate myself that I had a hand in that courtship's demise."

Eleanor grinned before her mouth formed an O. "How shall I get there, my lord?"

"His Grace's curricle, of course." His mouth twisted to the side. "Just do not tell Edmund until the evening of that you are invited. I wish for it to be a surprise."

Eleanor nibbled her lip. "Will he find it a welcome surprise, my lord?"

Lord Lendin patted her hand, his smile kind. "I assure you, he will." He turned, heading out the door with a wave of his hand. "Remember, mum's the word!"

Eleanor brightened, beginning to see just one of the reasons why Edmund and Lord Lendin were such good friends.

~

*E*leanor entered Edmund's study with her heart beating fast with anticipation, having arrived back at Ivy Grange only a half an hour before. She'd had just enough time to change out of her traveling dress and into a fresh lilac day dress before Fanny had knocked on her door and informed her of Edmund's wish to see her at her earliest convenience. Eleanor brushed her hands down the cotton skirt.

"How is your mother?" Edmund hurried to pull out her chair and she sat, her arm brushing against his. A tingle of warmth spread through her, leaving her nearly breathless. His heady scent of spices filled the air surrounding her. She'd missed it.

Edmund crossed his arms and leaned against the front of his desk.

"She's better now." The remembrance of her mother's state made her all the more relieved now that she was past the worst of it. "I arrived at my home to find my mother in the throes of scarlet fever. It was only through divine providence and the doctor's wisdom that she overcame the worst of the illness. She grows stronger by the day."

Edmund's countenance relaxed at her words. "I am glad she

is improving. No one should have to lose their mother in such a way.”

As he had. He sat in the chair next to her, both now facing the hearth, and sighed, resting his hands on the arms of it. She reached over and placed her hand on his, giving it a gentle squeeze in a show of silent support. Her heart raced at her own boldness. Would he reject it?

He tipped his chin, but his eyes lifted to meet hers, his movements hesitant. He turned his palm upward and intertwined their fingers, brushing her thumb with his. They sat in companionable silence for a moment, Eleanor’s hand tingling with the warmth of their connection all the while. Her pulse thrummed in her veins. Was he reacting as she was?

“And your home?” Edmund turned his eyes to her, a hopeful expression on his face. “Are things better there than when you left?” He didn’t let go of her hand, and she didn’t want him to.

It was Eleanor’s turn to sigh, a bittersweet sigh of acceptance. “They are not.” She hesitated, then told him of her mother’s words about Eleanor’s father and the subsequent conversation they’d had.

Edmund nodded thoughtfully every once in a while, listening with intent whilst she spoke.

“And so my mother contacted our solicitor before I left,” she concluded. “He assured us that our home would sell quickly and that he has begun to look for smaller homes we can afford. Mama is relieved.”

Edmund’s green eyes met hers. “And how do you feel, Eleanor?”

She gave a half smile at his question. “It is the right decision. I think.”

Edmund shot her a knowing look. “And yet?”

Eleanor tilted her head to the side. “I’ll miss it. I have so many fond memories there and know all of the secret places.

I'm glad to think we won't have to worry about money anymore and can keep the remaining servants who are so dear to us, but it will be difficult to leave the place I've held close to my heart for so many years."

A pensive expression settled on his face. "Eleanor, I...I missed you...when you were gone."

She blinked, her mind ceasing all function. She could only form one response. "Di-Did you?"

He brushed his thumb across her hand once more, his lips pulling into a line. "Very much. I—"

A scratch came at the door before Prumb entered the room. "Pardon me, Your Grace, but an invitation has just arrived from Lord Lendi—Pardon me. I was unaware you were speaking with Miss Clairbridge."

Edmund frowned, letting go of Eleanor's hand, which she quickly tucked into the folds of her skirt. "Leave the invitation. I promised I'd attend—though heaven knows why."

As the butler placed the missive on the desk, Eleanor stood. What must Prumb think of her being closeted with their employer in such a manner? She felt obliged to follow him out.

As expected of a gentleman, Edmund rose as well and bowed as she bid him goodnight. The moment was lost. She could only wonder whether whatever he had been about to say might have changed her world.

❧

*E*leanor sat on the bed in her room as Fanny paced in front of her. Excitement rolled off of the red-headed maid in waves. It had been an hour since Eleanor's lessons with Rose had finished for the day, and only two days since her return to Ivy Grange.

"What about after yer lessons t'morrow?" Fanny paused and raised a finger.

Eleanor clasped her hands in her lap and tilted her head to the side. "Tomorrow? Well, I suppose..."

"It'll be perfect, ye see!" Fanny waved her arms. "Ye'll 'ave the afternoon to yerself and 'ave time t' prepare yerself before speaking with 'im in 'is study."

An afternoon would never be enough time for her to prepare the words she planned to say to Edmund, nor to rid herself of these half dreadful and half hopeful thoughts, but she let Fanny continue.

"No one should be there to interrupt ye, and if they try, they'll certainly get an earful from me!"

At this, Eleanor stifled a laugh. "Thank you, Fanny. Your help is most appreciated. I do hope my words are well-received tomorrow." Eleanor bit her lip, nerves causing her fingers to tremble ever so slightly.

"Don't ye worry about that, Ellie, they will be. Cook's been crowin' about ye both for nigh on a month! Says it's only a matter o' time before ye get married."

Eleanor's eyes widened. "Do all of the servants know?" She didn't want anyone to believe she was dangling herself before Edmund or that she attempted to rise in the ranks of society.

"Most are unaware, I think." Fanny sat next to her on the bed and placed her hand on Eleanor's arm. "All who knows below stairs are prayin' for the two of ye to make a match of it. Ivy Grange's ne'er been so bright as it is now, and ye're the reason for it!"

With that encouragement, Eleanor straightened her shoulders. She could be brave—for herself and for them.

CHAPTER 22

The next morning, Eleanor strode to the schoolroom, palms sweating. In only a matter of hours, she would be laying her heart open to Edmund, and she could only hope that he would be gentle with it. All of their interactions up to the present day had led her to believe he shared her feelings, yet would he act on them?

For the next few minutes, she attempted to focus on preparing the day's lessons instead of the man her thoughts so often drifted to.

"How d'you do, Miss Clairbridge!" Rose ambled into the room, eyes ever curious as she surveyed the room, her blond curls drawn up with a pale-blue ribbon and her hands clasped in front of her, enthusiasm evident in both her expression and stance.

"Good morning, Rosie." A smile broke over her face at the sight of the dear girl. The idea of being Rose's aunt was a bolstering one. Eleanor would risk her job if it meant a lifetime with this sweet child.

They took no time in sitting down to work, the hours

passing quickly given the ease with which Rose completed her lessons.

Before Eleanor knew it, Fanny knocked and entered bearing a tray. "Pardon me, Ellie, but Mrs. Brinder tol' me to bring ya yer luncheon."

Eleanor glanced at the small clock on the far wall. "Goodness! I suppose it's that time already." She rose and gestured for Rose to do the same. "We'll pause in our lesson for now and continue after we've eaten and you've rested. Working minds need energy, after all."

Eleanor moved to take the tray from Fanny as Rose made her way to Eleanor's desk, where they usually enjoyed their repast. "Thank you, Fanny." Eleanor grasped both sides of the tray, yet Fanny held on for a moment, garnering her attention.

"We'll have to come up with a new plan, Ellie," Fanny whispered, her tone disappointed.

"And why is that?" she whispered back.

Fanny gave up the tray. "Word below stairs is that 'is Grace 'as gone to London for a few days. 'E 'ardly gave word to any of us, and dinna say why 'e was goin'."

"That does pose a problem," Eleanor murmured, swallowing. Her chest squeezed at the idea of having to hold in her feelings for a longer period of time, yet there was nothing for it. She would have to wait until he returned. "If you have a spare moment today, will you meet with me? I need to decide what to do next."

Fanny nodded. "I'm a wee bit busy today but—I 'ave an idea! I'll meet ya in yer room at yer evenin' meal."

～

"Absolutely not." Eleanor slumped onto her bed that evening, her words conflicting with the sprout of excitement in her stomach at Fanny's outrageous suggestion that Eleanor approach Edmund at the Lendin ball.

"It's the best option ye 'ave." Fanny pointed at her hand. "Ye've said yerself that ye wish to tell 'im as soon as can be, and that's as soon as ye'll be able to. Lord Lendin said he'd be there."

"He might return earlier than that, or he might even decide to forgo the ball. And it's not as though I have anything suitable to wear to a ball." Eleanor shook her head. When she'd accepted Lord Lendin's invitation, she hadn't thought about how mortifying it might be to show up at a ball in one of her drab everyday dresses. She hadn't even been thinking about clothing! This plan was proving more complicated than they'd thought.

Fanny gestured to the armoire in the corner of the room. "We could add some frills t' one of your better gowns, I'm sure." She strode to the piece of furniture and threw the doors open.

"They are too worn..." Eleanor protested feebly.

Fanny pulled Eleanor's light-blue gown out and held it before her. "This one's not."

"That's my best dress, but I really am not sure we'll be able to make it look presentable." Eleanor eyed the darkened hem of the gown, spotted with stains from the last party she'd worn it to. She shrugged without confidence.

Fanny continued to eye the dress, shifting it about in order to look at it from all sides before nodding to herself. "We'll be able to make it real nice." She took the gown off of its hanger. "We'll need to start soon, else we won't 'ave enough time."

Eleanor straightened on her bed, eyes widening. She was aware by now that once Fanny set her mind to do something, she would. "The ball is at the end of this week! That only gives us four days."

Fanny paid her no heed, only folding the gown over her

arm with a grin on her face. "I've done more work in less time, and I'm 'appy to for my friend, but we will need 'elp."

As heartening as that might be, was it wise, bringing more people into this? What if things went horribly wrong and Eleanor was left shamed? Surely, the less who knew of her plight, the better.

Then her mother's admonition rose to mind, and Eleanor lifted her chin. Edmund's hand had felt so perfect in her own. "Whom do you have in mind?"

~

The next evening, Eleanor sat in her bedroom embroidering small white flowers on the modest neckline of her blue gown, Mrs. Brinder and Fanny on either side of her. Mrs. Brinder had been more than happy to help with Eleanor's predicament.

"This ribbon will look just marvelous around the waist." The housekeeper held up a cream-colored silk ribbon.

Eleanor sank the needle through the fabric of her gown and pulled it back up, glancing at the housekeeper with appreciation. "Are you sure you don't mind my using it?"

Mrs. Brinder waved the question away, a warm smile on her face. "I've many like it, dear. The milliner and I are close friends, you see, and she always gives me those she cannot sell. See why?" She pointed at a small black mark on the silk. "Ink. It is easily hidden, considering how small a mark it is, and yet no one would buy it. I can get the stain out with milk. I've had this ribbon nigh on three months and have yet to wear it. Its purpose will be served much better with you, dearie."

"It will look lovely." Eleanor smiled. "I am grateful to you—for the ribbon, of course—and also for your help."

Mrs. Brinder set the ribbon aside and began to thread a needle, speaking as she did so. "Many seek perfection and fail to realize the worth in the imperfect. And you need not thank me, dear. I am happy to be of service."

Eleanor couldn't help but feel glad now that most of her old acquaintances had turned her away when they'd found that her family lacked money. Though it had been a hardship, it had allowed Eleanor to make true friends. Now, she not only had the years-long friendship of Teresa and Eliza, but also the unexpected friendship of strong, resourceful women like Fanny and Mrs. Brinder. Eleanor finished one flower and started on the next, her heart aflutter with conflicting thoughts and emotions.

"Oh! I almost forgot." Mrs. Brinder reached into her apron and fished around in it. After a moment, the woman gave a satisfied hum and pulled something out. She opened her fist, and Eleanor let out a gasp. Her lost locket was lying in the palm of the housekeeper's hand. "Mr. Roskilly found this in the garden the other day. He said something about the piskies having taken it to exact their revenge, if I remember correctly. While I'm not sure about that, I recognized it as yours."

Mrs. Brinder handed the locket to Eleanor, who flipped it over to look at the familiar inscription. A joyous laugh bubbled from her throat as she rubbed a thumb over the smooth gold.

"Thank you." She clasped the locket around her neck.

Mrs. Brinder gave her a maternal smile, and Fanny clapped her hands before the three of them continued their work, Eleanor's heart full with the friendships she'd made at Ivy Grange.

Half of her was excited, eager to surprise Edmund and once again attend a ball, and another part of her dreaded the event. She fought against the budding fear that it might end up being almost exactly the same as the only other ball she'd attended, the one at which Miss Pottan had so cruelly deflated her already weak confidence.

Her mother's words whispered in the back of her mind. *No*

one can tell you your own worth or value. There will always be those who wish to tear you down in life, and you mustn't let them. You must rise above their words and continue on.

Eleanor calmed her nerves. She could not see into the future, but she would not fret over possibilities. If Miss Pottan did decide to confront her, then Eleanor would heed her mother's advice. That was exactly what Eleanor would do. Continue on.

~

*E*dmund smiled to himself as he gazed out the window of the carriage. The past few days had been filled with business and meetings with his solicitor, and he was glad to finally be on his way back to Ivy Grange. It wasn't as though he had much of a choice regarding his quick return, however, as he'd promised Lendin he'd come to the ball he was throwing this evening. Edmund knew well how his friend would react if he failed to show after having given his word.

Once, at Oxford, Edmund had spent the day studying and had lost track of time. He had been so caught in his work that he'd completely forgotten he'd promised Lendin they'd meet at the quadrangle near the fountain before walking to a nearby penny university.

Not an hour later, Lendin had barged into his room and plucked the quill from Edmund's hand, setting aside Edmund's books—he hadn't thrown them, for he enjoyed books rather too much to treat them in such a fashion—with an exasperated expression on his face. He'd then all but pulled Edmund from the room, Lendin heaving a sigh of lament as he did so.

Edmund chuckled now as he thought of it, for it wasn't difficult to imagine Lendin breaking into Ivy Grange to drag him to the ball if necessary. Edmund had never truly enjoyed balls, as they tended to remind him of the accident, and he'd much rather spend time with Eleanor and his niece after the days spent apart from them, but Lendin was counting on him to be there. Edmund pulled his pocket watch from his waistcoat, flicking it open and raising his eyebrows. It was later in the day than he'd thought.

The minute he arrived at Ivy Grange, he'd have to prepare for the ball. His lips turned down at the corners. He wouldn't even have time to greet those he most wished to. Edmund sighed inwardly and tucked his watch away.

He'd simply have to see them tomorrow.

CHAPTER 23

*B*efore his mirror an hour later, Edmund straightened his tailcoat and exhaled a small sigh, mentally preparing himself for the uncomfortable evening ahead. Matchmaking mothers would be sure to send their marriageable daughters in his direction, and he would be forced to retreat to the library, as always.

He strode from the room and down the main staircase, his steps quick as he approached Prumb and asked that the carriage be readied. Prumb nodded and walked off with an almost mischievous smile on his face. One that Edmund had no time to interpret. He stood to the side of the foyer as he waited for the carriage to be brought around, clasping his hands behind his back.

A light tapping sound reached his ears, growing louder with every second. He turned, only to see Eleanor practically running down the stairs. His breath promptly left him. Her head was tilted down, eyes on the steps as she neared the base of the staircase.

Her hair was pinned beautifully, with two dark curls left free to frame her face and a spray of tiny white flowers tucked into it. She appeared to be wearing her pale-blue gown, but it had been altered since he'd last seen it. Embroidered flowers at the hem and neckline matched the ones in her hair, a ribbon of the same color was tied around her waist, and her golden locket hung from her elegant throat, the pendant gleaming in the candlelight.

Her rose-colored slippers peeked out from beneath her gown as she stepped from the last carpeted step and onto the floor of the foyer. Completely at a loss for words, he lifted his eyes to hers.

She spoke quickly, cheeks flushed in a most charming way. "Lord Lendin invited me to the ball, and he said you were going too. He said I was to keep it a surprise."

Edmund leaned back with a smile of admiration. "It *is* a surprise...a most pleasant one."

"Might I ride with you in the carriage?" She flushed even redder. "If you'd rather not arrive together, then certainl—"

"Yes." Edmund's voice was hoarse, breathless—not from exertion but from the mere sight of her.

As Prumb returned, they both turned. "Beg pardon, Your Grace, but I've had the curricle brought 'round." There was a definite twinkle in his eye.

Bless him. They'd cause quite the stir if they arrived at a ball without a chaperone or third party, but the curricle would make a chaperone unnecessary, given its open design.

"Perfect." Edmund grinned, approaching Eleanor and extending his arm. "Are you ready?"

Eleanor took his arm lightly and gave a nervous smile. "I am."

As he escorted her down the front steps of Ivy Grange, her hand wrapped around his arm and the lantern light shining upon them, his smile would not fade. He knew now, that there was no better place for her—no place he'd rather have her— than at his side, always.

The ride to the ball was filled with excited energy, and Edmund fought to keep his gaze from flicking to Eleanor as he held the reins.

"You look absolutely lovely." His heart thumped like a wild rabbit loose in his chest. It hadn't slowed since they'd left Ivy Grange.

Her arm brushed his as she shifted in her seat. "Thank you." She was quiet for a moment before replying over the sound of the horses' hooves. "You look quite handsome as well."

Edmund peered at her from the corner of his eye, noticing the wine-hued blush that suffused her cheeks in the starlight. She'd have to show him that mushroom she spoke of to see if they were truly the same color. Certainly, it wasn't possible, but his heart beat even faster beneath his ribcage.

He returned his eyes to the road, warmth spreading from his chest throughout his body despite the comfortable evening breeze. Edmund would have loved nothing more than to have taken her into his arms at that moment, but his attention was quite occupied with driving the curricle, so he contented himself with the idea that he'd ask her to waltz. Lendin's mother was sure to have a few scattered throughout the evening's chosen dances.

"Eleanor…" He hesitated as her gaze landed on him. "Might I have your first dance?"

It seemed Edmund had no reason to worry, for Eleanor responded directly. "Certainly," she murmured. "I would love nothing more."

Edmund couldn't keep his lips from pulling into a smile at her response.

$\mathcal{E}$leanor accepted Edmund's assistance down from the curricle after they'd arrived at Lendin's estate, his hands only lingering on her waist for a brief moment before he offered her his arm. She bit her lip as they walked up the stone steps leading to the front entrance. Would she look rather plain in her humbly embellished gown compared to the other guests with their newly tailored fineries?

They were greeted by Lord Lendin and his mother as they stepped into the foyer, and Eleanor was immediately put at ease by their warm smiles.

"So this is Miss Clairbridge, the famed governess Henry's been telling me of." Lady Lendin grasped Eleanor's hands, flicking her gaze between Eleanor and Edmund. "I'm sure Edmund is fortunate to have you. We are certainly glad that you could attend this evening's festivities."

Eleanor's cheeks burned as Lady Lendin released her hands and faced Edmund more directly. The woman placed a maternal hand on his cheek. "It is always good to see you, dear boy, although I should scold you for how long it's been." She placed both hands on her hips. "Fortunately for you, I have far more pressing matters to attend to this evening, so I will save my chiding for a later time."

Lord Lendin stepped forward to greet them next and bowed over Eleanor's hand before shaking Edmund's.

Edmund led her into the ballroom where countless others already stood, chatting amongst themselves and making merry. The room was beautiful, with candles glowing in every corner and intricate chalk designs on the light-wood floor, placed there in order to keep dancers from slipping. A large chandelier hung in the center of the ceiling, crystals dripping from it like dew from the morning blades of grass.

A familiar voice caught her attention. Were her ears deceiving her? She glanced to the side.

"Eleanor!" Teresa Witherby, or—Eleanor supposed—Teresa Wicker now, was gliding toward her, smile wide. Immediately, she pulled Eleanor into a tight embrace, her blond curls tickling Eleanor's cheek. "I cannot believe I am in the presence of my dear friend again! I had begun to wonder if I'd only hear of you through your letters. This"—Teresa released Eleanor and stepped back, pulling a familiar blond man forward—"is my darling husband, Thomas. Mr. Wicker." Teresa turned to her husband. "Thomas, meet Eleanor—Miss Clairbridge."

Teresa grinned as the man bowed, a smile on his face that told of a good nature. Teresa had first pointed him out at the Witherbys' ball.

Eleanor curtsied in return and shared a smile with Edmund, excited at the unexpected meeting with her friend. "Please meet His Grace, The Duke of Albemarle."

Edmund stepped forward and bowed, an easy smile on his face. Teresa and Mr. Wicker curtsied and bowed in return, eyes a bit wide at the unforeseen introduction to a duke. Before they had a chance to speak, the musicians struck up, signaling the guests to prepare for the first dance. Mr. Wicker begged their pardon and pulled his wife toward the line of dancers quickly forming, leaving Eleanor and Edmund alone with the promise that they'd be back to converse after the first set.

Warmth encompassed Eleanor's hand as Edmund gently wrapped her fingers in his own. "Shall we?" he asked.

Eleanor gave a single nod. She gazed into his mesmerizing green irises before following him to stand in the line with the other guests. As they faced each other, her eyes never left his. The beginning strains of music seeped through her reverie, making known to the guests what the first dance would be.

"A waltz," she murmured.

Edmund nodded and bowed before stepping toward her, grasping her right hand with his right and cradling her left with his left in the march position. She fought to breathe as he pulled her closer to him, his warm arm stretched across her back.

The scent of clove and nutmeg that accompanied him was enough to send her into a daze as they began the steps, spinning and moving with light feet. Eleanor hadn't much experience with dancing with handsome gentleman, let alone a duke, but she found she'd never danced so well. She anticipated where he intended to move with only a glance to his eyes and the small shift of the muscles within his arm where she held onto him. He grasped her hand, their arms held above their heads in an arch for several measures. They twisted and turned, then marched again, never looking away from each other as they continued the pattern.

His eyes were a darker green now, much like the forest when one ventured into the depths. And they were full of emotion. No doubt, so were hers.

As the music came to an end, they paused, though neither moved to leave the dance floor just yet.

"Edmund..." Eleanor breathed out his name, practically floating from the heady experience. His gaze was tender and held a warmth that took her breath away. "I ne—"

"Is that the governess?"

The question interrupted Eleanor, most fortunately, as she'd been about to confess her feelings in the middle of the ballroom floor with at least a dozen couples to overhear. Whilst glad that she had been spared the embarrassment of thoughtlessly making known such private emotions in public, that gladness quickly withered on the stem.

Miss Pottan sauntered up to them, a sneer on her face as she grasped her red silk gown in her hands.

Before Eleanor could speak, Teresa and her husband appeared beside them. Her eyes flashed with anger at Miss Pottan's pointed exclamation. "Miss Pottan." Her voice was cool.

Miss Pottan only tilted her head in some semblance of

acknowledgement before flicking her gaze back to Eleanor, moving closer with a glare. "Why are you here? You've no money, no beauty, nothing at all to attract a suitor. To think, a *governess* attending a ball. How ridiculous," she spat.

Eleanor was done with this woman's venom. Miss Pottan only sought to tear down others. Eleanor drew her shoulders back and held her head high, not allowing herself to stoop to Miss Pottan's level. "I feel sorry for you, Miss Pottan."

Miss Pottan's eyes widened and she sputtered. Obviously, she'd not been expecting Eleanor's words.

Eleanor went on. "It is clear to me that you are hurt, and that the well of your cruelty has been filled by your own unfortunate experiences. That you feel the need to treat others in such a fashion tells of your own struggles, however much you may try to hide them. I do not know what has led you to act in this way, but I sincerely wish that you will overcome your pain. It must be a great pain, indeed. Even so, I do not deserve your ire. Though it has taken some time, I have come to realize my worth, and your words do not affect me anymore."

As Eleanor finished her speech, the woman in front of her appeared pale, almost fearful. Miss Pottan's eyes were dull, no longer holding the fire they had. The woman seemed drained —and perhaps she was. She turned on her heel and stalked off, pasting a smug smile on her face.

Eleanor turned back to her friends.

Of all things, Teresa was beaming at her. "The way you handled that..." She paused as the group moved from the middle of the floor, shaking her head with a light chuckle. "You responded much better than I would have."

Eleanor gave a bashful smile, standing a bit taller than before. She'd faced Miss Pottan, and she'd done it in a way that would have made her father proud. She'd not been unkind, only honest, and perhaps Miss Pottan had needed the honesty.

"Everyone deals with pain in a different manner, and I've no idea what secrets Miss Pottan holds, nor what makes her act the way she does. I only know that pain is not diminished when one inflicts wounds on others."

Edmund's fingers grazed her own in a silent show of support. A small smile lifted the corner of his lips.

Even her dreams could never match the bliss that was this evening.

The conversation turned to more lighthearted topics, and Eleanor got the chance to hear about all that had been occurring in her friend's life. As Teresa spoke animatedly of her children, shared joy warmed Eleanor's chest. Mr. Wicker looked on with fondness while she spoke, clearly a doting husband with an abundance of love for his wife. The sight of that love and the pride in Edmund's expression whenever he looked at her—and he looked at her often—strengthened Eleanor's resolve. And her hope for her own future.

God would take care of her. He always had, though she'd lost sight of that. She wasn't just any creation—she was *His* creation, and He would never forsake her. With God with her, who could be against her? *She* certainly wouldn't be anymore. She'd learned not to be her own enemy.

"It's lovely to be all together." Teresa sipped from her wine glass, eyeing everyone in the group. *It truly was.*

The evening continued, with Eleanor being asked to dance by multiple gentlemen. Thank goodness, she remembered all of the steps. Lord Lendin even danced with her and told her of his school days with Edmund and the scrapes they had gotten into, making her abdomen ache from laughter.

Eleanor finally had her coming out—sort of, anyway—and it had been everything she wished for. Would she get her prince too?

CHAPTER 24

Sitting beside Edmund in the curricle on the way back to Ivy Grange, Eleanor couldn't keep the smile off of her face. She'd seen Teresa again, danced with Edmund, laughed with Lord Lendin, and even faced Miss Pottan without fear. Now was the perfect time to tell him how she felt.

She shifted her body toward him in the seat and took a breath, her heartbeat picking up its pace. "Edmund..."

He tilted his head toward her, flicking his eyes between the road ahead and her face. "Eleanor?"

She placed a gloved hand to her cheek, sure she must be burning. "Well, I've wanted to tell you for some time now—"

A squeak sounded at her side. A flash of fur caught her eye, and a shriek burst from her lips. A shrew—the bane of her existence—ran across her lap! Eleanor swatted at her skirt, attempting to sweep the thing off. It leapt to the floor of the curricle. She stomped her slippered feet, shivers running up and down her stockinged legs.

"What's wrong?" Edmund slowed the horses as she burrowed into his side, clutching at his coat and ducking under his arm.

"A shrew!"

The fabric of his fine garments muffled her response, but his laughter rumbled through his side. "It must have gotten in at the ball." Edmund craned his neck. "There, it squeezed out the back. It's gone now."

And there had gone her chance at telling him how she felt. If only she could remain buried in his coat forever. Truly, it was becoming a more pleasant thought by the second, with his arm wrapped around her shoulder.

"As much as I enjoy having you close, I can't imagine that position is incredibly comfortable." Edmund's voice was soft in the night air.

She sighed and raised her head from where she'd pressed it into his chest. "You might think not, but I would be content to be there for an entire day." Her mouth dropped open. Had she really just said that? "I mean..."

Edmund only gave her a small smile, directing the curricle down the long drive toward Ivy Grange. "Perhaps someday, you'll have the chance to be."

Had *he* really just said *that*?

The curricle pulled to a stop in front of the main entrance to Ivy Grange, leaving Eleanor little time to wonder. Edmund hopped down and swiftly moved to Eleanor's side to assist her. The footman, John, came to see to the horses and curricle as Edmund escorted Eleanor inside. They had barely laid off their wraps before Edmund pulled her through the hallway, whispering, "Come with me."

Eleanor hurried to keep pace with him, glancing at Edmund with curiosity as the muted sounds of their footfalls filled the air. He led her down another hall before they reached the large oaken doors of the library. Eleanor followed Edmund inside, the familiar scent of books reaching her nose. He stopped only a few meters into the room, Eleanor right beside him, before turning toward her with an earnest look on his face.

He reached out slowly and grabbed both of her hands in his. What was this? Eleanor tilted her head up. His eyes were warm, yet there was a touch of fear in their depths.

"Edmund?" She whispered the question, her heartbeat picking up its pace with his proximity. He held her gaze, and sparks seemed to fly through her fingertips at his touch.

"Eleanor...I have tried in vain to hide my feelings, but I find that I cannot hold them within any longer, nor do I wish to." He took a breath.

Eleanor's pulse raced in her ears. Could this be?

"I do not know how I ever lived before meeting you. Ever since catching you from falling on that street in London, I have been drawn to you. Your kind eyes, your warm smile, your lively spirit. I have tried so very hard to remain unmoved by your charms, but you are the beautiful moon, and I am the tide. I cannot help but be affected by your brightness and the way I am pulled to you."

Eleanor's heart lifted in her chest with every word Edmund spoke.

"With each passing day, your light waxes, and I can't help but draw nearer. The strength of my affection is such that it can no longer remain hidden. I love you, Eleanor, and can only hope that your heart may beat the same rhythm as mine."

It seemed as though she floated above the ground, in a daze. She must be dreaming, and what a dream it was. Everything about it was too good to be true. Eleanor closed her eyes tight for a brief moment, then reopened them.

Edmund still stood before her, a look of such caring on his face and a melting warmth in his eyes. Her eyebrows raised ever so slightly. It was not, in fact, a dream. It was very much real. Edmund had just confessed his love for her, and here she was, making him wait for a response.

She sucked in a quick breath. "Edmund, you've no idea how I've longed to hear you speak such words. I never imagined that you might return my affections."

He shook his head, eyes wide. "Oh, Eleanor!"

She squeezed his hands, hurrying on. "At first, I tried to distance myself from you because of the fear of unrequited love that stemmed from Miss Pottan's terrible words and my own feelings of inadequacy. As my feelings for you grew and I came to realize my own value, I wondered if you might ever feel the same. I now find my feelings are too strong to deny, and as you do not wish to, neither do I." She laughed aloud, joy filling her being. "What you say about the moon and tide is true for, as the sea reflects the moon's gleam, I've been hoping all along that you might reflect my own feelings. I love you, Edmund."

Edmund took a deep breath, his exhale shaky. Eleanor's heart beat loudly in her chest as she stared into his eyes. Time seemed to still. Then his lips found Eleanor's. She melted into him as he held her close, one arm around her waist and the opposite hand at her cheek. Eleanor wrapped her arms around his neck, her pulse racing with joy as she leaned against him. The warmth that always emanated from him wrapped around her, making her dizzy in a most pleasant way. She had no idea how long passed before Edmund pulled a little away, breathless.

"Will you, then, grant me the greatest honor of being my wife?" A sudden uncertainty dimmed his smile.

Eleanor's eyes welled with tears of happiness as her mouth upturned into what she was sure was the widest smile she had ever given. "Yes, Edmund, I will." She beamed, watching as his uncertain expression fled at her words.

Eleanor had barely spoken her response when Edmund wrapped his arms tightly about her waist and lifted her from the ground, spinning in a circle as she laughed, unimaginably happy. He gently set her back onto the ground, and his breath brushed her face in a light caress.

This time, she would surprise *him*. She peered up into his eyes for a tender moment before her lips met his in a sweet kiss. She did her utmost to infuse it with all of the love she had for him and all of the excitement she held for the future.

Edmund rested his forehead against hers, and they reveled in their shared love and full hearts. "You make me happier than I ever thought I could be, darling," he whispered.

Eleanor placed a hand on Edmund's where it cradled her jaw, leaning into his touch. "And you have given me the love that I never thought I'd have," she whispered in reply.

When the thumping of expeditious footsteps sounded in the hallway, they broke apart. Short arms wrapped around Eleanor's waist as a small someone barreled into her with a squeal of delight. Edmund took hold of Eleanor's arm to steady her, and the sight of Rose's rosy upturned face greeted her.

"You're meant to be abed, dearest," Edmund chided gently, a smile of amusement on his lips.

Eleanor couldn't help the grin that broke across her face as she beheld the little girl in her billowing nightgown, feet bare on the carpet. Eleanor wrapped her arms around her.

"I woke when you returned, and Prumb told me you went to a ball! Say it is so, Miss Clairbridge! Say you're marrying Uncle Edmund!" She bounced up and down.

"Did Prumb mention marriage as well?" Edmund asked in a curious tone.

The moment Edmund spoke the man's name, he appeared in the doorway. "Do you have need of me, Your Grace?"

Edmund shot him a knowing look, one eyebrow raised and lips upturned. "I suppose you happened to be walking past the library at the exact moment I stated your name, eh, Prumb?"

Prumb smoothed the invisible wrinkles out of his jacket and stood with all of the dignity he could, his reddening cheeks the only thing that betrayed him. "Quite right, Your Grace," he replied quickly, putting on a casual air.

Rose skipped over to Prumb and grabbed his hand with her small one, giving a toothy grin. "Prumb said you were getting married but that we had to wait to come in!"

Prumb reddened further at the girl's accidental reveal of their eavesdropping.

"Did he?" Edmund eyed Prumb with a teasing grin.

"Well, Miss Rose—I—we only wanted to know if you would finally ask her to marry you…" Prumb studied them with pleading eyes as Rose swung her hand and Prumb's between them.

Edmund let out a chuckle and folded his arms. "You could never resist her charms, Prumb. 'Tis no matter. I would shout the news throughout the halls and down the stairs if it wouldn't wake the entirety of the staff."

A warm laugh erupted from Eleanor before she turned her attention back to Rose. "Yes, dearest, we are getting married." Her own excitement bubbled inside her. Her dreams had come true.

Rose clapped her hands. "I've been praying every night for it. I'll have a mama again, and you won't ever have to leave."

Eleanor chuckled and took one of Rose's hands in her own, squeezing it affectionately. "You'll never have to worry about me leaving, dearest." She brought her other hand to where her locket hung around her neck and grasped the warm metal, her heart full with love and happiness.

EPILOGUE

*E*dmund sat on the settee in the drawing room, his beautiful wife by his side with Rose settled comfortably in her lap. In the almost four months since they married, not a day had passed that Edmund had not given thanks he had married her. She was reading a story with his niece, her melodic voice washing over him in sweet waves. Her chestnut curls framed her soft face, and joy brightened her eyes. She was a vision, as she always had been.

Her mother sat across from them in a leather armchair, deftly poking a needle in and out of the fabric held within her embroidery hoop. She, too, had a smile on her face. When Edmund and Eleanor had gotten married, they had agreed that her mother would come to live with them at Ivy Grange. She was a complete delight to have around, and Rose had come to spend much of her time with the woman. Edmund often found them out in the gardens, enjoying the last flowers before autumn truly set in.

"And then Elizabeth said, 'I would love to.'" Eleanor lifted a hand up to her mouth to cover a yawn as she paused in her reading.

Edmund smiled. He knew well enough that his wife would continue to read despite her obvious fatigue.

"I think it's time you head to bed, Rosie. You must get your rest in order to be ready for your lessons tomorrow." Edmund spoke the words with an affectionate smile.

She nodded with drowsy eyes and turned in Eleanor's lap, wrapping her small arms around her in an embrace before hopping to the ground and stepping closer to Edmund to do the same.

Eleanor's mother stood, having put her embroidery aside. "Come, little one. I'll take you to your room." She flashed a knowing look toward Edmund and Eleanor.

Edmund gave her a grateful smile as Rose took her hand and they walked from the room together. Eleanor closed the book in her hands and set it on the table beside the settee.

Edmund softly grasped one of her hands in one of his own and brought it to his lips, bestowing a loving kiss there. "Do you remember when I traveled to London before Lord Lendin's ball?" He attempted to hide his excitement.

Eleanor lifted an eyebrow at him, mouth tilting up at the side. "I do."

Edmund grinned, no longer able to hide his eagerness. "Well, it wasn't only business, darling. You see, I've kept a secret from you."

"A secret?" Eleanor blinked, her eyes widening as a smile graced her lips.

Edmund's gaze dropped to them briefly, but now was not the time for that. Not yet, anyway. "Yes... The truth is, I am the one who bought your London townhome."

Eleanor's mouth dropped open as she took in his words.

Edmund continued. "I knew then that I could never see you separated from a home you so cherished, and you'd told me your mother wished to sell it, so I bought it. Since then, I've been having it restored to its former glory."

"What?" She covered her mouth.

"It's taken quite some time, but it is finally back to the beautiful home it had been before your father died. I haven't had anything changed, of course, for I know how each piece has a memory attached to it, but the paint is no longer chipped, the dust is no longer in the air, and the wallpaper is no longer peeling, among other things."

Eleanor merely stared at him.

Had he done the wrong thing? "Darling? If it displeases y—"

Edmund's words were cut off as Eleanor sealed his lips with a grateful kiss, shifting closer to him on the settee. Edmund gladly returned her kiss. There was no telling how much time had passed when they finally separated. Her kisses never failed to daze him.

Eleanor brushed her fingers gently over his cheek, as soft as the beat of a butterfly's wings. The subtle scent of her lavender perfume cascaded over him. "What did I ever do to deserve you, Edmund?" she whispered.

He often asked himself the same question about her. They sat in contented silence for a brief moment.

"Thank you," she murmured, twining her fingers into his hair and shifting it around with delicate movements. "I would love to visit it as soon as I am able." She yawned again, removing her hand from his hair in order to cover her mouth.

"You've seemed rather tired of late, darling. Should I be concerned?" Though he wasn't sure he should be, he *had* been concerned about Eleanor lately. She had been disappearing for brief periods throughout the day and had seemed to lack her normal robustness. Should he call the doctor?

Eleanor squeezed his hand and stood. He immediately followed suit.

"There is no need for concern, darling, but I do have something to tell you, as well." Excitement gleamed in her eyes.

He raised his eyebrows, yet thank goodness, there didn't seem to be anything wrong.

"It is true that I have felt a bit ill lately. Well...I had the doctor visit to see what the matter was, and he was very pleased to declare that...I am with child."

Edmund froze for a moment, thoughts drowned out by the blood rushing through his ears. Then he wrapped his arms around her, lifting her from the ground and spinning in a circle, reminiscent of his actions when he had proposed.

Her soft laughter sounded as he spun her, and a huge grin spread across his face. *I'm to be a father. Me. We're having a child.* As he set Eleanor down, he stared into her bright blue eyes, shining with love. Taking her hands in his own, he kissed her knuckles, his excitement and elation overflowing. "I cannot possibly put into words how happy this news makes me."

Eleanor beamed up at him, her cheeks a rosy hue, her skin practically glowing.

He moved his face closer to hers. "Rose will have a sibling. She'll be overjoyed, I'm sure."

Eleanor nodded lightly and pressed her soft hand against his cheek. "Darling?"

"Hm?"

"If the babe is a boy, I was thinking we might name him Philip."

He gazed into her beautiful eyes, briefly remembering how he had made the foolish promise to himself to remain unwed. One of the best decisions he had ever made was marrying the woman who now stood before him. "A wonderful idea, dearest. If the babe is a girl, perhaps we shall name her Ruby?"

Eleanor's eyes gleamed as she nodded, brushing her thumb across his cheek.

"I love you." His words were a whisper.

Eleanor tilted her face up toward his, her breath against his skin. "I love you, too," she whispered in response before their lips met, a shared joy for the future tying their hearts further together.

Did you enjoy this book? We hope so!
Would you take a quick minute to leave a review where you purchased the book?
It doesn't have to be long. Just a sentence or two telling what you liked about the story!

Receive a FREE ebook and get updates when new Wild Heart books release: https://wildheartbooks.org/newsletter

Don't miss the next book in the Saving the Spinsters Series!

Arranged with the Earl

1818, Cumbria, England.

Loftus Cromwell, Fourth Earl of Hardwicke, strode toward the conservatory, the only place in this blasted house in which he could find peace. Frowning portraits stared at him from their places on the walls. His jasmine needed tending, and his melissa needed to be watered. What other plants needed attention? His booted footsteps marked each distracted thought.

"Loftus."

He stopped in his tracks at the sound of his brother's voice, a frown pulling at his lips. As he turned toward that blood relation of his, the other man grimaced. Loftus was used to the reaction by now. He cleared his throat and eyed the man's rumpled cravat. He was wearing the same coat as he had yesterday. "Gilbert." He checked the time on his pocket watch, then slipped it back into his green waistcoat. "You're awake...early."

Gilbert stood taller, his light-brown hair disheveled from what Loftus assumed was the previous evening's carousing. "It's one in the afternoon. Don't act so surprised." His voice was thick, as though he'd woken up only ten minutes before.

Loftus tilted his head, eyes narrowed. "Indeed. Is there something you wish to speak with me about? I was just—"

"Going to the conservatory? Yes, I thought you might be. Really, Loftus, must you always be tending to your plants? It's dreadfully embarrassing to have a brother whose sole interest is in leaves and vines. You wouldn't believe the ribbing I got about it last evening from Lord Templeton." Gilbert propped his hands on his hips and shook his head, light flooding in from the window behind him.

Loftus stretched out his arms, irritation bubbling within him. "What care I for Lord Templeton's opinion? His reputation is as clean as a chimney sweep's after twelve hours of labor."

"You know, this continued behavior of yours isn't what Father wanted." Gilbert crossed his arms, his dark-blue eyes flashing. The corridor seemed to narrow around them. "He thought your foolish hobby would go away. When he sent you off to war, he thought you'd come back a hero. Not like..." Gilbert raised a hand in a gesture toward Loftus's face. "This."

Loftus's hands tightened into fists at his sides, his jaw clenching. "There was every possibility I wouldn't come home at all." Indeed, perhaps his brother would have been better suited to the fight. "But I agree. I wish he would have let me be. I would never have had to see what I have seen, nor to see what I have to every day when I look at myself. You do not realize how difficult Badajoz was. It is not only the physical marks that I have but the—" He swallowed past the thickness in his throat. "Do you believe I want these scars?"

"You still won't understand, do you? You needed to secure

the line. No woman would have married someone as obsessed with plants as you, which is why Father sent you away." He eyed Loftus, a pitying twist to his mouth. "But now the situation is doubly impossible."

Loftus's heart sank. Must his brother state the obvious? "It's been three years since I came home from the war to find that my brother was no longer as I knew him, and you have remained that same changed man—that same stranger in my home. Will you ever return to the kind sibling I knew?" He couldn't keep the longing from his voice.

Their father's death had done something to Gilbert. Perhaps he attempted to find solace in vice and hide away from his grief in drink and cards. Perhaps it was the uncertainty of his own future now that his dock—their sire—had been washed away. Gilbert had always idolized the man, after all. Whatever the case, Gilbert had only grown more distant over the years.

Gilbert stepped forward, his handsome visage animating. "I *am* trying to be kind. To give you what you want...peace and your plants. Father taught me about how to run the estate when you were recovering, you know...before he died, that is." His brother looked away and shrugged. "If ever you wished to relinquish your title, the estate would be in good hands. It can be a lot of weight on one's shoulders, I understand." Gilbert shifted on his feet. "The title needs heirs to continue the line. You'll never marry, whereas I—"

Anger and disappointment mixed in his stomach. "I am not relinquishing my title. I do not care what you believe, brother. I will be married, and I will carry on our family's name." For his brother to suggest such a thing only proved how much he had changed. Loftus might be scarred, yes, but did his brother really think so little of him? It only served to make Loftus more determined to prove him wrong.

Gilbert's expression twisted. "Do you truly believe a woman of the *Ton* will marry you?"

Loftus raised his hand. "Enough! Go back to sleep before the next round of spirits takes you off."

He turned on his heel and departed, heading for his study instead of the conservatory. He'd need to send a note to his solicitor. As much as Loftus didn't wish to marry, he'd need a wife and heir if he was to keep his cad of a brother from becoming the next to inherit. Loftus wasn't about to let Gilbert run Blackfern Manor and the surrounding lands into the ground—not with his record of debts.

Surely, his solicitor could find some woman who wouldn't mind a marriage of convenience in exchange for land and title—even if that marriage happened to be to a man with a face as marred as his.

Catherine Blynn sat down at her vanity, her maid reflected in the looking glass as she pulled back Catherine's long blond hair. Each tug and push of a pin readied her for the evening to come. She slid her round-rimmed spectacles higher up her nose and examined her well-proportioned face. She was pretty, she supposed, though no diamond of the *Ton*. Gentlemen asked her to dance—that wasn't the problem. What *was*, was that they didn't seem to enjoy listening to what came out of her mouth thereafter. That was, of course, besides the fact that she was four-and-twenty. Would anyone ask her to dance tonight?

"Do you think this one will be like the last?" She met her maid's eyes in the mirror, tension threading through Catherine's shoulders.

Susan pinned a few violets here and there. They were a good match for Catherine's light dress. "I can't see 'ow it would be, miss. Ye were engaged at the last ball. Ye won't be at this one."

Catherine's arms tingled where the bruises had been. When she'd been betrothed, Lord Balfour had certainly left his mark on her—and not in a good way. "What if he's there?"

"'E may well be, but 'e can't 'arm ye no more, miss, and thank the Lord for that!" Susan blew a wayward strand of dark hair from her face, ruffling the edge of her white cap in the process. "I don't know why yer parents arranged that match in the beginning, 'twas so terrible."

Catherine sighed. "You know as well as I, Susan. I am nothing but a pawn to them—simply a thing to be traded to get connections and status."

Susan set the hairpins aside and moved to the jewelry box, reaching in to pull out Catherine's pearl necklace. "Well, I'm mighty relieved that Lord Balfour called off the betrothal."

Catherine nodded. While the scolding she'd received from her parents had been horrible—them blaming her for his calling it off—she'd much rather face their wrath than spend a lifetime with such a man as he.

The door burst open, and her mother entered the room, a storm of silk and jewels. A scowl was on her face, framed by golden curls. "Catherine! How are you not yet ready? We must be going immediately if we are to be on time for the ball. Come!" She reached for Catherine's hand and pulled her from the seat, Susan clasping the necklace onto Catherine's throat as they hurried out of the room and down the hall.

Not long after, Catherine was unceremoniously pushed into her family's carriage, and they were off to the ball, her heart thumping louder with each *clop* of the horses' hooves upon the ground.

If Lord Balfour was there, would he speak to her? Would he attempt to reconcile? She shuddered. Kenneth had never pretended to be a good person nor a loving betrothed. He only wanted her dowry. He had made it clear her eccentricities would not be tolerated. Her hand lifted to her cheek of its own volition, a phantom sting on the skin.

"You must be on your best behavior tonight." Her father furrowed his eyebrows, his voice gruff. "If you're to ever make a match, the Ton must forget about your failed engagement. Let us hope Lord Balfour hasn't been spreading the news to all of his friends."

"Yes, Father." Catherine ducked her head, her voice quiet.

His black mustache twitched, and his brown eyes flashed. "None of your eccentricities. If you make a fool of us again, there will be consequences. I don't know what you did to make Lord Balfour call off your engagement, but you won't get out of another one, I tell you. Your mother and I have worked too hard for this."

Catherine lifted her chin. "I didn't do anythi—"

"It was surely your bluestocking tendencies that sent him running. What an ungrateful child you are." Her mother sniffed, turning her head to look out the window. "We have done so much to ensure you could marry a titled man, yet all you do is complain."

Catherine wasn't the one who wished for a title, and she was hardly a child at the age of four-and-twenty. Yet she bit her tongue.

The carriage ambled down the busy London streets, eventually stopping in front of Lord Fifett's large brick townhome. Candles were aglow in every window, and footmen stood at attention on either side of the front door, waiting to greet guests.

Catherine followed her parents into the house and was welcomed by the hosts, a large man and woman with great smiles on their faces and bright eyes. Catherine's shoulders loosened. How did these people come to be friends with her parents? She bobbed a curtsy.

"Welcome! We're so glad to have you here." Lady Fifett spread her arms out and gestured around the expansive foyer at the few lingering guests, nodding her head in the direction of the ballroom. "There are many people to meet, for it is a crush this evening." She leaned toward Catherine as though imparting a secret. "There are many young men as well."

Heat rose in Catherine's cheeks, and she clutched her skirt with both hands. Lady Fifett studied her for a moment, then turned her head to a nearby servant. "Where is Roger?"

The man straightened. "He is—"

"I am right here, Mother." A man who looked about a few years older than Catherine entered the foyer through a side door, a drink in hand. His hair was the color of rust, and his features pleasing, with a smattering of freckles along his nose and cheeks.

"Ah, so you are." Lady Fifett's smile widened as her son neared. "Come, meet the Blynns and their daughter, Catherine."

The man—Roger—moved across the marble floor and bowed at the waist. "It's a pleasure to meet you all." He picked up Catherine's gloved hand, his face hovering over it. "Might I have your first dance, Miss Blynn?"

Her eyes were wide. Never had she so quickly secured a dance—and the man seemed genuine too. "If I might have the pleasure of knowing who I am dancing with."

Roger's chin dipped. "Ah, please forgive me.' He looked past her to her parents and then his gaze darted to hers once more. "I am Lord Fortescue."

Catherine nodded. "I'd be pleased to dance with you, my lord."

Her mother's tight voice sounded from behind her. "You'd better let him escort you to the ballroom, Catherine, for I am sure we are the last of the guests and the dancing is soon to begin."

Catherine allowed herself to be led away from her parents, her shoulders easing as the distance apart from them increased.

"Might I say, you look lovely, Miss Blynn." Lord Fortescue leaned forward, his head tilted in her direction.

A flush heated her cheeks. She mustn't say anything her parents would disapprove of.

"Thank you, my lord." She settled on giving him a smile. Surely, her parents wouldn't find fault with that.

As he led her through the doorway into the ballroom, he took one last sip of his drink and handed the glass to a nearby footman. He turned to her and said with brandy on his breath, "Let us join the throng, then."

The first dance was a minuet, which Catherine knew very well. She promenaded with Lord Fortescue, then danced in slow circles while other couples watched. Whenever the dance brought them close, his eyes brightened and her steps were lighter. He was a fine dancer, truly. He held her gloved hands in a soft yet warm grasp.

When the dance was over, he bounced on his toes. "Would you like to take a turn about the room?"

Catherine lifted her lips, though hesitation pulled back on the reins of her enthusiasm. This was how Lord Balfour had acted when she'd first met him. Her stomach tightened. "I would, thank you." No matter her anxiety, she wasn't yet prepared to return to her parents. They'd always find fault in her, no matter what she did.

Lord Fortescue wrapped her hand around his arm and circled the ballroom. The dancers in the middle skipped about with their partners, the sound of their feet tapping beneath the steady thrum of the musicians' instruments.

"Why is it we've not met before?" Lord Fortescue cast her a sidelong glance. "I've never seen you around London."

Catherine fingered her pearl necklace. "I attend events, but

I do not stay at them for long, if my parents have any say." And she wouldn't say more, though they normally blamed Catherine for their leaving early—saying her behavior was causing them embarrassment.

Realization crossed his face. "You must have to get up early for callers, then. It's no wonder your parents wouldn't have you stay out too late."

Let him think what he would. Catherine wouldn't have him believing her to be some sort of oddity among her sex—which is what her parents would claim, if he asked. "What of you, my lord? I haven't seen you about either."

"I've just returned from a stay with my friend in the country." A half smile crossed his face.

"Indeed?" Catherine tilted her head, interest coloring her tone. "What area, my lord?"

"He has an estate in Kent. It's beautiful there. A perfect place to escape the city crowds. They're too akin to peacocks for my tastes."

He plucked a glass of lemonade from a footman's tray and offered it to her, pausing right before the glass left his fingers. A look of concern crossed his face. "As much as I wish to keep you in my company, I should return you to your parents. They are looking in our direction with rather undecipherable stares. Your mother, in particular, has quite the scowl." Lord Fortescue frowned. "I've no ill intentions toward you, Miss Blynn. I promise, I will not steal you away."

Catherine took a sip of her lemonade. This man seemed to share her same views, and he was good company so far. "Do not fear, Lord Fortescue. I do not mind, for it would be a blessing if you would."

He reared his head back. "What?"

"'Tis nothing, my lord." She waved his concern away. "You may take me to them. I would be most grateful." She placed her hand on his arm, and they moved toward her parents, sliding around giggling groups and men slapping each others' shoulders.

"I do not want our acquaintance to end." Lord Fortescue tilted his head down to whisper in her ear. "Might I take you for a ride in my barouche tomorrow? We could go to Hyde Park."

"What time of day?" She hated to go during fashionable hour. It was so slow then. It was nothing more than people parading themselves around for the sake of being seen—absolutely ridiculous.

"Anytime you like." His breath brushed her ear, sending tingles down her spine.

Her parents, of course, would wish for her to go, but this time, Catherine wished to as well.

"Meet me at two." She gave him her address as they stepped to her parents' sides.

"What is this?" One of her father's dark eyebrows rose in question.

Catherine cleared her throat. "Lord Fortescue has invited me for a ride in his barouche tomorrow."

"How wonderful!" Her mother's face transformed in an instant from a dislike for Catherine to an eagerness to see the outing go well. "Thank you, Lord Fortescue, for doing our daughter such an honor."

Lord Fortescue's eyebrows furrowed, his mouth twisting to the side as he bowed. "'Tis an honor she accepted, madam. If you'll excuse me, I must check on my mother." In a blink, he was gone, and Catherine's parents stared her down as though she held the weight of the world on her shoulders.

Her mother grabbed her arm, her lips pulling into a thin line. "You must make him like you, Catherine. Our family depends on it."

Her arm began to ache as her mother's nails dug into Catherine's skin—her cold blue eyes without emotion. "Yes, Mother."

Finally, the woman released her, only for Catherine's father to move closer, a furious look on his face. "While you were dancing, your mother and I were trying to find you prospects. As it is, Lord Balfour has slandered our name because of you."

Catherine's mouth dropped open. She took a step back, her heart racing. "I—I didn't do anything to discourage him, Father—I promise. I always bent to his whim as you told me..." Her voice was a murmur. How could her father be blaming *her* for Lord Balfour canceling their betrothal? It had been *his* decision, not hers.

"What does it always come down to, girl? What is it that always gets you in trouble?" He didn't wait for her to answer. "Your behavior!" He huffed, pulling on the lapels of his coat. "You can never act as your mother and I have instructed. Instead, you spout what that governess taught you and what my sister taught you after that. It's a good thing we replaced the former and sent the latter away, or I suppose you'd be even worse than you currently are, eh? My sister never learned, and neither will you, it seems. No man wants an odd wife, Catherine, and Lord Balfour's been telling all who will listen that's exactly what you are. Says you drove him away with your vulgar ways."

Tears stung the back of Catherine's eyes. Her father was keeping his voice low, but she felt as though many eyes were upon her. Now that Lord Balfour had spread these rumors, perhaps there were. "I was always refined in his presence, Father." And she had been. She'd never been her true self around him—not that she wasn't refined in her normal behavior, but by the Ton's standards, she was not yet the pure gold that could be made into a ring. It had been difficult, yes, but necessary, according to her parents.

So, then, why would the man use her behavior as a reason for canceling their betrothal when it clearly hadn't been? Unless... There had been one time Catherine had stoked his ire to a greater degree than others. The anger on his face was burned into her mind, and she'd received more than one slap for denying him what he wished.

Catherine met her father's eye, her stomach churning. "I know why Lord Balfour canceled our engagement."

Her father crossed his arms. "We already know the reason."

"This isn't about my unladylike behavior, Father. Lord Balfour broke our engagement because of my Christian behavior—the behavior that he views as meaningless."

"What are you talking of?" Her mother narrowed her eyes.

Catherine's heartbeat increased. This was not something she was comfortable talking about—especially not in the middle of a crowded ballroom—but her parents were sure to force it out of her one way or another.

She lowered her voice to a whisper. "During our betrothal, Lord Balfour wished to...lie with me...in a carnal way. I told him I would not do so."

Her father's eyes widened, and her mother clutched the jeweled pendant at her neck. Catherine's shoulders fell in relief. At least they cared about this.

"Why did you deny him?" Her father's voice was all fury as the words spewed from his mouth.

Catherine's gaze lost its focus. Her limbs went numb. "You... want..."

Her mother shook her head. "You foolish, foolish girl." Her voice was all venom.

Catherine came to her senses, her gaze flicking from her father to her mother. "You would have me go against God and... and *lie* with a man before marriage? I cannot disrespect Him in such a way. I cannot disrespect *myself* in such a way."

The music seemed to get louder. Her father rubbed a hand down his ruddy face. "You could've entrapped him, Catherine. Don't you see? He'd have to marry you then. You'd be titled, and all of the fellow merchants would be crawling to me, asking to merge businesses. Lords would finally be willing to work with me."

Her mother waved her fan in an erratic motion. "I would finally be able to show to the other ladies that not only do I have the wealth they do, but the relations, as well. We told you what to do in the simplest of directions, yet you couldn't even follow those. Our only hope now is that Lord Fortescue doesn't hear of these rumors before you can convince him to marry you."

Catherine felt sick. Never before had she known her parents to be willing to stoop to such levels in order to get what they wanted. Inwardly, she sighed. Lord Fortescue, though she hadn't interacted much with him, seemed kind and genuine. He didn't deserve her manipulative parents for relations. On the drive tomorrow, she would do what she hadn't done in some time with a suitor—be herself. If that scared him away, then at least he was safe from her parents' schemes.

ACKNOWLEDGMENTS

I'd like to acknowledge my Heavenly Father for His help in writing this book. Without His guidance and words in my ears —as well as the urging to continue—it would not have been written. I'd also like to thank the dozens upon dozens of publishing houses and agents that rejected my work. Without you, I would not have found such a wonderful publisher. I truly believe that God guided me to this one. Of course, I'd like to thank my publisher, Wild Heart Books, for their endless help and support with the publication process. They have helped me to understand what it takes to publish a book and how the process goes, for which I am very grateful. I am very thankful for my editor, Denise Weimer, who helped me to figure out the little mistakes and errors in this book and the things that didn't quite make sense. With your help, I took this book from a rock and shaped it into a stone. Lastly, but certainly not least, I'd like to thank my friend Terra Taylor for beta reading this novel. Your kind comments are what helped me to continue on my novel-writing journey, even when the rejections would strike at me daily. I hope you find success with your own!

The idea for this book popped into my head in 2021. I had been reading a lot during the time. I had been binge-reading historical romance novels ever since I finished *Pride and Prejudice*, in fact. I suppose it's no surprise, then, that my own story began to form in my head. I had written and self-published three poetry books. Writing a novel couldn't be so difficult, right?

Wrong.

I thought I'd have it out within the year. Perhaps I would have, had I decided to self-publish it. That's not to say, of course, that it would've been any good. The amount of rewrites this thing has gone through is inconceivable.

Though rewrites were necessary, this story came easily to me. I knew who I wanted Eleanor and Edmund to be as people. I wanted my audience to be able to relate to them. Though they are characters and, therefore, fictional, they still hold human flaws and emotions. They have insecurities, just like you and I.

I also wanted the story to tell of truths that aren't too often spoken of. Eleanor struggles with the idea of her own worth, allowing others in her life to decide whether she is valuable or not. She also struggles with the idea of her father no longer being alive and his quickly fading memory. She worries that if she loses her home, she will no longer remember him. However, even if we have lost everything relating to a person who was once in our lives, our memories will always hold them close to us in spirit.

Edmund struggles with the idea of allowing himself to love again—fearing the loss of another loved one. What he comes to realize is that the love and contentedness that comes from love is worth far more than the pain of it being taken away. The reward of love in a life outweighs the eventual outcome of death. If you, dear reader, have learned or understood any of this, then my job has been done.

I must say, I had a pleasant time doing research for this book. I learned a lot about fungi and when specific mushrooms were discovered. It was interesting to find out that the Regency waltz position is different than the Victorian waltz position—for I previously had no idea. (Thank you, Denise.) As I mentioned above, there was much that had to be done in order for this book to be the polished and bound thing it is now, so I found out a lot in the in between. My favorite fact from the book is probably the one about the mushrooms that Eleanor's father tells her in the flashback (the one where she gets the locket). I also especially enjoyed writing the scene when Edmund comes to pick Eleanor up on the dirt road in his carriage and they see one another once again.

I hope you've enjoyed reading my novel, and I would be ever so glad if you could leave a review on Amazon or wherever you prefer to leave your reviews. I delight in reading every one.

If you wish to follow my progress with books and keep up to date on new releases, please follow me on Instagram on my page, @authorjackiekillelea, or on my Facebook page, @AuthorJackieKillelea. I also have an author website at https://jackiekillelea.weebly.com/. If you are interested in other books I've written, you can find them on Amazon.com. Thank you!

ABOUT THE AUTHOR

Jackie Killelea is a born and raised small-town girl from Connecticut with a degree in English and Creative Writing. She started off her writing journey with poetry, soon shifting into novels and becoming hooked. On days when she's not busy with her nose in a book, she can be found typing away with a piece of chocolate in hand.

After failing his former flock, Reverend Ian McCormick is determined to start anew in Stone Creek, and he's been working harder than ever to forget his mistakes and prove himself to his new congregation—and to God. But when he meets a young woman seeking acceptance and respect, despite the rumors swirling about her sordid past, Ian finds himself pulled in two directions. If he shows concern for Sophie's plight, he could risk everything—including his position as pastor of Stone Creek Community Church.

Will the scandals of their pasts bind them together or drive them apart forever?

~

A Summer at Thousand Island House by Susan G Mathis

She came to work with the children, not fall in love.

Part-nanny, part entertainer, Addison Bell has always had an enduring love for children. So what better way to use her creative energy than to spend the summer nannying at the renowned Thousand Island House on Staple's Island? As Addi thrives in her work, she attracts the attention of the recreation pavilion's manager, Liam Donovan, as well as the handsome Navy Officer Lt. Worthington, a lighthouse inspector, hotel patron, and single father of mischievous little Jimmy.

But when Jimmy goes missing, Addi finds both her job and her reputation in danger. How can she calm the churning waters of Liam, Lt. Worthington, and the President, clear her name, and avoid becoming the scorn of the Thousand Islands community?

~

Revealing the Truth by Lorri Dudley

His suspect holds a secret, but can he uncover the truth before she steals his heart?

When Katherine Jenkins is rescued from the side of the road, half-frozen and left for dead, her only option is to stay silent about her identity or risk being shipped back to her ruthless guardian, who will kill to get his hands on her inheritance and the famous Jenkins Lipizzaner horses. But even under the pretense of amnesia, she cannot shake the memory of her sister and Katherine's need to reach her before their guardian, or his marauding bandits, finish her off. Will she be safe in the earl's manor, or will the assailant climbing through her window be the death of her?

British spy, Stephen Hartington's assignment to uncover an underground horse-thieving ring brings him home to his family's manor, and the last thing he expected was to be struck with a candlestick upon climbing through the guest chamber window. The manor's feisty and intriguing new house guest throws Stephen's best-laid plans into turmoil and raises questions about the timing of her appearance, the convenience of her memory loss, and her impeccable riding skills. Could he be housing the horse thief he'd been ordered to capture—or worse, falling in love with her.